EXCEPTIONAL

M. J. FABULA

MILTON & HUGO L.L.C.
4407 Park Ave., Suite 5
Union City, NJ 07087, USA

Website: *www. miltonandhugo.com*
Hotline: *1- 888-778-0033*
Email: *info@miltonandhugo.com*

Ordering Information:
Quantity sales. Special discounts are granted to corporations, associations, and other organizations. For more information on these discounts, please reach out to the publisher using the contact information provided above.

Library of Congress Control Number: IN-PROCESS
ISBN-13: 979-8-89285-134-3 [Paperback Edition]
979-8-89285-135-0 [Digital Edition]

Rev. date: 05/10/2024

Content warning:

This story contains events related to a school shooting and its aftermath. There are scenes that deal with mental health, trauma, and misogyny, which may be too difficult for some readers.

Dedicated to the six men and women who tragically lost their lives in the tragic shooting in Isla Vista, CA on May 23, 2014: Veronika Weiss, Christopher Michaels-Martinez, Katie Cooper, George Chen, Weihan Wang, and Cheng Yuan Hong.

CHAPTER

1

"So glad you found that secret spot," I said to my best friend, Lizzy. "Lunchtime is going to be so much better from now on."

"Don't mention it, Jessica," Lizzy said. "I'm just happy we don't have to deal with all the popular jerks at our school at lunchtime anymore."

Lizzy and I were making our way back to the main campus from this hidden spot on the beach adjacent to our high school, Manzanita, before third period started. Along the way, we discussed the latest books we'd read as well as the comics we bought yesterday.

"I'm really loving this latest Protectors series," I said, referring to Wonder Comics' flagship superhero team. "Twenty-eight years strong, and Scott Lowe and the rest of the Wonder crew still continue to impress with more amazing material every year. Spectacle may have started the superhero genre, but Wonder brought it to a brand-new level, saving comics in the process."

"I couldn't agree more," Lizzy said. "They could still improve on how they portray some of their female superheroes, though. Like, how does Mistress Mystic fight like she does in a miniskirt and high heels? Don't give me any crap about 'But at least she can fly and has magic powers,' either. Too many female superheroes in comics dress in skimpy outfits like hers, for no reason other than to appeal to the male gaze. Come on, we're in the twenty-first century, and the comics industry still has a hard time remembering that half of their fan base is women and girls?"

I clapped my hands as the two of us continued walking. "A+ rant, Lizzy," I said. "I used to think that it was so cool how Mistress Mystic could fight in those clothes. But now that you put it that way, my mind has changed."

"Happy I could change your mind, Jess. Easy enough for me, but changing one mind is better than none." The two of us laughed at the same time. "How's your English paper going, by the way?"

"Ooh, I'm so glad you asked. I can't believe I didn't tell you until now, but you inspired me to write about the topic I chose. I still remember that day you texted me about Sarah Everard's murder in the United Kingdom and how it opened my eyes to the fact that we women and girls aren't safe anywhere on this planet, not even here in the developed world. My English teacher, Mr. Bradley, assigned us to report on a major non-COVID global issue from this decade for our semester papers, and when I was thinking about what to do my project on, the tears you shed when you shared the Everard news with me came to my mind. So I thought, *This would be the perfect topic to write about for my English paper. I'm certain Lizzy would be proud of me for doing so.*"

"Aww, that's so sweet of you." Lizzy placed her hand over her heart. "I'm honored, Jess."

As we stepped onto our school's central plaza, several deafening pops suddenly filled the air, cutting our conversation short. At the same time that other students around us ran in different directions, Lizzy and I scrambled for whatever cover we could find within the wide-open space we were in. A tree, a wall, an adjacent building, anything.

But before we were able to find safety, Lizzy's body tumbled backward. A shriek erupted from my vocal cords, and I felt like everything around me came to a standstill.

"Get up . . . please get up, Lizzy!" I yelped with desperation as I cradled my best friend in my arms.

I didn't know how I managed to dodge all of the shots that came flying in my direction, but somehow, I wasn't even scratched. That didn't mean anything to me with Lizzy currently fighting for her life after multiple bullets penetrated her upper body. Despite everyone throughout the plaza panicking, screaming, and running all over the place, all that mattered to me right now was that Lizzy's life was on the line.

After some unknown amount of time, the atmosphere of panic subsided, and the drums of gunfire were no longer audible. Everyone started to come back out to the school plaza, and the atmosphere on campus became much different from what it was only a few minutes ago.

It took the longest time for paramedics to arrive at the campus of my beachside high school. My mind couldn't make out whether first responders were taking way longer than they should've to come to my wounded best friend's rescue, or if it just felt that way. Afraid of messing up the emergency response, I left Lizzy in the care of the paramedics. With several others injured or wounded, I was far from the only one worried about a friend's life. Still, with anxiety clutching me in its arms, I fixed myself next to the ambulance that the paramedics were taking Lizzy into; it was as if my feet were stuck in cement. I couldn't let the ambulance depart without getting whatever information I could from the paramedics about Lizzy's condition.

"Excuse me, do you know if my friend is going to be okay?" I asked.

"I'm sorry, miss, but we don't have time to answer any questions at the moment," said a female paramedic. "All we can say is that we're taking her to the nearest hospital. We hope to take care of what we can as fast as possible."

A few seconds later, the ambulance departed. All I could do was stand as still as a statue and gaze at it in shock as I tried to process what had happened over the last few minutes. Powerlessness crushed me, evoking emotions in me that I never had before in my sixteen years of life.

One hour after the first shots rang out, I got word from school security that classes were canceled for the rest of the day. Normally, I would've taken the ten-minute walk home from school, but because of how shaken I was by the surreal terrors that I witnessed toward the end of lunchtime, I was mentally in no condition to walk home, so I gave my parents a call to tell them about the situation and ask them to pick me up. Both of them said they would leave work early in order to be by my side for the rest of the day. My two other best friends, Orlando and Charlotte, texted me that their respective parents already picked them up and drove them home, so even if I might have been okay to walk back home, I wouldn't have felt comfortable doing so alone and without them.

The entire time I waited for my parents, I remained fixed in the same position I'd been standing at since the ambulance picked up Lizzy. Every nerve in my body was frozen, too numb to feel like walking away from my current location. It wasn't until Mom and Dad arrived that my nerves thawed, at least as much as my ongoing state of shock would allow them to. Somehow, Dad's car was able to find a spot to pick me up just a few spaces behind the line of ambulances in front of them. When I saw his blue car around an hour after I heard the first gunshots at my campus, I half-ran to my parents, who promptly got out of the car to give me the biggest hug of our lives.

"Jessica!" Mom shrieked as I sank into her and Dad's arms and quickly received a kiss from each of them. "So glad you're safe."

"So glad you two are here, too," I said to my parents as I started to tear up. "I wish I could say the same about Lizzy."

"Oh no, is Lizzy okay?" Dad asked.

"She was shot several times. Her wounds were so serious that she had to be taken to the hospital. I can't even say if she has a chance of surviving, but I wish I could . . ." My parents gave me another tight group hug before we got into the car, needing to head back home sooner rather than later so as to not interfere too much with the ongoing emergency response.

Lunch was as difficult for me as it could get after we got back home. All I could eat was two bites of the salad that my parents bought me, and that was it. I had much more water than food, and even then, all the water I consumed wasn't enough to quench the never-ending thirst I had ever since I watched those bullets strike Lizzy's chest.

Being an introvert, it was already typical of me to spend several hours alone in my room doing my favorite solo activities, such as reading comics or texting friends. But things were different today. I didn't want to do anything more than stay in my room, like a timid turtle hiding inside its shell. No amount of sunny Southern California weather could motivate me to go outside right now. I wasn't even in the mood to read any books or comics or watch any TV shows like I usually was. The only thing on my mind was how Lizzy was doing, and if she was still going to be okay.

My phone buzzed to notify me that I just received a text message. The sight of the name in the notification—Veronika Manchester, Lizzy's mom—sparked my anxiety, as I texted her a few times here and there after my early departure from school to offer her and Mr. Manchester any comfort that I could in this trying time for them. Before I opened the text, I clung to the slightest semblance of hope that there was still an aura of life left in Lizzy. That the damage from the bullets that hit her chest wasn't as bad as it looked. That fate had chosen her to continue on. Until I read the text and saw words that I did not want to see.

Veronika Manchester

Hi, Jessica. I wish I could give you some positive news, but sadly, our Lizzy is no longer with us. I'm so, so sorry. We appreciate you keeping in touch on this most difficult day for us. Let's get through this together.

They can't be serious, I thought. *Why her? It doesn't feel fair at all.*

The sight of Mrs. Manchester's text shook me so much that my fingers were physically unable to type a reply to it. All I could do was pound the wall next to my bed as tears burst out of my eyes. My sobs and the banging on my wall were loud enough to catch my parents' attention, provoking them to walk to my room to check on me.

"Jessica? Cupcake?" Dad said. "Were you able to hear about—"

"I got a text from Lizzy's mom," I said. "She said . . ." My sobs erupted again as I tilted my head down in sorrow. "She's gone . . . I can't believe I'm saying that . . . it's just not fair." My voice was too choked up for my parents to understand clearly enough, but they could still recognize what I said.

"No . . . I'm very sorry, darling," Mom said. "She was such a wonderful girl. Why her, of all people?"

I would've told Mom "I thought the same thing when I read the text" if my emotions hadn't been so overwhelming. But all I could manage out of my mouth were the most agonizing bawls of my life. My parents pulled me into another group hug, and none of us left it for a while.

This couldn't be real. Lizzy couldn't be dead. There was no way that text from Mrs. Manchester could be true. There had to be something that the doctors who tried to revive Lizzy could've done to save her life.

Something.

I normally didn't watch the news; most of the topics they reported on were too much for my sixteen-year-old heart to handle. But with this latest shooting affecting me and my community, I felt the need to stay informed about what was going on as we Manzanita students headed into a new normal on the first day after the tragic shooting we witnessed yesterday afternoon.

Reports indicated that ten people were killed in the Manzanita High School shooting and fifteen others were wounded, leading me to think about who else lost friends and loved ones and which of the other murdered individuals I might have shared a class with. But the real freight train that hit me was when they broadcast the name of the shooter himself:

Garrett Lowe, the son of renowned comic book mogul Scott Lowe.

Scott Lowe was the brain behind Wonder Comics, one of the two most famous superhero comic book companies in the world (the other being Spectacle Comics, the very first superhero comic book company). Known for the idealism of his works, Lowe was also said to display an all-loving demeanor in real life. Knowing this brought a tightening pain into my head as it tried to piece together how the son of the world's most famous comic book writer could be the suspect of a mass shooting at my own high school. Heck, until this report aired, I wasn't even aware that Garrett Lowe attended Manzanita. I never saw him around campus, so either he was fantastic at hiding himself in preparation for his murder rampage, or we just never hung out in the same areas or had the same classes.

The media coverage of the Manzanita shooting would've fit better in a crime procedural show than an actual news report. It helped that the shooting provided them with the perfect ingredients for a compelling news story.

"Exposed to the glitz and glamour of Hollywood from a young age and recently accepted into USC's prestigious film school, eighteen-year-old Garrett Lowe decided to create his own horror movie by murdering ten students and injuring fifteen more in a shooting spree on the beachside campus of Manzanita High School," the female reporter on my television noted. "Like other mass shooters in the past, he posted an online 'manifesto' on YouTube a few days ago. Titled 'Reckoning,' he described in the video how he would execute the shooting rampage that he went on yesterday afternoon."

As the news started their segment about the "manifesto" and broadcast Garrett Lowe's mug shot, I turned off the television and got on my computer to look up Garrett's "Reckoning" video on YouTube. When I entered "garrett lowe reckoning" into the search bar, that same "Reckoning" video was not only the very top search result, but it was also the actual, original video itself, not a repost of the video by a news channel for their latest report.

As much as I admired Scott Lowe, this was the first time I ever heard about his son, so seeing Garrett Lowe's face—a round, well-polished face free of facial hair and topped by a head of smooth black hair—was something new for me. He did bear a slight resemblance to his comic book mogul father, though.

"Hello. I'm Garrett Lowe," he said to begin the video, speaking to his phone camera from the driver's seat of his car. "I am now eighteen years old. I graduate from high school in three weeks. And yet, I've still never had a girlfriend."

Right away, I could tell that something was very wrong with this man based on the tone of his voice and the way he talked. The backdrop behind his car—the beach and the ocean hanging out in the background on a clear, sunny day—only added to how eerie the video was.

"For the past four years, I've had to suffer through a never-ending whirlpool of loneliness, pain, and depression. All because all the cool kids at school would refuse to give me the time of day. All because no cute girl would ever hang out with me. How can you girls not see how perfect of a man I am? How can you not be attracted to this handsome face? My likable personality? This awesome car that I own?"

The rest of Garrett's video consisted of nothing other than more rambling from the driver's seat of his car. Every single second of it was just as grueling as the seconds that came before them. "All the girls around me would show so much love and affection toward other guys," he complained. "But they would never show any toward me. They would always choose other guys over me. Arrogant douchebags instead of kindhearted, gentle souls like me."

Garrett then dropped the title of his now-infamous video to further drive in his incredibly warped message. "But now, the day of reckoning awaits. I will have my satisfying revenge against all those who have wronged me. And the girls who rejected my awesomeness will suffer the consequences for refusing to choose me."

He let out a brief laugh, the kind you'd only hear from comic book and cartoon villains. Chills flowed down my spine listening to it, and my body felt like a cold midwinter day in the Midwest. It was the most unimaginable nightmare come to life. *What could've driven someone at my school to develop this type of hatred toward others?* I asked myself.

"Tomorrow, at lunchtime, I will make my way to the center of campus at my high school, Manzanita High School. I will unleash the wrath of my precious handgun. And I will *murder*. Every. Little. Pretty female *shit*. That I can find."

Wow, I thought. *How can Scott Lowe have raised this kid? It doesn't feel possible that someone like this could be related to the world's most brilliant and groundbreaking comic book writer.*

"I wish it didn't have to come to this. I wish it didn't have to be this way," Garrett continued, with a sarcastic tone this time. After spouting another sinister giggle, he moved back to the chilling voice he was using for most of the video. "But I must bring justice to all you popular kids.

All you spoiled, obnoxious jackasses who pushed me away to live the lives of happiness and pleasure that you've stripped me of—I will create a bloodbath out of all you assholes. And I will punish you for your crimes, just like you deserve."

And then, at long last, he concluded his venomous rant. "All you jocks who have won the hottest girls' hearts for being the biggest jerks in the world, you shall get your comeuppance tomorrow. And all you girls who chose to avoid me and not hang out with me, you will pay for doing so. You refused to show me love, and now I will make you suffer in the most painful way possible."

After around seven minutes of nonsensical ranting, Garrett Lowe concluded his video with one more twisted laugh. In all, he made three such laughs through the course of those seven minutes. Being raised around Hollywood movies and your father's superhero comics must really get to you.

After finishing up the video, there was nothing but a sick feeling in my stomach—a feeling of discomfort that I had never felt before in my life. My mind couldn't fathom the thought of this troubled kid being a real live person. People like this were supposed to exist only in the movies. Though, as the local news said, he did create his own horror movie yesterday afternoon. Talk about life imitating art.

Despite the pangs of terror and shock lingering throughout my body, I decided to look through the rest of Garrett's YouTube channel to uncover some of the other videos that he made before his shooting spree. In one video, he enjoyed a beautiful beach view, until he caught a happy couple cuddling and kissing and ranted, among other things, "There they go again, kissing each other. Absolutely disgusting of them. Just infuriating."

Many of his other videos included glorifications of his perceived greatness, sporting titles such as "I'm a Boss." In other videos, he flaunted various expensive items he'd acquired from his life growing up around Hollywood, like a multi-thousand-dollar TAG Heuer watch he bought on a trip to Paris for the international premiere of the latest movie about Beacon, Wonder Comics' flagship character and franchise. There were videos in which he ranted about how wretched he viewed humanity to be, and others peppered with offensive slurs aimed at people with mental disabilities, including the R-word.

And then, of course, there were all his videos where he complained about how miserable his life was, sulked over the rejection he claimed he'd had from his peers, or whined about never getting any girls. Oftentimes, all three in one video.

In one video that I watched, Garrett filmed a girl around his age in the distance, walking along the beachside walkway that lined my high school. "Look at this fine, perfect blond vixen," he narrated, speaking in the same creepy voice he used in his "Reckoning" video. "Look at that incredible body, those amazing legs. This is the girl of my dreams. Why does she not like me? Why can't I ever have her?" He zoomed in on the girl's face, and—oh my God, the girl in that video was me.

The Manzanita High School shooter was secretly stalking me. I couldn't believe he had a crush on me, either. I'd never even met or talked to the guy before in my life, for heaven's sake. And he had to creep on me while I had short shorts and flip-flops on, too. I felt so violated.

The fact that the Manzanita shooter liked me gave me a sense of guilt. *Am I one of the reasons that Garrett Lowe sank into a massive hole of darkness that he responded to by gunning down several innocent classmates?* I thought to myself. *Would Garrett not have shot ten people at my school dead if I had talked to him to see what was going on with him? Would Lizzy still be alive if I had helped him in his darkest moments?*

As if the videos that I watched weren't enough to frighten me to an unimaginable degree, my mind pondered the possibility that they might be only the tip of the iceberg regarding the dark material on Garrett Lowe's YouTube channel. Videos that provided a gaze into the mind of an emerging teenage sociopath. I couldn't imagine what it must feel like to watch the rest of those videos. Anyone with the guts to watch all of them would've hated the world in an instant.

I didn't know why I thought it was a good idea to watch that awful "Reckoning" video. Let alone discover the rest of the dark, dreadful videos populating his YouTube channel. As dusk approached, I knew I was bound to lose a lot of sleep that night.

It wasn't enough that I had to cope with the aftermath of the shooting and the pain of watching my best friend die in front of my eyes, but I also had to deal with the lingering shock from viewing Garrett Lowe's YouTube videos, in which he stalked me and made creepy comments about my body. The resulting roller coaster of emotions from the past two days spoiled my appetite during our family dinner. It was noticeable enough to my parents that I was having a hard time with my favorite family meal, Beyond Meat–brand vegan schnitzel. Typically, I would've eaten it all in five minutes or so, but not this time around; all I could manage was half of my vegan schnitzel and two bites of my salad.

After an awkward meal in which I hardly uttered a word, I just wanted to take a walk on the beach by myself. I told my mom and dad that I was going to sleep, but really, I slunk out of the house for a bit at 11:00 p.m. I was in dire need of alone time, and watching the waves of the Pacific Ocean rise and fall late at night was the perfect form of mental remedy for my introverted self.

With classes canceled for all of next week to give students some time to mourn and deal with any trauma they were experiencing, I had more freedom than usual to stay up late and sleep in the following morning, so however long I stayed up wasn't as consequential as usual. Plus, the closest beach to us, West Beach, was only ten minutes away from our house, and I didn't plan on being away long enough for my parents to start being suspicious about me being out so late at night. I still needed my sleep, even on an extended weekend. I may have been going through plenty of crap, but like my favorite superheroes, I was going to be brave and face whatever fears might have crept up on me.

Once I settled on a spot on the beach that I liked, I set down my beach towel. I took off my Rainbow flip-flops and put my hoodie up to keep myself concealed. I sat back, relaxed my shoulders, and observed and listened to the ocean waves.

Normally, the sound of the waves would be a boon to my mental well-being. Even after sixteen years living near the ocean, they never got old. But I'd been in such anguish over the past forty-eight hours that even the sounds of those waves felt meaningless to me now.

Although the lights around my neighborhood were almost all off, lights coming from other corners of town were obscuring the night sky a bit. But they weren't enough to block the brightest objects in the night sky, including the most notable object tonight: a shooting star. It was no ordinary shooting star, either. It had a glittering rainbow-colored glow to it, something I'd never seen from any shooting star before.

I knew it was the most cliché thing to make a wish when a shooting star passed by, but as they say, desperate times call for desperate measures. So . . .

"Shooting star, please bring superpowers to this world. Superpowers like what heroes and heroines have in comic books," I said to the shooting star, speaking to it as if it was a living, breathing being. "I'm tired of feeling helpless. I'm tired of people having no way out of hopeless situations, having no one to save them." And as a tear seeped out of my eye, I finished, "We need superpowers in this world. We need superheroes. People who can come in and save the day with ease."

After the shooting star exited the late night sky, I put on my headphones and opened up the Spotify app on my phone. As if trying to be more cliché, I decided to play the song "Save the World" by Swedish House Mafia. Now my body was able to relax a little bit and feel more soothed.

There was no better song to express my mood over the past forty-eight hours than that one. And through every second and word of the song, I clung on to any faint hope that my Wonder Comics fantasies would indeed become a reality.

CHAPTER

2

In response to Thursday's events, Manzanita High School canceled all classes until the following Thursday to give students and faculty members more time to grieve. Even other schools in the Santa Barbara Unified School District canceled all their classes for that entire time period. Manzanita's campus was now a temporary crisis counseling center, and everything going on with me and my community felt so unreal. Classes still happened online while the pandemic was going on, and they did the same whenever there were major wildfires in the Santa Barbara area; this time around, there were no classes or other school activities at all. The only event coming up at Manzanita before the resumption of school was the memorial service being held on Tuesday in honor of those who lost their lives in the shooting. Thank goodness for this Memorial Day weekend; more time for me to get through the seven stages of grief. As well as catch up on all the newest comics, of course—the perfect escape for me from the harsh, unforgiving world known as real life.

The first thing I did when I woke up Saturday morning was think back to the wish I made on the shooting star the previous night. I knew it was ridiculous for someone my age to think that something like that could magically come true. But still, was it possible that I now lived in a world of superheroes where people used their powers to ensure that no criminal or dictator could ever hurt anyone again?

Don't be ridiculous, Jessica, my mind told me. *That kind of shit only happens in fairy tales and Disney movies. There's no way it could have come true in real life. Real life is nothing but a never-ending series of events where mass murderers get their way and prejudice toward women, minorities, homosexuals, and the disabled is a way of life. It's an awful world out there; why bother thinking that any semblance of hope will make life better in these tough times?*

But hey, it didn't hurt to find out. Positive moments can emerge in our supposedly cruel world, after all. We just don't hear about them enough in the news.

Following a rather silent breakfast by myself with my parents at work, I stepped out onto the grass of my front yard, barefoot and still in my pajamas. With no one outside on the street but me, it was a perfect time for me to confirm if, indeed, I had superpowers.

I took up a relaxing pose before making a few emphatic hand motions, trying to imitate the action of firing a beam or ball of energy out of my hand, making sure to aim skyward in case I was able to do so. But nothing came out. All I did was look silly, and I would have gotten more than a few glances if there were people around the neighborhood.

But wait. Perhaps it wasn't the ability to shoot beams of energy that I gained. Maybe the shooting star granted me super strength.

As silly as it was, I put my arms around my next-door neighbor's car parked by their curb. A slight tinge of hope sifted through my veins . . . but my 100-pound body still felt every ton of weight packed into all that steel. With all the force I could, I continued to try to lift the car in my arms, but I still didn't feel more powerful than a locomotive. At least my neighbor wasn't there to give me weird looks at me for my pathetic attempts to lift his blue Volvo up into the air.

Instead of outwardly exhibiting my obvious inner disappointment, all I could do was giggle like a weirdo. But I still wasn't willing to give up on the possibility that my wish may have come true. So I stepped back into the grass of my front yard and relaxed every nerve in my body, attempting to tap into something again. After a few seconds, I started to feel lighter. My neighbor's Volvo began to hover off the ground as I turned my focus back to it. Soon enough, my feet came off the earth, too. I couldn't explain what was happening around me, but it felt great.

Not only was I levitating in the air, but so was a multi-thousand-pound object in front of me. This kind of phenomenon should only be possible in the depths of space or on the moon.

Still afloat in the air, I made sure to place my neighbor's car back on the street, using my mental power to let it gently descend onto the road. I didn't feel like going back down to the grass myself; it was the most liberating feeling not just being up in the air like this, but also knowing that I did gain not just one comic book power, but several of them. That my wish did indeed come true.

While still in the air, I raised my arms to the sky and got into my best flying superhero pose to test out if I could fly as well. Once more, I relaxed and tried to tap into some part of my mind that would allow me to move through the air. After a few seconds, I started to feel myself gliding through the air, like I was paragliding without the actual paraglider. I was so giddy about being able to fly like my favorite superheroes for the first time that I giggled like a little girl during my first few seconds above the ground.

I only glided within the vicinity of my house so as to not catch too many people's eyes. I started off slow since it was my first time flying, but picked up a bit more speed as I spent more time airborne. As I surfed through the air, I truly felt like a comic book hero. I could only imagine how my favorite Wonder heroes would've felt, seeing me become one of them.

When I returned to the ground, I became curious to find out if others at my school gained comic book powers, too. If my wish for a world of superpowers did come true after all. My immediate instinct was to contact Orlando and Charlotte first to see if they now had powers themselves. Before doing so, I went back into my house and took some time to brush my long blond hair. After a few seconds of brushing, I slipped on my Rainbow flip-flops at the doorstep, then headed out the door and to Charlotte's house. I flew there, of course, now that I could come to their houses in style using my new comic book powers. The thought of others in the town looking up at me and noticing how strange it was that a human could fly without the need for assistance didn't matter to me; I was enjoying my first experience with self-powered flight too much to care about that.

Both Charlotte and Orlando lived walking distance away from where our high school was, but farther from the beach than me and in different neighborhoods. Thus, going to their houses made for a nice test drive for my brand-new flying ability. I always enjoyed my hometown's natural beauty, but being able to soar through the air blessed me with even better views of the city than ever before. Even the views from UC Santa Barbara's Storke Tower that Larson once described to me couldn't beat this.

Charlotte was in her backyard, and from above, I could tell that she was practicing the routine for the big piece that I was to lead at the end of our dance show next month. Until I made a surprise appearance on the grass, her expression was stoic throughout; I couldn't tell if it was because she was so focused on her practice routine or because of the emotional turmoil from the past few days.

"Oh, geez, you scared me there, Jessica," Charlotte said. "Did you forget what knocking on the door means?"

"Oops, sorry about that, C. C. I should've texted you first to let you know, but I'm a little too giddy right now," I said. "By the way, as aspiring Manzanita Dance Troupe captain, I must say that your turns and flow look much more polished than the last time we went over that piece."

"Thanks, Jess. Been practicing this on and off for the past thirty minutes, so I better have made some improvement at this. If we're going to have an extended period of time off from school, I might as well spend whatever time I can to keep my dance mind fresh. The people of our town could use something to escape our current reality, and for me personally, this is the best way to do that."

"I appreciate the dedication from you there, Charlotte. You're going to help the dance troupe nail it in the next show."

"It's an honor to hear that from an aspiring dance troupe captain. Thanks again, Jess. Do you mind going over the whole thing with me again, by the way?"

"Oh, I'm not here to practice that piece with you, as much as I would like to. We can save that for when we return to school on Thursday."

"Okay, I guess that's fair. What did you want to come over here for? Does it have to do with why you're feeling so excited?"

"Yes, in fact. I know this is going to sound bizarre to you, but . . . I have superpowers now. That's how I was able to get to your backyard without needing to go through your front door or some random secret back passage. I can fly through the air, change the gravity around me . . . hopefully many other things, too."

". . . okay," Charlotte said, rolling her eyes.

"Really? That's your only reaction?" I teased Charlotte. "All the time you've spent around me and my obsession with superheroes and comics since we were kids, and that's all you say?" I giggled a bit as a further tease.

"If you were looking for a more enthusiastic response, my apologies. I just have trouble believing that you gained superpowers. It's scientifically impossible for anyone to gain abilities exceeding human capabilities, you know."

"Let's see if you have trouble believing this, then." With no obvious source of propulsion except whatever mysterious new magical forces now fueled me, I took off into the air like a rocket launching into space. I kept my eyes on Charlotte the whole time as I performed some somersaults and flips into the air like a Blue Angel, even performing a few aerial dance moves for good measure. Then when I descended back onto the ground, I alerted Charlotte, "You might want to be vigilant here. This might feel a little weird for you."

I ascended back into the air in a slow, gentle fashion, but this time, Charlotte floated up with me at the same time. She flailed her arms and legs around as if she was trying to find something to cling to while climbing up a dangerous cliff.

"What's happening . . .?" she asked.

"Oh, yeah, my gravity power allows me make things and people float off the ground now."

"I'm not going to fall and break any bones, am I? I don't want to suffer an injury that will force me to sit out our dance show; you know how I'd feel if I had to miss out on it . . ."

"You don't need to worry about that, C. C. I got this under control." I brought Charlotte and myself back down to the ground, as gently and slowly as I got us up into the air. When she got back onto solid earth, Charlotte's eyes were as wide as before.

"Okay, there's still no way for me to believe you have superpowers now," she said. "It's got to be some sort of divine intervention. Or maybe some sort of unusual natural phenomena going on through town that has somehow reached us for some reason."

"Whatever you say," I said with a shrug. "What about you—do you have any comic book powers now, Charlotte?"

"I'm thinking . . . no."

"Do you think you could perform some test to see if you can do anything extraordinary?"

"Pfft . . . please. I don't even know how I would be able to determine if I have any fancy powers or whatever strange thing is up with you. I need to get to studying for upcoming tests and finishing up school projects, anyway. Might as well make the most out of these days off that the school has given us."

"I guess that's fair. See you at the public memorial on Tuesday, C. C. I'll be heading to Orlando's now; I need to show him my powers, too. And see if he has powers himself as well." After sending Orlando a quick text to inform him that I was coming to his house, I took off into the air.

"You don't feel like walking to his place?" Charlotte called out.

"Nah, too boring for my tastes," I said to her, more loudly now that I was airborne. "I might as well take advantage of these new powers today, y'know."

"Whatever you say, Jess," Charlotte said, also with a louder tone. "Good luck on Tuesday if they ever bring you up to speak."

Even with the new view of his house that my new flight ability gave me, I didn't see Orlando outside like I did with Charlotte. So instead of landing in his backyard, I headed to the front of his house. When I landed by his doorstep, I delivered three knocks to his door before he opened it.

"Hey, Jess," Orlando greeted me. "You sure got here quick."

"That's because I can fly now, Orlando," I said. "Check this out."

Beaming a smile to Orlando, I relaxed again, following up with a calm ascent off the ground. I quickly noticed his gaping face before I performed a few loops through the air around his neighborhood, much like I did at Charlotte's place. And just to show off more, I stopped myself in the air for a bit so I could pull off another one of those emphatic hand gestures I had made earlier. This time around, something did magically come out of my hand: a light-yellow ball of energy that soared through the sky, like something straight out of *Dragon Ball Z*. The sight of it led me to deliver a few more energy balls from my hands, my gestures having more enthusiasm than the first few times.

As my flip-flops touched the ground again, Orlando maintained his gaping look. "Wow . . ." he said. "You're a superhero now."

"Yep, pretty much," I said. "Just in case you were skeptical about me saying that I have cool comic book powers now . . . well, there you go. Though, the magic energy balls were new."

"I hope you have many other awesome powers, too. Like controlling the weather, or reading minds, or maybe even warping time and space!" Orlando sounded like he was trying to out-geek me, a comic book and pop culture enthusiast for as long as I could remember. "But I'm getting ahead of myself. How'd you get your powers, anyway? What's your superhero origin story?"

"Well, you're going to find me silly for saying this . . . but I think my powers came from a wish I made last night when I saw a shooting star light up the sky. I made a wish for superpowers to become real because I got sick of people having no choice but to be helpless in the face of tragedies like the shooting. And so, here we are. I'm a Wonder character now. Or a Spectacle character to anyone who prefers their stuff over Wonder's."

"Wishing on a shooting star?" Orlando laughed. "Wasn't that cool when we were, say, five?"

"Hey, I was desperate, Orlando. It was a natural reaction for me to feel after watching Lizzy die in front of my eyes, so I couldn't help but resort to a classic childhood habit to make myself feel better."

"Oh man. You saw Lizzy get shot in the middle of all that chaos? I knew that she had been killed by the shooter but . . . wow. Not to sound insensitive, but that's a classic superhero origin story if I ever heard about one."

"It's okay, Orlando. You know I've read more than enough comics to know what you mean." A smile started to grace my face and the two of us laughed together. It was quite a nice feeling to experience with our first time seeing each other since the shooting. "Anyway, how have you been since the shooting? I haven't really had the time to speak with you much because of all the stuff I've been going through lately with Lizzy's death and all."

"It's been a hard few days for me, too. For all of us in general. It's heartbreaking that we lost so many of our fellow students. That Lizzy's no longer with us. She taught me so much about the world, helped me to become a more understanding person toward others. I'm not sure I'd be who I am today without her around." Orlando began to tear up, and then said, "I don't have much more to say."

My eyes flushed red and come close to shedding their own tears as I leaned in to give my closest guy friend a soft, comforting hug. For all the years that the two of us had been friends, it was the most compassionate hug I ever experienced with Orlando. The hug could've gone on for longer, but then it got interrupted when my phone buzzed in my pocket.

Despite my general reluctance to tune in to the latest news cycle, I turned on my phone's news notifications setting to keep in touch with the latest events happening in town and at Manzanita in response to the shooting. And the breaking news story that popped up on my phone was just about the least pleasant thing I could see right now.

BREAKING NEWS: Manzanita High School shooting suspect Garrett Lowe escaped from prison using new fire abilities he mysteriously gained this morning

Normally, I didn't turn on news notifications for my phone, but recent events made the past few days an exception. In this case, I was glad to have been informed fast of such an urgent situation.

"What's going on?" Orlando asked, surprised by the sudden end of our hug as I scrolled through my phone with desperation to find out how Garrett escaped.

"Garrett Lowe's escaped," I replied with jittery intensity in my voice. "Yes, the same Garrett Lowe who's the son of Scott Lowe. The same guy who shot dead ten of our classmates, including Lizzy, out of revenge for girls supposedly rejecting him. The police were able to catch and arrest him, but now he's broken out of prison."

"Oh my God . . ." Orlando's tone of voice didn't sound pleasant, either. "Does the news article mention where he went?"

I scrolled down the article to look for updates on Garrett's whereabouts. "It says that he fled to Leadbetter Beach. God, that's where my dad's surf store is located . . ."

"Well, I suppose you know what to do now that you have superpowers, Jess," Orlando said. "Do you think you'd be up to it? You just discovered your powers today, at least as far as I know, so I'm not sure about how well you'll fare with this being your first superhero fight."

"I wouldn't have it any other way, Orlando," I answered. "And whether Garrett wants to kill my dad, or some of our friends, or even those popular jerks, I can't have him take another life. I'm happy to call this my battle."

"Come back safe, Jessica. I'll be rooting for you."

"Thanks, Orlando." From there, I was off to Leadbetter Beach as I propelled skyward.

I wished for superpowers to become real so that I wouldn't have to feel helpless anymore, knowing that we would now have superheroes to save us from murderous criminals like Garrett Lowe. My wish came true, and I ended up gaining powers of my own. This was my chance to be a superhero. My chance to avenge the loss of my best friend and the carnage that my high school had to suffer at Garrett's hands. And I was not going to blow it.

CHAPTER

3

Approaching Leadbetter Beach from the air should've given me a majestic view of the Santa Barbara beaches. It wasn't a pretty sight this time around, however, as beachgoers ran in many different directions from streams of fire that ignited on and off, evoking unpleasant memories for me of watching students run for cover on the day of the Manzanita shooting. Those flames weren't coming from a flamethrower, either—they were coming from a person. A person whose entire body was on fire.

I dove down to where the flaming person was attacking innocent beachgoers. Before I could unleash my first attack at him, he caught a quick glimpse of me and shot a stream of fire at me. I dodged out of the way, but not without flinching. Right as he saw me, the fires surrounding his body faded away, revealing his face. As much as I refused to think so, my worst nightmare was right there in front of my very eyes.

"Garrett Lowe," I snarled at the young man.

"Actually, you can call me 'Rage' now, babe," Garrett said, walking toward me with a sinister smirk.

I wanted to deny that this was the same psychopath who gunned down ten of my fellow students and took my best friend's life. I wanted to believe that Santa Barbara police were able to restrain Garrett and keep him in the county prison. I wanted to believe that he was still just an angry kid with a gun and a callous attitude, possessing no special powers like mine. But nope. There he was, standing in front of me. And now he gained his own comic book powers, too.

"What are you doing here?" I asked Garrett, my eyes narrowing into a scowl. "You're supposed to be rotting in jail, deprived of the infamy you sought like every other mass shooter before you."

"Just finishing what I started, bringing justice to those who ruined my life," Garrett replied. He unleashed another torrent of flame at a pair of blond girls, provoking shrieks from both of them and causing them to sprint away from their beach spot. I didn't recognize the two girls; they most likely didn't attend my high school, and they looked like they were college age. But based on what he stated in his "Reckoning" video on YouTube, Garrett didn't seem to mind targeting any pretty girl he saw around him, whether or not he had some personal connection with her.

"And what are you doing here? Auditioning to become Santa Barbara's resident superhero?" Garrett chuckled and said, "I see you got fancy powers, too."

"And unlike you, I'm going to use them for the right purposes. That starts with putting you back in your place."

"Pfft, you need to quit reading those superhero comic books, Jess. We don't have heroes who rescue others from the vilest humans and other perils in this world. Violence and carnage are the way of humanity. That's just the way real life is—there are no Hollywood endings, Jessica Summer."

"Oh, look who's talking. The son of the world's most famous comic book mogul himself. Do you even read any of the comics that your dad creates? Or watch any Wonder movies?"

"Hey, at least I know how to differentiate between fiction and reality. You don't seem to want to, Jessica. You prefer to live in denial of the sad state of our broken society."

"That doesn't mean I can't maintain hope. I can tell that you like me a lot, which I'm guessing is why you decided to attack near my dad's surf shop. Don't get me started on that video where you stalked me, either." Garrett didn't react at all to a single word that I said. "Instead of fulfilling your fantasies about me, how about I suggest a date with my friend, karma." I floated up into the air and hovered above the sand with my arms spread out as each of my hands emitted a ball of yellow light.

To my surprise, Garrett didn't show immediate interest in fighting me as he turned his attention back to the crowd of panicking beachgoers. Specifically, he brought his focus to a tall, lanky guy with wavy brown hair in a white tank top and gray board shorts and a petite girl with golden blond hair dressed in a seafoam-green bikini. Even as they dashed away, I recognized their faces right away, and it already worried me that Garrett was going after them.

"Actually, how about I take care of some unfinished business first?" Garrett said to me. "There are two certain people who I've wanted dead more than anyone else in this godawful world. So glad they're here today; perfect timing for them to meet my wrath."

Those two kids—Darren Owens, the star wide receiver and resident jock of my graduating class at Manzanita, and his best friend Melissa Snyder, the queen bee of our class— were the bane of my existence at school. Normally, I couldn't stand them and the arrogant popular kids that they hung out with, especially with how much they liked to mock nerds and outcasts like me. However, knowing the specific types of people that Garrett was targeting according to his "Reckoning" video, I couldn't let him hurt these two.

As Melissa and Darren ran by each other's sides at the same pace, Garrett caught up to them from behind and struck Darren in the right shoulder and the side of his chest bared by his tank top with a fireball the size of a basketball, causing him to tumble down and clutch his shoulder. The fireball provoked a shriek from Melissa, who flinched and started to run off further into the distance as Garrett continued to chase after her. Fortunately, I knocked him off his feet by firing a quick energy ball at him before he could strike her, sending him flying a good distance before plummeting back onto the sand.

Now in the clear, Melissa stopped where she was, with Darren writhing in pain some distance across from her but still able to stand up. With Garrett down on his shoulder, she spotted my face, unable to comprehend what was going on around her.

"Did you just save me from that fiery madman?" she asked. "With . . . whatever it was you just did?"

"Yes. That was me," I responded. "And that fiery madman was the mass shooter from last Thursday. He broke out of prison today, and declared his intention to slaughter as many pretty popular girls as possible in a YouTube video he posted a few days ago. And he's targeting you and Darren in particular because of your popularity."

Melissa rushed to me to give me a big hug. Even though I just saved her life from the Manzanita shooter, and I was quite glad to have done so, this hug would've been a lot nicer if it wasn't with the biggest bitch in my class.

When our hug ended, Melissa said, "Sorry, I forgot your name. I don't believe I see you around often. Do you even go to my school?"

"Jessica Summer," I answered. "And yes, I go to Manzanita, too."

"Oh yeah. The loser geek girl whose dad owns the local surf shop." Ah, there was the Melissa Snyder I was more familiar with.

"And I don't need you to introduce yourself to me as Melissa Snyder. I can tell that quite a lot of people at our school like you." There was no time for any further trash talk between pop culture nerd and class princess as we had more important issues to deal with. "Anyway, where's Darren? I hope he's okay."

Darren dashed to where we were standing, but it was no ordinary wide receiver sprint. He reached our position in what must've been a fraction of a millisecond. While his overall physical condition was okay, the damage that Garrett inflicted on him was evident from the dark smears on his chest, shoulder, and tank top.

"Sorry I kept you waiting for a bit, babes," Darren said. "I would've gotten here sooner, but it took me a bit to recover enough from that fireball that hit me. Really hurt like a bitch."

"Dude . . . how did you get here so fast, D. O.?" Melissa asked, referring to Darren by his nickname on campus. "It's like you . . . appeared in a flash."

"I can't explain why, and I don't know how I just did that," Darren replied. "But it looks I can run like Sonic the Hedgehog now." With a more arrogant tone, he continued, "Man, I'm going to be even more of a stud on the football field next fall! Imagine how much more the chicks will fall in love with me with this sweet new speed I have."

"Yep, you're certainly an asshole version of Sonic the Hedgehog now." Maybe I shouldn't have spoken up there, because I just provoked

Darren to say something crude about me, something he often did when he saw me.

"Hey, fancy seeing you here, Blondie," Darren said. "Lovin' the hot pink nail polish; it goes well with your pj's." Melissa sometimes forgot I existed, but Darren recognized my face and my hair in an instant. It had to be a guy thing, man.

"No time for another cutesy comment, Darren," I said. "We have more serious issues to deal with here." As if everything going on around me wasn't stressful enough, I had to deal with not one, but two guys voicing their over-the-top affection for me. And one of those guys just tried to kill the other. Talk about an eventful morning.

Speaking of the other guy, the disgruntled senior at our high school who now went by Rage reemerged in front of us, having gotten back on his feet. He ignited his entire body on fire, now a living, walking being of flame.

"Dude . . . what did you burn me for?" Darren said to Rage. "Do you ever consider chilling out? It can be nice for your mental health."

"Darren Owens and Melissa Snyder." The looks on their faces indicated that they were stunned to find out that Rage knew their names. "I've been waiting to get my revenge on you two. The two most popular and most obnoxious kids at my school who get all the glory that I deserve. I wish I would've been able to shoot you two dead two days ago . . . but like they say, better late than never." The flames surrounding Rage's body intensified, as did his scowl.

I caught Rage glaring at Melissa as he spewed a stream of fire in her direction. By reading his first move on time, I jumped in front of Melissa to protect her and instinctively deployed a bubble of transparent energy in front of my body for the first time, neutralizing Rage's flames. At this point, it seemed that my powers became second nature to me; even though I was using them for the first time, it helped having knowledge of how superpowers tended to work from all the comics, shows and movies that I'd read and watched in my life, allowing me to grasp my new abilities with relative ease.

For each stream of flame that Rage aimed at Melissa, I flickered the energy field surrounding me on and off. I could feel my confidence building in this fight, even with the dread and trauma that Rage incited in me. The fact that he was my idol's son was the last thing that crossed my mind whenever I saw his smug face.

Rage decided to shift his attention toward Darren, but as he unleashed a torrent of flame at him, Darren dodged out of the way in a flash.

"You'll have to try a little harder to catch me," Darren bragged. "I can zip like lightning now, don't you see?"

Rage continued to hurl fireballs at Darren's feet, but none of them came close to touching him. Darren zigzagged through the sand, his jolts too much for Rage to keep up with. His supersonic antics distracted Rage enough for me to fly from behind and land a fist on the back of his head once the flames around him disappeared due to his apparent exhaustion from his fruitless attempts to hit Darren. I didn't pack the most strength, but the momentum and speed at which I approached Rage were enough for my fist to leave a tingling imprint on his head.

"Damn, that felt good," I said.

Rage clutched his head where I struck him and turned, maintaining focus in his glowering eyes. "Not half bad, Jessica Summer," he said. Then he let out another terrifying laugh. "Now let me get back at those two shitheads. You're standing in my way, babe."

Darren dashed back with Melissa by his side to the beach spot where they sat before Rage attacked, doing so in a split second with the help of his new super speed. Still unlit, Rage chased after them, but not before I channeled a long beam of yellow light at him, knocking him off course again. I could've caused some considerable damage around me with that attack, but luckily, almost all of the crowd that was at the beach left, giving me enough space to be careful with my powers. In an ironic twist, Rage made my job a lot easier by scaring off most of the beachgoers.

Before I could execute another attack and finish the job, a stream of flame struck my waist, eliciting a piercing shriek from my vocal cords. For a brief moment, I soaked in the sting of pain. Then Rage leaped at me and landed a punch on my nose.

"Sorry, hot stuff," he said to me. "I regret having to inflict pain on the girl of my dreams. But you've left me no choice, Jessica."

Rage's brief talk gave me a chance to fight back. Taking advantage of my ability to fly, I swooped up and unleashed a furious kick to the back of his head from behind. Despite my lingering pain, I managed to give Rage a decent knock with my golden-yellow aura empowering my kick. But then Rage set himself aflame again, turned around, and rammed me, sending me flying forward.

My body crashed into one of the beach parking lots, but I was still able to battle back. I got back up and fired more energy beams at Rage, but he was able to absorb the beams with the flames hugging his body. The fiery aura surrounding his body grew larger, enabling his punches and kicks to hurt even more.

With my greater variety of powers, I did my best to retaliate and counter Rage's attacks. But my abilities didn't have the same oomph that they did before. As our fight continued, my body lost more fuel, allowing Rage to inflict more burns on me.

"You just got your powers, too. How are you starting to manhandle me?" I asked.

"Simple. You can't underestimate the power of anger and hatred," Rage said. "Regardless of how long I've had these powers, those feelings are enough to make me a force to be reckoned with. Just as a handsome epitome of perfection like me should be."

I shouldn't have been losing ground against this madman, but I was. As the fight returned to its original site on the sands next to my dad's surf store, Summer Sea Shack, a menacing fireball rushed toward me, enormous enough to knock me down onto the sand.

I wanted to battle back; I couldn't let this monster get away. But my body had a difficult time even lifting a finger, as if I was bathing in a pool of ash.

"Ah yes, I have new life in me," Rage said, lighting his right hand on fire just to show off and display his new power. "With these flames, I can bring real punishment to all the slutty girls who've rejected me. They can now suffer just as I've suffered; just like they will for all eternity when they are sent to Hell."

"And *you* don't think you'll be going to Hell for all the lives you've taken, all the families you've brought untold grief to?" I rebutted.

"I'm just getting started, my princess. Now, where is that blond slut and her football pal . . ." Rage scoured the beach around him, trying to find Darren and Melissa. However, it appeared that they'd left; I didn't see their beach towel anywhere, nor did I see any of their other belongings. Given the near-death experience they just went through, I wouldn't have blamed them for wanting to go back home.

Although I was aching like I never had before, I still had room to deliver a sly comment toward Garrett. "Darren can give Trailblazer a run for his money with his speed now," I said, referring to Spectacle Comics' iconic speedster hero. "So I'm sure you can imagine why you failed to catch him and Melissa."

True to his new villainous identity, Garrett's rage literally ignited as his body lit aflame again. He threw out his frustrations at the nearest bikini-clad girl he could find, but not before I could alert her.

"Look out behind you!" I cried to the girl, who was sitting by herself. Thanks to my warning, she scampered away from the waves of flame that Garrett blasted at her. As his face morphed into a more stoic expression, Garrett turned his head back to me.

"I may not have gotten those two obnoxious jerks this time around, but I have bigger plans in mind," he said. "I will make sure that humanity finally shows its love to Garrett Lowe, now also known as Rage. Just as they're supposed to. Just as they should have. And you will be by my side to witness my rise to glory, Jessica Summer."

"And how exactly do you plan to do that, Garrett?" I asked, still unable to get back on my feet.

"Oh, you'll see. And when you do, it will be wonderful." And with a twisted kind of steely determination, Garrett ran off.

—∞—

When I got back up, I walked to the patio that graced the exterior of Summer Sea Shack, taking a seat to rest while my pain continued to linger. I second-guessed choosing to come here, knowing the possibility of my dad coming out and seeing me wounded and bruised, but this was the closest resting spot I could find. I didn't have the energy to walk anywhere else. Plus, Summer Sea Shack was a comfortable, familiar place for me. It wasn't just the shop that my dad owned; it was also a popular hangout for Manzanita students. In fact, many kids at my school recognized me as the daughter of the guy who ran Summer Sea Shack.

Sure enough, just before I got to Summer Sea Shack, there was my dad, walking in the distance through the sands of Leadbetter Beach rather than where he usually was in his office. When he saw me, he stopped walking and spread out his arms to signal an embrace, and I walked into his arms, slower than usual due to my aches and pains.

"Jessica, are you okay?" he said. "There was screaming, and a commotion outside, but by the time I came outside I couldn't tell what exactly was going on . . . what happened to you, cupcake?"

"It was the shooter at my school," I replied, the tone of my voice noticeably low. "Garrett Lowe, Scott Lowe's son. The police arrested him after the shooting, but he escaped. They couldn't restrain him because he now has deadly fire abilities. And he came over here to kill two of my classmates from Manzanita with his new powers. I gained powers of my own, too, and I used them to save my classmates. But then he beat me to a pulp."

"You two gained superpowers? Is that why there were fireworks going on at the beach?"

I took up a cross-legged meditation pose, relaxing my body and my gaze as Dad and I started to rise up into the air, with a golden-yellow glow that I emanated for the first time surrounding me as I did so, making me look like a *Dragon Ball Z* Super Saiyan. To further prove to Dad that I had comic book powers, I projected a small, bright yellow beam of light upward from my right hand.

"I hope this isn't making you feel weird, Dad," I said while we remained afloat.

"It isn't," he said. "Watching you hovering in the air like this, it all feels . . . incredible. Just make sure no one around you is looking."

"Eh, lots of people at the beach are sure to have witnessed the duel I engaged in earlier. So this may not look as strange to them as you might think." I returned the gravity around us to normal, leading the two of us to make a gentle descent back onto the sand beneath us.

"You weren't kidding after all," Dad said. "All those comics and movies you fell in love with, and I never imagined you would become just like their characters. I never thought I would say that my daughter's a superhero . . . but here I am."

"*Tried* to be a superhero would be a more accurate way to put it," I said with regret. "I tried stopping Garrett, Dad . . . but he got away. And now I fear he may do even worse things than what he did last Thursday. Who knows what he could be up to next?"

As my eyes started to redden, Dad wrapped me in his arms, and I returned the favor. The thought of Dad seeing me like this by his store was nerve-wracking at first. But now I was glad he could come over to comfort me after what I just went through.

"Let me take you home, Jess," Dad said. "We can buy a few things to treat those burns along the way."

"Well, it is a good thing that your work is just a short walk away from where we live," I joked. I planted a kiss on my dad's forehead before he drove me to the closest pharmacy to our house.

After Dad and I purchased the items we needed to treat my burns and bruises, we got back home, headed to my parents' room, and met up with Mom, who took weekends off from her job as a marine biologist, save for the occasional morning where she performed clarinet tunes for a local coffee shop called Dart Coffee Co. Dad already informed her through text that he would be leaving work earlier than usual in order to get me home, and that I needed treatment for a number of injuries. But before Mom could greet us, she was taken aback by how bad my injuries were.

"My goodness, what happened to you, darling?" Mom asked when she saw all the wounds on numerous parts of my body.

"Long story," I replied. "But to sum it up, the shooter who attacked my school Thursday escaped from custody at the county prison, and I tried to stop him, only to suffer a really bad beating from him."

Mom paused for a few seconds before trying to find her words again. "I heard about that earlier on the news . . . So awful to hear . . . and only two days after he went on his shooting rampage and killed Lizzy, too . . ." She briefly paused in order to let the news settle in. "Why would you try to pick a fight with a man as dangerous as him? You were being a bit reckless there, don't you think?"

"I had to put a stop to him so that he wouldn't take any more lives like he did at my school. I was confident that I had the power to stop him because I got all these incredible abilities like what my favorite superheroes have. If you don't believe me, check out the news."

"Oh goodness, that was you on the news today? I saw a story about a flying teenage girl who got into a fight with the Manzanita shooter after he mysteriously gained the ability to control fire and tried to attack Leadbetter Beach. Reporters were describing it as something straight out of a superhero movie. You were the teenage girl in that fight?"

Shrugging my shoulders—though only slightly due to the pain I was feeling in parts of my shoulders and arms—I answered, "Well, it's not like I was going to avoid the headlines after members of the local media were bugging me and Dad on our way to the pharmacy . . . Apologies, that was not the best time for sarcasm there. But yes, that flying teenage girl in the news was me, Mom. I have superpowers now."

Before Mom could fully process what I just said, I opened the window of my parents' room and jumped out of it, causing a brief but understandable freakout from her. From my parents' window, I ascended into the air and performed a quick flight over the neighborhood, returning to the room in around four seconds. When I returned to the room, the same golden-yellow aura that I generated at the beach while demonstrating my powers to Dad surrounded my body once more. Even if I did cause my mom to panic a little by leaping out our window, that was a pretty awesome stunt I had just pulled off, especially while still battling the pain I had from my burns. Yet another reason to be stoked to have comic book powers.

"Geez, you scared me there for a bit, Jessica Alexandra Summer," Mom said with her right hand over her heart. "I thought—"

"It's okay, you never had anything to worry about, Mom," I said. "Although this cool yellow glow I now have is new. I feel like I'm getting it from the sun." I took a look at my arms and feet to examine the solar aura that surrounded me before it slowly faded out, causing my wounds to stand out again.

"She can shift gravity around her too, hon," Dad said to Mom. "And fire bright balls and beams of light as well, she told me."

A glimmering smile took shape on my mom's face, which was a pleasant surprise for me since I wasn't sure how she would react to hearing that I now had comic book powers—if she would have an adverse reaction to me having potentially dangerous superhuman abilities. "I never thought I'd see the day that my daughter would get to live her superheroine dreams," she said. "Of all the people in the world, I couldn't be happier that you, of all people, would obtain extraordinary abilities that shouldn't even be real. But we do need to get back to reality for a bit: What were you thinking, Jess?" I shuddered a bit hearing those words as Mom's tone of voice started to display more concern. "You could've been killed; we could've lost you after you lost Lizzy . . . Having abilities like that can come with serious consequences, you know."

"After what he did to my school and to Lizzy, I had no choice but to play the role of superhero against Garrett," I answered. "If I now have incredible powers, I have to find a way to make the most of them. And that was the best way I felt I could harness them after hearing of his escape from jail. My first superhero battle didn't go as I dreamed it would. But I did what I could, and at least I prevented Garrett from claiming any more lives."

"Well done on your part, cupcake," Dad said. "But your mom has a point. You can't assume you'll get away with everything just because you have superpowers now. It's like they say in one of those comic franchises you love so much—what was that line again, Jess?"

"Those with power must not be reckless," I told Dad. "It's the most famous line of the Beacon comics. And it's something I plan to keep in mind as I learn to adjust to these new powers. I promise you."

"That's a good sign to hear that declaration from you," Mom said. "I bet Lizzy would be proud to see who you are now." My sadness reemerged for a brief moment upon hearing the mention of Lizzy's name.

"Thanks, Mom; it means a lot to hear that," I said. "Now let's get to patching up my wounds."

"Yeah, let's," Dad said.

As my parents started the process of wrapping bandages around my burns, I took the time to reflect on how amazing it was that I could now do things that normal humans could never be capable of. Of all the people in the world who could receive powers from a silly shooting star wish that I made the night before, I was one of those people. It sucked that my school's shooter was one of those people, too, and that he was an even greater threat than before as a result. But since both of us had powers, that made us even, just the way it should be.

I would've loved to be more ecstatic in informing my mom that my greatest comic geek fantasies had come true; alas, current circumstances didn't permit that. Still, the emergence of my newfound extraordinary abilities granted me a sense of empowerment that I never would've imagined having in my life, especially in the minutes and hours that followed the Manzanita shooting. Having abilities that would help me fit into the Wonder or Spectacle Universes like a glove gave me the optimism for the future that I'd needed since the tragic events of May 23.

My very first superhero battle wasn't the instant success that the comics and movies led me to expect. But I just discovered my powers for the first time today; in no way had I gained full mastery over them yet. So it was natural that there was a lot more work for me to do before I could feel confident enough with playing the role of hero. On the bright side, I did save numerous lives from Garrett Lowe's latest mass murder attempt two days after he murdered ten of my fellow students. While I didn't completely stop him and return him to jail, preventing him from taking more lives still made my first attempt to be a superhero a success to some degree. It was a good thing that Garrett got too obsessive over targeting two particular people that time around. I got lucky that he didn't take any additional lives, but I wasn't sure I would be as lucky the next time around. Especially now that he'd become a lot more than a delinquent freak with a gun and a callous attitude.

CHAPTER

4

During football season, the atmosphere in my school's stadium would've normally been bursting with passion and excitement. On Tuesday afternoon, one day after Memorial Day, there was nothing but an eerie silence with the occasional peppering of loud crying, including mine. Not even the ocean view that blessed our stadium was enough to soothe the moods of mourning students and faculty members. It was an unusual experience that none of us had ever experienced as students.

Not only did my feelings of anguish and the aches and pains from my battle on Saturday continue to linger, but so did the shock from watching Garrett Lowe's pre-massacre manifesto and the venomous doses of misogyny that he infused into it. It was fair to say that the video only piled more trauma onto the trauma I'd already been feeling since last Thursday, and I was still wondering why I even watched it in the first place. Four days after watching them, I couldn't get the thoughts of Garrett's collection of deranged YouTube videos—my trip into his dark, troubled world—out of my head. They were only making me feel more nervous, as if I couldn't be nervous enough about having to make a speech in front of my whole school in memory of my slain best friend. And that went without mentioning how much of a shadow his escape from prison was casting over the memorial, bringing a sense of fear and concern to go with the pain and sorrow that his hatred and violence had brought us.

Four people spoke before me during the course of the hour-long memorial: a staff member, a teacher close to one of the murdered students, a fellow student, and the mother of another one of the slain students, who made a passionate plea to Congress for improved gun control and stricter federal gun laws. I was the last to speak, and having to wait only worsened my anxiety about speaking to everyone in attendance. I had a lot of pressure on me to make my speech worth listening to. And I didn't write anything in preparation; I was just going to speak whatever I could from my heart.

When Principal Warden called me up to speak, my eyes were already red and dotted by slight tears. I was wearing a black polo shirt and black trousers, dressing for this memorial in the same manner that I would for a more traditional funeral. I planned to wear this same outfit to Lizzy's private funeral on Wednesday night.

"I never imagined I would be up here, speaking in front of all of you during a period of immense mourning," I started my speech, with my voice already in full funeral mode. "It's all so unreal. And it's just not right. It's unfair, really." I said that last sentence as my widened eyes began to shed more tears.

"We here at Manzanita have the blessing of attending high school right by the beach. We have a campus that makes it onto lists of the top ten U.S. high schools with the most breathtaking views. Why? I ask. Why did our beautiful campus have to be the site of an act of senseless violence? Why did this have to happen to an amazing community of people like ours? Why did we have to lose ten of our own? We did nothing to deserve this."

After a brief pause to settle myself down, I continued on. "My best friend, Elizabeth Manchester, had her life taken in this heinous shooting spree," I said. "So to anyone else who lost a friend or loved one on May 23, and to anyone with a friend or relative currently fighting for their life as a result of this tragedy, I grieve with you. Just remember that you are not alone in your period of mourning." Applause followed before I moved on with my speech, and I took a moment to appreciate the sympathy from my school community.

"If the trend of media reports on mass shootings is any indication, the news will put forth the name of the shooter, but not the names of the innocent victims that the shooter took. I am here to ensure that the names of these wonderful souls won't be forgotten, ever. These ten innocent men and women were all very important people who were near and dear to us, and we must make sure they remain in our memories, even in death. Elizabeth Manchester, Jennifer Martinez, Nicholas Chow, Michelle Anderson, D'Shawn Carter, Rose Nguyen, Corey Jeffers, Derek Garcia, Lindsay Harris, Ellen Sugiyama, our hearts are with you and your families. And we promise that the brave people of Manzanita High School, young and old, will never forget any of you. Thank you."

I departed the podium to one more, louder round of applause from the crowd. I came very close to collapsing from grief, but not before some of my teachers lent me their arms in support to save me from completely falling and offered me some much-needed hugs. As I took my seat again, I thought about the massive applause I just received, which gave me a sense of accomplishment in speaking out the names of the ten lives lost to ensure that our school retained them all in our memories. Saving the best for last indeed.

As if being at Lizzy's private funeral the day after a public service of mourning at my school wasn't stressful enough, the fact that I failed to stop Rage's escape from prison cast a large shadow over the ceremony. The news of the Manzanita shooter's breakout was already common knowledge among those at the funeral, triggering every single negative emotion you could think of for each individual there, as if we weren't grieving enough already. After executing the latest mass shooting in America, using his new flame powers to escape from prison, and almost pulling off another murder spree, it was worrying to me what Rage would have in store next.

This funeral was bound to be a major source of discomfort for me, but the fact that I was standing out as a result of all the bandages draping the parts of my body Rage burned only added further discomfort for me. My fight with Garrett naturally made local news headlines, so at least people here were aware of where I got all my burns. Heck, the hugs I received from friends and family ached more than I would've liked as a result of my burn wounds.

Among those attending the funeral were Lizzy's parents, grandparents, and other family members; my parents and my older brother Larson, who was a junior at UCSB; Orlando's family, including a couple of members of his large extended family; Charlotte's immediate family; and myself. Orlando and Charlotte were also best friends with Lizzy alongside me. And never would I have imagined the three of us and our families gathering in mourning for our best friend. Together, the four of us attended comic conventions; held birthday parties; hit up local beaches; visited Wonder World, mine and Lizzy's favorite theme park in the world, a couple of times; and caught the midnight premiere of every single Wonder movie that had been released in theaters since 2019, to the dismay of our parents who didn't enjoy driving us to the movies on school nights. But this kind of scenario for our friendship would've never seen the light of day in my still-developing brain.

Never in my life did I imagine that I would be attending my best friend's funeral while I was still in high school, before even getting my driver's license. Because I was only sixteen, I never thought much about what my friends' funerals or my own funeral would look like. The thought of Lizzy's funeral occurring in the circumstance that it was right now had never crossed my mind once. How much more for Mr. and Mrs. Manchester? They didn't deserve to be going through the same things that the parents of the Sandy Hook and Parkland kids did after the shootings that claimed the lives of their own children. And neither did the parents and immediate family members of the nine other shooting victims.

It was easy for me to spot where Lizzy's parents were sitting, as Mrs. Manchester was wearing a black veil similar to the one that Jackie Kennedy wore at her husband's funeral following his assassination. It was difficult for me to have the guts to speak with them considering what they'd gone through. But I would've been insensitive by not doing so.

"Jessica," Mrs. Manchester shrieked, having sobbed a good bit. "It's so nice to see you!"

"Oh my gosh, same," I answered as I wrapped her in a big hug. "I'm so, so sorry for what you two have gone through. I can't imagine what the past few days have been like for you."

"We're sorry for you, too," Mr. Manchester said, also hugging me. Soon enough, the three of us gathered together in a group hug. Due to our overwhelming emotions, we remained in this hug for several seconds.

As I was hugging and sobbing with Lizzy's parents, I could feel a white, silvery glow flashing from my body, as opposed to the golden-yellow glow that I'd generated before. Lizzy's parents were so wrapped in our three-way hug that they didn't even notice the aura emanating from me. It must've been another one of my powers that I hadn't discovered yet, but I brushed it off like it was nothing; I had more important things to focus on, anyway. There wasn't even time for small talk between the three of us, as it would've been too difficult for us to proceed with the rest of the funeral.

—∞—

"It's obviously been tough for you guys these past few days, and for the Santa Barbara community as a whole. So I've worked hard to ensure that Ms. Manchester earns the best tribute to her life that she possibly can." So said the mortician to start off funeral services before we paused to hear Mr. and Mrs. Manchester's chosen tribute song. The surrealness of it all settled deeper into me, reinforcing that, yes, I was sitting here in a church, at sixteen years of age, attending my best friend's funeral. I needed to breathe and feel all the objects around me to recognize that all of this was indeed happening in real life.

When the song finished, it was Mrs. Manchester's turn to speak, with her husband by her side, holding her arm for support.

"Lizzy was an incredible beam of sunshine in our lives," she said. "She brought joy to countless others, too, including everyone in this room. And now, just like that, she's been taken away from us in a circumstance we could've never imagined. It's difficult beyond words for me to be up here, but I will try my best to speak about what made our only child so wonderful for us."

Mrs. Manchester took a deep breath, then exhaled. "It's the cruelest irony that Lizzy lost her life to someone with an extreme hatred of women, because in spite of her age, she was the most passionate women's rights advocate that my husband and I ever knew," she said. "In so many ways, she was wise beyond her years. A precocious writer, a straight-A student, an activist with the most optimistic attitude in the midst of some of the darkest times in human history. Her presence was a gift to this world. And that only makes her sudden loss all the more impossible for us to fathom."

Mrs. Manchester then started to choke up. "Our Lizzy's sudden passing has left a hole in our hearts that can never be mended," she continued. "And now, we are left with so many questions. Lizzy died far too young, and as such, I encourage all of you in this room to maintain our daughter's memory for the rest of your lives." Her tears intensified so much that she started to have trouble forming words as she ended her speech. "That's all I'm able to say for tonight. Thank you." Mrs. Manchester began to sob into her veil as her husband escorted her back to their seats, a soft round of applause blanketing them along the way.

As difficult as I knew this would be for Lizzy's mom, that was as beautiful of a speech as she could have made. It touched me so much that I felt I had a tough act to follow with my own speech.

This was the second time in the span of as many days that I was dedicating a mournful speech to my slain best friend. It was every bit as difficult and overwhelming as it was the first time around. And just like my speech for the public memorial at Manzanita, this eulogy was 100 percent unscripted.

"I still can't believe that I'm here, mourning my best friend's life at sixteen years old," I began, already choking on my first words. "Lizzy and I had known each other since we were toddlers. I always imagined that the two of us would grow old together, raise our families together, be the maid of honor at each other's weddings. I thought I was seeing the next J. K. Rowling in the making, a passionate fan fiction writer about to begin her first novel, one that I knew would have tremendous potential in the literary world. But I guess it wasn't meant to be." I needed to sniffle and take a pause before I could continue my eulogy.

"I'll never, ever forget you, Elizabeth Drew Manchester. I'll never forget our first-ever trip to San Diego Comic-Con last year, the countless sleepovers we had, the annoying laugh you'd always make, that time I sobbed on your shoulder reading *Looking for Alaska* for the first time. I won't even forget the very first time we met when we were three years old; that's how far back our friendship goes. Little did I know back then that it would be the beginning of something wonderful. And now . . . it's heartbreaking beyond words to have that something taken away just like that. Lizzy, I will miss you greatly, and life after you is going to be extremely difficult. But you will remain in my memories, always. You will remain in all our memories. Thank you for touching so many lives during your short time on this green Earth."

When I concluded my speech, the funeral audience delivered a round of applause for me. Then came the most difficult part: the viewing of Lizzy's body.

As the mortician opened the casket to reveal Lizzy's dead body, my cries became shrieks, or more accurately, a combination of the two. Upon seeing the corpse, I covered my mouth, then slid both of my hands over my eyes to avoid seeing it anymore. If not for Lizzy's parents' tears, which were indescribable to me at that moment, my own weeping would've filled the entire room. My legs collapsed to the ground, no longer able to straighten themselves. A few arms picked me up, giving me the support I needed just to stand up. I didn't know whose arms, because my emotions were too overwhelming for me to look behind. But I passed on my gratitude to those individuals, whoever they were.

I couldn't remember anything else that happened the rest of that night. It all passed by like a blur, my grief too much for me to recall anything after the casket viewing. No one my age should have to go through what I just went through. And it sure sucked that this was an experience for plenty of young Americans and American families before me.

CHAPTER

5

On Thursday, classes at Manzanita High School resumed for the first time since the shooting. While restarting school may have felt like a return to normalcy for me, it still wasn't right to return to campus.

What was normally a lively, laid-back high school that was blessed to enjoy classes and recess right by the beautiful Pacific Ocean was instead enveloped in an unusual silence. People's voices were softer everywhere I went, and tears were shed every now and then. And because of the news of the Manzanita shooter's escape from jail, a palpable fear hovered over our campus too, knowing there's a possibility that Garrett Lowe might try to pull off another attack. He already targeted two of our students for murder on Saturday, after all.

In the midst of this uncharacteristic sadness and anxiety, however, there was also plenty of heartwarming empathy and condolences going around. It was common for us to offer our closest friends in each of our classes hugs of sympathy, something we usually didn't do to start each school day. We were even hugging students that we didn't know very well, including those that were close to the shooting victims. So you could imagine how many hugs I received, even from students I'd never met.

But as much as I welcomed the extra love, my emotional state was still uneasy, anxiety-ridden, and guilty as a result of what I discovered on Garrett's YouTube channel six days before. The events of Lizzy's funeral and the public memorial the day before didn't make things any easier, the sobs and images of those two gut-wrenching ceremonies still fresh in my mind. Seeing the campus plaza for the first time since the shooting also triggered difficult flashbacks in my mind; it was where I found myself at the moment of the shooting, and where I watched Lizzy get shot and die in front of my eyes.

In the aftermath of losing my best friend, I was grateful to have two other very close friends in Orlando Gabriel and Charlotte Chen. Seeing each other at school for the first time since the shooting, we huddled together in the biggest group hug of our lives. Though we did see each other at Lizzy's funeral, I got a very different vibe seeing Orlando and Charlotte at school again. It wasn't enough to make my situation feel any better, but being around them sure helped.

"I can't believe I'm seeing you two here again," Charlotte said, her voice choked up. "It feels like a lifetime since the last time we were here together."

"How are your burn wounds feeling, Jessica?" Orlando asked as we broke away from our group hug. "I heard about what happened to you on the news. I hope our hug didn't aggravate anything."

"Still some progress to make with them, but they're getting better," I replied. "Nothing that Nurse Morris can't take care of."

Wanting to lighten the mood, Orlando joked, "I was tempted to ask you two how your week off was, but then I realized that it sucked too much to be worth discussing. Except for Jessica gaining cool powers, of course. Powers literally straight out of our favorite comics and movies." Charlotte's body language still screamed skepticism.

"Which reminds me, did either of you two gain comic book powers yourselves?" I asked Orlando and Charlotte.

"Let me see for myself," Orlando answered. "I've been excited to find out; I don't recall discovering anything since you came over to my house on Sunday." He assumed a fighting stance in the middle of the plaza, let out a light exhale, and then started to execute some very over-the-top martial arts moves. Complete with the full allotment of exaggerated grunts and screams, of course, including Liu Kang–esque shrieks here and there. He even did his best imitation of a Liu Kang-style bicycle kick—the fighting move, not the soccer move—during his little martial arts show. He didn't display any special auras, super-reflexes, or super-speed, though. With a large crowd of students still making their way through the plaza, many of them flashed some brief stares at Orlando, wondering what all the fuss was about. Charlotte was befuddled herself about what he just did, too.

"What was that supposed to be, Orlando?" she asked.

"I was just imitating what I've seen from Power Rangers episodes," Orlando said. "Eh, I suppose that doesn't actually count?"

"Well . . . not really," I answered. "Technically, I guess you could say the Power Rangers are superheroes, but they tend to rely on fancy fighting moves, mystical objects, and giant mechas to take down their enemies. But I wouldn't consider them to have any superhuman abilities that they can use without special assistance."

"Ah, drat," Orlando said in disappointment. "Oh well, at least I tried. How about you try, Charlotte?"

"I'm still not sure about this," Charlotte said. "But okay, I'll give it a try, just to make sure. Don't want you two bugging me about it all day anyway."

Charlotte relaxed herself while standing, trying to tap into . . . something. She attempted to fire things out of her hands, performed some martial arts moves, and even did some fancy gymnastics and handstands from her dance routines, all in a calmer and more low-key manner than Orlando's way-too-flashy extravagance. No special powers emerged from her, either. But she didn't seem to mind.

"It doesn't look like you have any comic book powers either, C. C.," I said.

"Dang it. I would've loved to have a pair of superheroes for best friends," Orlando said.

"You wouldn't mind being the lone muggle in our group?" I asked.

"Hey, nothing wrong with being ordinary. There's something cool that I would feel if I was a regular person with two superhero friends."

"To be honest, it's kind of a relief not having any special powers," Charlotte said. "Glad I don't have to worry about firing off anything dangerous or accidentally hurting anyone now."

"I wouldn't blame you there," I said to Charlotte as the three of us walked to our respective homerooms. "If I've learned anything from comics and movies, it's that powers like mine can either be a blessing or a danger to those around you if not used and handled carefully. And how fast one manages to grasp their superhuman abilities varies by person. I can't quite say I've mastered my own yet. But then again, I've only had them for five days."

As we made our way to our homeroom classes, I started to feel several stinging sensations throughout my body. They weren't at random spots, either; they were where each of my bandages were.

"Hey, are you okay, Jess?" Orlando asked. "Maybe you should've stayed home with all those burns and bruises you still have."

"Don't worry, I'm still fine, Orlando," I replied without sounding legitimate. "I can get through this. No way I was going to skip our first day back at school. Though I am surprised that these burns haven't healed up as fast as I expected."

It was inevitable that it was going to be a difficult and awkward day. As if the aftermath of his shooting wasn't enough to create an eerie vibe that none of us had ever experienced before, Garrett Lowe cast an even greater shadow over the school with his shock breakout from prison, coupled with the fact that he now had comic book powers himself. So after my homeroom teacher, Mr. Thompson, recorded my attendance for the day, I headed over to the principal's office to inform Principal Warden of the difficult news. I didn't care if I missed the first few minutes of my first period geometry class, either; speaking with the principal was a much greater priority right now with the safety of our school at stake.

Principal Warden tended to be difficult to get in contact with most of the time. But to my delight, he was available to speak to at the moment, having just wrapped up the announcements for the school day—ones which naturally came with a lot of difficulty and paid tribute to the victims of the shooting as well as those who suffered wounds that were grave enough to keep them in the hospital.

Before Principal Warden could utter a single word, I was quick to speak up first. "Thank goodness you're available, Principal," I told him.

"I'm glad we could talk with how hard times have been at our school, even more so with Garrett Lowe having escaped from prison."

"Likewise, Jessica," Principal Warden said. "Thank you for meeting up with me today."

"No problem, Principal. When I heard that Garrett broke out last Saturday, I rushed to where he was at Leadbetter Beach to try to stop him. I was able to prevent him from murdering two students, but I let him get away. And now he's on the loose, planning who knows what. Possibly something even worse than his shooting spree last week . . . he's even more of a threat now that he's developed fire-based superpowers."

Principal Warden remains quiet for a few seconds before speaking. "Thank you for informing me, Ms. Summer. I can't put into words how hard it's been for me to process the news of the shooter's escape. This is a devastating development for our school and for the town of Santa Barbara as a whole—a community which is normally peaceful but is now grieving. Our school must do what we can to keep Mr. Lowe subdued, and I will make sure to discuss this issue with the rest of the school staff. Thank you for your proactiveness, Jessica."

"My pleasure, Principal Warden. Garrett—who also now uses the name Rage as his new alias, like a comic book supervillain would—murdered my best friend Lizzy Manchester last Thursday, so it's my duty to play a role in preventing him from causing any more carnage and destruction. I can't let him claim another life."

"Ah yes, Lizzy. She was such a wonderful and wise student to be around. Such a tremendous loss for our school, even for those who didn't know her well. My condolences to you as well as Lizzy's family, Jessica. Her loss, and the loss of those nine other students, have left holes in our school that cannot be replaced. All of them such wonderful students that we were lucky to have."

"Thank you for your kind words, Principal Warden. And best of luck to you in taking care of the school in these dark times."

"You're welcome and thank you, Ms. Summer." Putting his right fist over his chest, he continued, "My heart will continue to be with you and all the other students who lost a friend or loved one last Thursday."

As I walked out of the office and to first period, which started in around five minutes, I couldn't help but note that Principal Warden didn't react at all to the news that Garrett gained superpowers. He also didn't say anything about me using my own superpowers to stop him, something that was common knowledge now that it's made several rounds on the news. Did Principal Warden not say anything about those important details because he was secretly as much of a comic book geek as me and thus didn't find superpowers being real to be that out of the ordinary? Or was he shocked about the fact that there were individuals with comic book powers now living in our very town? Garrett and I weren't the only ones, either. By now, Principal Warden very well might have witnessed Darren using his powers—knowing Darren, this was highly plausible—or perhaps even another student with superhuman powers that I didn't know of yet.

Thinking about this was a little odd, but it might have been more important than I was giving it credit for. This was Manzanita's school principal that I was talking about. And if there were more of us students with comic book powers, or even staff members with extraordinary abilities, then whatever response Principal Warden had to the presence of such beings would be crucial for our school's students.

—~—

"*This* is your new secret lunchtime spot?" Orlando said, looking around him at the sand surrounding the three of us and the majestic Pacific Ocean in front of our eyes.

"What, you're surprised to know that our school has hidden spots like this?" I said to Orlando. "If we're lucky enough to go to school by the beach, we might as well take advantage."

I sat down and slipped off my flip-flops so I could dig my bare feet into the fine white sand surrounding us. Normally, settling my feet into beach sand would be the greatest feeling in the world for me, but because of the bandages covering the burns that Rage inflicted on my feet, I didn't experience the full enjoyment of such a sensation. It was still wonderful though, especially on my toes, which were luckily untouched by Rage's flames.

As Orlando and Charlotte sat at each of my sides, we all took a few minutes to soak in everything around us with each of our senses. The clear blue sky and beaming sunshine, the gentle sea breeze, the waves tumbling down ahead of us . . . it was the perfect live ASMR experience for the three of us given all the troubles we went through over the past week.

"Wish we had found out about this place earlier," Charlotte said, breaking the silence. "It's so amazing how we can get to enjoy views like this."

"Lizzy discovered this spot by herself some time ago and introduced it to me last Monday. Never did I think that, three days later, she would never get to see this wonderful secret area again. So it's a little bitter for me returning here."

"It doesn't need to be bitter, Jess," Charlotte said. "I see bringing us here for the first time on our first day back at school as honoring Lizzy's memory. I don't think there's any better way you could've done so, girl."

"That is a great way to put it, Charlotte. Thanks."

As I lifted myself to keep my muscles warm in preparation to practice my big finale piece for the dance troupe's next show, a sharp sting of pain hit my waist, provoking a harsh grunt from my vocal cords. The burns and bruises I received from my fight with Rage five days ago didn't heal as fast as I was hoping.

"Are you okay, Jessica?" Orlando asked.

"I'd like to say I am, but not as much as I'd like to be," I replied. "I wish I could stay with you guys for longer, but I need to head to Nurse Morris's office. These burns still hurt like hell."

"Sorry to hear that, Jess," Charlotte said. "Hope she can give you the treatment you need. We'll continue to enjoy these wonderful surroundings in the meantime."

"Thanks, C. C. You and Orlando enjoy yourselves for the rest of lunch."

I had a bitter taste in my mouth as I stepped back onto Manzanita's campus. I could use all the therapy I could get from Southern California's natural beauty for the rest of lunchtime, but alas, reality was kicking my rear end again, reminding me of the turmoil that resulted from this past Saturday. Just as an ardent comics aficionado like me would have dreamed growing up, my life had been following the plot of a superhero origin story over the past week, from the death of a longtime companion to the surprise discovery of new superhuman abilities. But superhero life wasn't always as awesome as we made it out to be. As I was reminded last weekend, every superhero had their low points every once in a while. Not everything came easily for them despite the amazing feats they could perform that normal humans couldn't.

Of all the awesome comic book powers I could get, why couldn't I have received total invulnerability or a healing factor?

CHAPTER

6

The injuries that I got from fighting Rage peppered several parts of my body—my feet, my arms, my neck, and my face (no burns there, at least). So I expected to be in the nurse's office for a while, most likely for the rest of lunchtime. I didn't even mind being a little late for my third-period French class for the sake of extra treatment for my aches and pains. Our school nurse was wonderful and was beloved by virtually the entire Manzanita student population, so at least that alone made my time there worth it to some degree.

"How are your burns feeling now, Ms. Summer?" Nurse Morris asked.

"They're getting better, but not better enough, I think," I replied as Nurse Morris applied a wet cloth to the burns inflicted on my right foot. "I've had almost a week for my wounds to heal, so of course the pain had subsided a bit. Still more work to go, though." Ugh, I was so smart to battle Garrett in my pajamas and flip-flops that day; not exactly the ideal outfit for combat.

"No offense, but you were kind of silly to use your powers to get into a little fight," Nurse Morris said. "Or whatever it is that you can now do." She then mumbled to herself, "Don't be silly, Kendra, superpowers can never be real; the news was just playing around with you with their usual overexaggerated headlines . . ."

"It wasn't a little fight, Nurse Morris. I was trying to stop the Manzanita shooter that day. He escaped from prison and gained the ability to control fire. I had to stop him."

"There are more responsible ways to use . . . those fancy moves you can now pull off, Ms. Summer. You could cause a lot of unnecessary destruction doing those things in a fight. Let the police take care of despicable criminals."

"Even after they allowed him to break out of prison? I'm certain that only I would've been able to stop him. And I couldn't. But imagine how much worse the situation would've been had I not come."

"Now, don't be so much of a braggart, Ms. Summer. You shouldn't let your flashy new . . . magic get to your head like that."

"Okay, maybe I can agree with that, Nurse Morris. 'Those with power must not be reckless,' as the Beacon comics famously say."

"Just another reminder to always trust your wise adult guardians. People your age really need to do that more often." Well, look who's being the braggart now. Good ol' boomers . . . "Say, have you seen a short blond girl around who can somehow magically heal other people's injuries in an instant, or something like that?"

"No, I don't believe I have. Why do you ask?"

"Well, those of us here at the nursing office worry that she might put our jobs in jeopardy if every single kid throughout the school starts to see her for healing. I don't think that would be fair for all of us who work here. We put in a lot of effort every day to treat students' injuries, and have been doing so for so many years."

"I wouldn't agree with that, Nurse Morris. Even if there was someone around who could instantly heal others, I'm sure there will be a few kids who would choose to seek your services first. They might feel more comfort receiving treatment from you, they might have too strong of a bond with you to receive treatment from anyone else, they might not even know anyone with magical healing abilities." After a brief pause, I continued, "Since I started school here, I've found you to be an incredible nurse. Manzanita wouldn't be the same without your work, Nurse Morris. You'll always have my full trust."

"Thank you. I'm happy to hear that," Nurse Morris said. I was uncertain about how sincere she sounded, but I preferred to take it for what it was worth. I didn't see why she wouldn't see the sincerity in my own words. Where would I have been without her help when she treated an ankle injury that I suffered practicing with the dance troupe just before my first ever dance show at Manzanita as a freshman three semesters ago?

I heard a nasty grunt of pain come from the bed across from me. A pale-skinned kid in a white shirt with long, scruffy brown hair was sitting there, clutching his left shoulder blade.

"Really bad sporting injury?" I asked him.

"Funny that you ask . . . that's what I tell people who ask me about it, especially because I'm on the baseball team," he answered. "But in truth, I got this pain from the shooting. Took two bullets in this part of my body. I thought the pain would have subsided by now, but it turns out that's not the case." Another sting of pain ripped into the pale-skinned boy like a kidney stone in the shoulder blade.

"Wow. I'm sorry to hear that. First day back at school, and I've already met someone who was hurt by the gunman. I hope you didn't lose a friend to the shooting, either."

"I didn't. I got lucky that I didn't lose anyone close to me, or lose my own life. That could've been any of us. Out of curiosity, why do you bring that up?"

I took a big exhale before speaking. "I lost my best friend that day. I had to watch her succumb to several gunshot wounds in front of my eyes. As much as I'd like to forget it all happened, the memories are still fresh in my mind. Every single second of them."

"Damn." The scruffy-haired kid paused for a few seconds before he could find his words again. "I don't know what to say about that. I can't imagine what going through something like that must be like. And I hope I'll never know."

"Well, I hope so too, for your sake. For now, be lucky that you're still here, kid. Because you never know how many days you still have left on this beautiful planet."

"We learned that the hard way exactly a week ago." I nodded my head in response to the scruffy-haired boy's statement. Then I got off my bed, ready to head to French class.

"I'm going to let Nurse Morris help you out now," I said to the scruffy-haired boy.

"Thanks," said the boy. "I appreciate that. Hope you get better soon."

"Same with you, kid. I'll try to deal with these burns on my own. Nurse Morris has done a fantastic job treating them today, so I think I'll be good for the rest of the day."

"It pleases me to hear that, Jessica," said Nurse Morris. "Thanks."

"See, I told you that I still have my full trust in you, Nurse." I flashed her a smile as I headed out the door into the school hallway, keeping my eyes on her as I walked out. Nurse Morris smiled back at me, giving me confirmation that I still had her trust despite her apparent skepticism toward people with comic book powers.

Fourth period was always the part of the school day that I looked forward to the most because it was when my favorite class, dance, took place; it was the time of day where my Manzanita Dance Troupe teammates and I practiced our performances and routines for the dance shows that we had at the end of every school semester. But dance class now felt different. And not just because of all the gossip that my teammates tossed among one other before the start of class about the newfound presence of comic book powers at our school, or the fact that it was our first dance class since the shooting. I wondered how many of my teammates were already aware that I had such powers, given that they almost certainly knew by now with how much I'd been on the news.

Even as a high school sophomore, I'd been challenging for a spot as one of the captains of the dance troupe next year. As a result, our upcoming dance show next month was putting unprecedented pressure on me to perform well. The fact that I was dealing with so much grief and uncertainty due to the events of the past week only added more pressure and anxiety for me—not just with the show itself, but also in the practice sessions leading up to the show.

To start off class, our dance instructor, Ms. Newton, requested that we gather together for a group prayer. In a somber tone, she expressed,

"As you all know, today marks our first class together since the horrific shooting at our school last Thursday that claimed the lives of ten innocent boys and girls. My thoughts and prayers continue to be with those who lost close friends and loved ones in this horrible tragedy. You may know that Jessica and Charlotte were among those who lost someone near and dear to them. So Jessica, Charlotte, feel free to come to the center of our group circle. Our hearts are with you through these difficult times."

Having a big spotlight shined on you wasn't the most comfortable situation in this kind of circumstance, but it humbled me that Ms. Newton was dedicating this group prayer to me and Charlotte in particular. It made me think back to when she sent me a condolence text on the night that followed the shooting; she was the first teacher at my school to do so.

I'd never found myself in the center of a group hug this huge, so I felt a bit nervous about the collection of everyone in the room squeezing me too hard. But as Ms. Newton and my dance teammates gathered around in a circle, all those nerves dissipated in an instant, and there was nothing but a soothing, heartwarming sensation passing through me as my arms draped over Charlotte's shoulders while everyone else's wrapped around me.

After our emotional ceremony to start class, it was off to work. We started our practice with the big modern dance piece that I was leading in our upcoming show next month. This piece was my baby, much like a painter's first ever piece of artwork or an author's debut novel. Since the first week of spring semester, I'd spent countless hours revising and perfecting the art and choreography of my signature performance. I liked to think of it as my showcase to prove my worthiness of dance troupe captaincy.

As I got into position in front of everyone else, I said to my teammates, "Five, six, seven, eight," snapping to each number of the count. It felt good to get those words out with how much I needed this practice as a means of escapism.

The piece that I was leading and practicing for was a free-flowing modern dance piece set to an acoustic instrumental version of a popular 1990s song. Because we'd practiced this piece so many times by then, I didn't have to express each individual move out loud to my teammates, instead saying them in my head. Numerous terms for dance moves come from the French language, so I had a lot of fun saying words like "chaîné" and "glissade" in my mind through the course of our latest rehearsal for my big piece. Big thanks to the schedulers at Manzanita for placing my French class right before my dance class.

As much as I enjoyed practicing with the dance troupe, today's class was more exhausting for me than usual. Because I was still ailing from my burns and bruises, I felt I was overexerting myself and trying too hard to drag myself through the number. The typical repetitiveness of our routines only made class feel like more of a burden that day.

In the middle of our third run-through for the piece I led, I stepped off the floor, wanting to talk to Ms. Newton.

"Is something wrong, Jessica?" asked current dance troupe co-captain Megan Miller, a soon-to-be-graduating senior who I'd be replacing as co-captain if I was able to win the role.

"Sorry, Megan," I replied. "It's just that . . . I've been trying to get through all this pain. But it's starting to become too unbearable. I'm not sure I can keep going; you girls might have to be on your own for the rest of today. I'll go talk to Ms. Newton."

"Okay then. Get better soon, Jess."

When I stepped away from my team, I sulked, watching my girls go on without me. Some energy drained out of me, leading me to pause before I began talking with Ms. Newton.

When I walked up to our dance instructor, she asked, "Is everything okay, Jessica?"

"I wouldn't . . . really say so. I want to keep practicing with the rest of the team. Very badly. But I can't keep going through all these wounds I have. They've gotten better, just not better enough. And everything I've been going through because of the shooting and Lizzy's death isn't making matters much better for me, either. It really sucks having to step away from the team like this and watch them practice without me, but . . ."

Ms. Newton embraced me. "I understand how you feel, and I can tell that today was bound to be overwhelming for you with everything you've been going through," she said. "You can go for the rest of the day. We can take it from here without you."

"Thank you, Ms. Newton. I'll see you tomorrow. Hopefully I'll be better by then. Both physically and mentally." From there, I draped my bag over my right shoulder, slipped my Rainbow flip-flops back on, and headed out the door, ready to walk back home. Despite the pain I still had, it subsided enough that I could take the fifteen-minute walk just fine, albeit with occasional stinging sensations every now and then.

It really sucked going for the title of dance troupe co-captain and having to step away because of all the injuries I had. It was a massive setback not to lead my teammates in our first class back in over a week. But at the same time, I needed to take care of my health first. It didn't make sitting out the rest of a crucial dance practice hurt any less, though.

Some time before dinner, I had the obligation to chat with Lizzy's parents to provide them comfort in the midst of the reemergence of their daughter's murderer. Because of how much we went through at Lizzy's funeral, we didn't get to talk with each other much, and I was glad it had been that way. With all the time I had to soak in an early exit from school and think about what to discuss with Mr. and Mrs. Manchester, I found it to be the perfect opportunity to provide them a soothing light in this dark period of their lives.

Sitting on my bed, I dialed Lizzy's home phone number on my cell phone. It was a nerve-wracking wait, hearing the beeps on my phone and hoping that they picked up. When I first heard Mrs. Manchester's voice, my body eased itself.

"Hello? Who is this?" she asked.

"It's Jessica," I answered. "Sorry if you think I'm disturbing you, but I hope right now is a good time for us to talk."

"Jessica, hi! So nice to talk to you. I don't believe we've seen each other since—"

"Since . . . the funeral, yes." It felt like scalding water erupted from my mouth when I said that. "I wanted to check in with you and Jeff tonight. The fact that the Manzanita shooter is roaming about again must not be making things any easier for you, either."

Mrs. Manchester's voice lowered. "Oh yes. I don't have the words for that, to be honest. Jeff's here now, by the way; maybe he has more to say about it than I do." A slight mumble sounded through my phone; it appeared that Mrs. Manchester was passing the phone to Mr. Manchester, informing him that I was the one on the line.

"Jessica?" Mr. Manchester said through my phone. "Nice to hear from you. I heard you wanted to talk."

"Yes indeed," I said. "Like I was telling Veronika, not the easiest time for us right now, especially now that the Manzanita shooter has broken out of prison."

"And I heard that you tried to stop him from causing any further damage. We applaud your brave efforts, Jessica," Mr. Manchester said.

"Thanks," I said with a smile. "It helps that I'm now like the Wonder superheroes that Lizzy and I grew up loving, equipped with brand-new superhuman abilities. Of course, I'm sure you know that by now."

"We do, actually," Mrs. Manchester said. "We had to find concrete proof of your powers on the news to confirm them; it was too good to be true for us. But we're so lucky that Santa Barbara now has a superhero to defend us from hateful criminals like him. We can't believe that it's you, of all people. One of the biggest comic book geeks we know, alongside our daughter when she was still here."

"I know, right? It's funny how life works out, as unpleasant as it can be."

"It's horrifying to know that our daughter's murderer is out there somewhere, planning who knows what," Mr. Manchester said. "He killed our daughter and took nine other innocent young lives. All because of some deranged delusion that he wasn't getting what he believed he deserved from other girls. It's been devastating news for our entire Santa Barbara community, not just Manzanita High School, to hear about his escape. We couldn't be any more grateful that one of our favorite people in the world has become a shining light for our community in these dark times. Just like Beacon was for Muslim Americans in the days and years following 9/11."

"It's such an honor to be compared to one of my favorite superheroes of all time like that," I said. "Thanks, Mr. and Mrs. Manchester."

"You're welcome," Mrs. Manchester said. "That reminds me, we wanted to let you know that Scott Lowe himself got in contact with us not long after the shooting."

"No way! You're kidding. What for?"

"He's decided to start a collaboration with us on a project calling for a stop to gun violence in our country," Mr. Manchester replied. "He was devastated to hear about the heinous murders that his son committed at your school. So he wanted to make up for it by getting in contact with the parents and families who lost their loved ones in the shooting, including us."

"That is *awesome*," I said. "Hearing about that has made my day. Especially with how difficult my first day back at school was. I'm somewhat jealous of you two that you're now working with Scott freaking Lowe, to be frank."

"It's made our day sharing it with you, too," Mrs. Manchester said. "We've been so excited to share the news with you ever since he first called us up; we knew you had to be the first to know. We'll be happy to keep you updated on how our collaboration goes. Have a terrific rest of your day, Jessica."

"You too, Mr. and Mrs. Manchester. Hope to talk to you two again soon. Goodbye."

When I hung up my phone, it was as if something lifted me into the heavens. As jarring as recent times were, it was nice to hear about this wonderful piece of good news—some of the best news I could've ever heard in such times. Scott Lowe couldn't be any more different from his son. And I was glad that, just like with all the comics, movies, and more connected to his name and empire, he did what he could to be a light and inspiration in others' lives. Including the grieving parents of my best friend and fellow Wondnerd. (That was the popular term for the most hardcore fans of Wonder comics and movies.)

Real life may suck ass, but it is amazing to watch it write itself at times.

CHAPTER

7

On our way to our secret lunch spot after second period, Orlando, Charlotte, and I had the misfortune of passing by Darren Owens while walking through the hallway where the lockers stood. At least it was a sign that a bit of normalcy returned to my life when my nerves boiled over the sight and sound of Darren and his voice. It didn't make him any less annoying for us, though.

"Yo, hey, what's up, Blondie!" he greeted me. Then he pointed at me and said to his friends, "Didja hear that this chick saved me last weekend? Consider me lucky, man. You guys should all be jealous of me that a hottie like her saved my life."

I cringed at every single word he said, every stupid gesture he made. He seemed to be acting as if the shooting never happened, even after Garrett almost murdered him on Saturday.

"Oh, yeah, you're welcome," I said to Darren. "Sorry I forgot to mention that."

"Better not to give him the time of day, Jess," Charlotte said. "You know better than anyone that he's a total whack job."

I could've tried to ignore him, but I couldn't help but notice that the burns that Garrett inflicted on him had disappeared entirely, while mine were still present. As a result, I found myself staring at him, looking as if I was giving him a flirty gaze. Which I sure as hell would never do, ewww.

"Say, what happened to your burns, Darren?" I asked. "They sure seem to have healed fast. Did you develop super healing along with your super speed?"

"Nah, I wish; it would be super dope to have that though," Darren answered—emphasis on the "super," of course. "Melissa here healed them."

"How did she heal them? I wasn't aware that Melissa was an aspiring doctor."

"Oh, she just touched the areas where my burns were. And then, just like that, poof, they disappeared." Welp, now I knew who Nurse Morris was talking about yesterday.

"Wait, so you can now cure people's wounds just by touching them, Melissa?" I asked, flipping my attention to Melissa.

". . . yeah, I guess you could put it that way," she answered.

"Great. Because I got a lot of burns from Garrett, too, and they still hurt like hell." I removed the bandage on my right arm to show Melissa one of the burns I suffered that Saturday. Then, with the demeanor of a kindly old lady, I begged, "Would it be cool if you heal my burns, too? Please? I'll be nicer to you if you do."

"Eh. No thanks. I still prefer to avoid any association with losers like you." And so Melissa and Darren just walked away.

I guessed trying to act nice to Melissa Snyder didn't work out. Even in the times we were currently going through, and even after they just went through a near-death experience, she was still the same snotty bitch that she was before. And Darren Owens was just as cocky as usual, too. Some people never change.

After Orlando, Charlotte, and I finished our lunches, we typically stuck around our new hidden beachside spot and soak in the ocean and natural beauty in front of us. But this time around, we decided to walk around campus for the rest of lunchtime, looking to see how other students had changed since the night I made my shooting star wish.

"I would've loved to spend more time yesterday finding out who else at our school got comic book powers," I said. "But I had so many things to deal with all day long, to be honest. Past couple of weeks haven't been the easiest for me."

"Given everything you've been going through, we can excuse you for that," Orlando said.

"Thanks, Orlando. So did either of you two ever find anyone else at school who now has powers?"

"Well, I know Greg Nathan does," Charlotte answered. "I saw him heating up the air around him so much that it crackled into a bunch of lightning bolts above him. Now he's pondering whether to take on a superhero alter ego or not."

"Ooh, don't forget Maryam Asghari," Orlando added.

"Maryam Asghari?" I said. "As in the girl who showcases hijabi fashion on her YouTube channel? I love her! Both as a person and as a YouTuber."

"Yes. She demonstrated her powers in the latest video that she posted; I believe she said she has power over order and chaos, whatever that means. And for some reason, she's a redhead now. I've never seen her with red hair before. Or any Persian with red hair in general."

"Ah man. I wish I could've found the time to see her latest video. Watching her show off her new powers on YouTube would've been so awesome."

As we continued our curious search for other students with comic book powers, we ended up finding an elephant in the room—or rather, the campus: a tan-skinned, well-built kid who was able to uproot one of the trees dotting the outskirts of the plaza from the ground, sparking reactions of both amazement and shock in those around him. A few kids took their phones out to film him lifting up the tree with his own two arms. I recognized the kid: it was Victor Ullman, one of the linebackers on the football team.

Victor was one of the few Manzanita football players that I was cool with. Unlike many of the other football players—*cough, cough,* Darren and his friends—he was quite nice and likable. He usually didn't hang out with the other football players, either, likely because they didn't consider him manly enough to hang around them. Seeing him remove a tree from the ground all by himself made me wonder how much things had changed for him.

"Man, now why couldn't I have been able to do that?" I said to Victor as I walked up to him, thinking back to my pathetic attempts to lift up my neighbor's car with my arms while I was trying to find out for the first time if I had powers or not.

"Oh hey, what's good, Jessica?" Victor said, placing the tree back in its spot on the plaza perimeter. "My most heartfelt condolences to you. I heard about Lizzy—can't imagine what that must feel like for you or for Lizzy's parents."

"Thanks, Victor. I'll tell Lizzy's parents that you offered them your thoughts and prayers."

"No problem; I would appreciate that." Victor bowed his head down and let out a slight sigh. "I wish I could've done something to save her life. I may have stopped the gunman's rampage, but I didn't stop him from taking innocent lives . . ."

"Wait . . . come again?" I asked, looking for clarification.

"I saw the shooter that day. I saw the flashes coming from his pistol. I still have frightening visions of them every now and then. So when I found him, I locked my eyes on him and made sure to give him the greatest football tackle of my life. I was hesitant knowing that I could miss him and he could retaliate. But a few seconds later, there was the shooter, writhing underneath the weight of my body, giving police the room they needed to handcuff him . . ."

Close to tearing up, I gave Victor the biggest embrace that all 100 pounds of me could in one swift move—an embrace he was quick to reciprocate. As if Victor wasn't heavy enough as a football linebacker, he felt a lot heavier to me than he did before for some reason.

"I've felt the same way that you have, Victor," I said to him. "I tried to do what I could to save others around me, especially Lizzy. But I felt there wasn't much I could do. I felt so . . . powerless. All I could've done is rush others to safety and not much else . . . if only I had gained these powers a couple days earlier than I actually did, saving Lizzy and those other students who lost their lives or suffered severe injuries would've been a walk in the park . . . I wish I could've had the same courage that you did that day, Victor."

"It's an honor to receive such a compliment from you, Jessica. I must confess that you're the very first person at this school that I've told about tackling the gunman into the ground. I was uncomfortable telling anyone about it because I didn't want too much of a spotlight shined on me; it would've been too much for me to deal with. But knowing how close Lizzy was to you, it only made sense for me to tell you up front, Jessica."

"Thank you, Victor. We should all be grateful to you for your brave efforts during our school's darkest moment. That was a deed you should be proud of for the rest of your life. No need to be scared of the attention you might face from now on."

"That means a lot to hear that from you, Jessica. You've just given me more confidence in telling others about my actions that day. It's something to keep in mind if they ever call me to speak at our graduation, at least." I giggled at Victor's joke as we leaned into our embrace even more. As a result, I felt even more of Victor's exceptional strength.

After we unwrapped ourselves from our hug, I felt myself tingling a bit. I brushed off the sensation, though, knowing it was natural for that to happen when a scrawny, lightweight dancer met the body of a high school linebacker.

"So, you have powers too, Jessica?" Victor asked. "What awesome things can you do?"

"Oh, plenty of things." In the blink of an eye, I took off skyward, rising up to the same altitude where a drone would be sailing above the school.

"Ah, so you can fly. How unique," Victor snarked.

"You do realize I said 'plenty of things,' correct?" I descended closer to where I was standing next to Victor, Orlando, and Charlotte. "Heads up, by the way. That goes for you, too, Orlando and Charlotte." I fired a photon ball in Victor's direction, around the size of a baseball so that I didn't create a fuss by blowing up too many things and people in the vicinity. Although he reacted a bit late, Victor did manage to sidestep out of the way of my photon ball on time, and it detonated on the ground harmlessly, not causing any damage to property or hurting anyone.

"I told you heads up," I told Victor. "I wasn't trying at all to hurt you. That would get me in trouble, anyways."

"You call that a fair fight?" Victor asked. "I can't get you when you're in the air like that. Bring the fight a little closer, please."

"Okay then, if you say so. I wasn't asking for a fight, but hey, what's wrong with a little bit of fun every now and then?"

"These powers have to be useful for something." I flashed a smile at Victor's comment as my flip-flops touched back down on the ground. Right as I did, Victor picked me up in his arms and tackled me into the ground as if he was at football practice. While lying down, my body felt quite woozy—so much so that I couldn't even feel my burn marks.

"You call *that* a fair fight?" I echoed Victor's earlier words. "I only weigh 100 pounds, dude. No need to bring your linebacker habits to school lunch."

"I'd say it's fair*er* now," Victor teased. Seeing that he wanted to engage in a friendly duel with me, I slipped my Rainbows off and slid them to where my backpack was. Then I got into a combat stance, only for Victor to ram me with the force of an eighteen-wheeler, sending me flying a good distance backward. I could see the looks of concern on Charlotte's and Orlando's faces from where I ended up landing.

"He got you good, Jess," Charlotte remarked.

"Oh, come on, I still have all these lingering burn marks," I said to her. "He's not even dealing with me at full strength, you know."

At least I was now in my comfort range for fighting where I was standing. I tossed several small energy balls in Victor's direction, and none of them scratched him in the slightest. Even when I fired a larger, basketball-sized energy ball at him, he didn't flinch at all. As the energy ball dissipated helplessly, Victor stood with a smirk on his face. Either I shouldn't have been playing around with Victor while still feeling the lingering effects of my burns, or he was just way out of my league in terms of sheer power.

Deciding to take the fight into close quarters again, I zipped through the air in Victor's direction, about to land a punch, but all he did was grab my fist before I could strike him, stopping me dead in my tracks. With fantastic timing, a burly school security guard passed by us. Alas, we forgot that campus security had tightened significantly since school restarted, a natural response to the mass shooting that took place here twelve days ago.

"You know it's not nice to pick on a young girl like that, sir," he said to Victor. "Let alone someone as pretty as her." Ugh, even school security would hit on me. How wonderful. "Anyway, you two need to stop fooling around. You could cause some serious damage to school property or other students, fighting like that."

"We weren't fighting," I told the security guard. "We were just playing around with our powers. Just a little bit of playtime between friends."

"Sure you were. I've seen those movies with people like you. Causing destruction everywhere they go, no matter how heroic they are. I'm going to be keeping my eye on students like you. 'Cause it's my job." The security guard giggled, as if to ensure that he was being friendly with us.

The lunch bell rang, and I slipped my flip-flops back on before heading to my French class. Although I was a bit dazed by my playful duel with Victor, I had no problem walking to third period. A bit of pain in my burn areas, but no noticeable limps of any kind.

"I don't see what the fuss was about for him," I said to Orlando and Charlotte as I walked with them to our next classes. "Is he on very high alert because of recent events, or is he just scared of people with comic book powers for some reason?"

"Well, maybe the school wants to monitor those students carefully since they've never seen people with superpowers on campus before," Orlando said. "Just a matter of keeping students safe. But then again, this is the muggle talking, so maybe you might have more of a point, Jess."

"Victor beat you up pretty bad there," Charlotte said. "At least he's a good kid. Who knows what kinds of trouble other guys with powers will do? Not to mention all the students who have major trouble controlling their powers. It's a volatile situation having students with superhuman abilities on campus, no matter how you squeeze it."

"You have a good point there, C. C. I'm lucky I've been able to grasp my powers relatively well. Same goes for Victor, it seems. Anyway, see you two later." My third period classroom was a shorter walk from the school plaza than Orlando's and Charlotte's classes, so the three of us parted ways from there as I ended up the third student to arrive at my French class.

As I took my seat in the very front of the class and waited for my teacher, Mademoiselle Françoise, to arrive, I spent the next few minutes thinking about how much more interesting life at Manzanita High School would be now that there were several students on campus who had comic book powers like me. The thought of school activities and the Manzanita social scene looking much different with students having powers became very enticing for me. Several other questions about the emergence of comic book powers roamed around my mind, too. Were there teachers and other staff members at Manzanita who had comic book powers? Were there people with comic book powers in other states? In other countries? On other planets? Did comic book powers already exist on other planets and galaxies, or was our Planet Earth the very first one to witness its native species gain such powers?

At the start of the current decade, my peers and I witnessed the COVID-19 pandemic morph daily life and the shape of global society to a degree that humanity hadn't seen since World War II. The pandemic years were the most life-changing period in our existence, and we assumed that we would never go through a change that massive again. But in many ways—some good, some bad—it was quite clear that COVID was going to pale in comparison to the effects of my shooting star wish if it was true that people with comic book powers now existed throughout the world.

CHAPTER 8

I could still recall, detail by detail, every single event that transpired on that fateful afternoon of May 23.

I recalled Lizzy and I walking back onto the central plaza of our campus from our secret beach spot. I remembered hearing the sudden sounds of gunfire filling the center of campus. The sounds of screaming students following afterward. Watching fellow students around me running in a panic left, right, and all over the plaza. Three bullets piercing through Lizzy's chest. The shrieks I made when Lizzy was hit by gunfire. Taking quick sidesteps in a panicky attempt to dodge bullets. My pleas for Lizzy to get up from her gunshot wounds. What felt like the longest wait for emergency paramedics to come to Lizzy's rescue. A brief glimpse of a cold, angry face in the distance that appeared to be that of Garrett Lowe. And then the ringing of the school bell to signal the end of lunch, which sounded so much eerier than normal because of the circumstances that everyone found themselves in all of a sudden.

At least, that's what I was seeing in a dream.

I knew it was a dream because, right after the paramedics picked up Lizzy's limp body and carried it to the ambulance they were working in, I saw Garrett's face flash right in front of me. And then my eyes saw nothing but the inside of Garrett's luxury car, the same one in which he filmed his "Reckoning" video. There was the beach and the ocean in the background. And I heard Garrett describe his plan of chauvinistic vengeance again: "I will make my way to the center of campus at my high school, Manzanita High School. I will unleash the wrath of my precious handgun. And I will *murder.* Every. Little. Pretty female *shit.* That I can find."

In actuality, I didn't see Garrett's face on the day of the shooting. But in this dream, it looked like he was in the distance, at the far corner of the plaza, appearing to show some sense of satisfaction in his cold, angry face. Regardless of the fact that it was all in my mind, this dream felt too real, second by second.

The dream woke me up from the nap I was taking. It was the first time that I relived the shooting in my mind, perhaps because I'd been busy dealing with the new distractions stemming from my new comic book powers, witnessing people I knew at my high school developing similar extraordinary powers of their own, and some of the usual tribulations that come with being a teenager. The nightmare left me with a shivering sensation that even the warmth of the first day of June couldn't stop as I walked to my mom's room to ask her for help.

Mom was playing a song on her clarinet when I showed up in her room. As a marine biologist, she was quite fond of everything SpongeBob, so she decided to take up playing the clarinet as a hobby just for the sake of playing the same instrument as Squidward. To spend more time with her new hobby, she performed clarinet tunes at Dart Coffee Co. every other weekend. When I walked in, she finished up her latest tune, one of the pieces that she played at Dart Coffee's outdoor café.

"Hello, sweetheart," she said. "Have you been feeling better?"

"No, not really," I answered. "I had a very bad nightmare about the shooting, like I was reliving every second of it . . . and I saw the shooter in my dream, too."

"Oh gosh, that is terrible. I'm so sorry to hear that. Were you aware that it was a dream?"

"Yes, I was. It's just another grim reminder of how troubling everything has been for me lately." My tone dropped lower as I continued. "It's just so hard getting over these mental difficulties I've had lately, Mom . . . I just can't see them going away any time soon . . ."

"Well, you see, darling, recovery from tragedy is a lengthy process," Mom explained, placing her hand on my shoulder. "It's not always easy, and it takes a lot of time. Nothing is quick or immediate with the recovery process."

"I know, Mom. I knew this was going to be hard. But I just wish I could have some sense of normalcy for once. First the pandemic, and then the shooting. Even having comic book powers hasn't made my life any easier; I've been getting the feeling that members of my school staff are treating me like a wanted criminal because of my powers, as if I needed any more worries to deal with. I thought being like my favorite superheroes would make my life much easier and brighter. But it seems to only be adding more problems to my life." I put my head down and cover my face with my hands.

Mom placed her right hand just below my neck. "I know everything's so difficult for you right now, Jess," she said. "But this phase you're going through is just a normal part of anyone's teenage years. Of course, it's unprecedented that we have people with superhuman powers trying to fit into society nowadays. But whether it's your superpowers or something else that makes you feel too strange among the crowd, folks your age are always trying to look for an identity they feel comfortable with. You just need to embrace who you are, Jessica. Be proud of the fact that you have special powers. And anyone who looks down on you for being extraordinary, don't let their words and actions get to you."

The worried look on my face turned into a hearty smile. "So you're not going to look down on me because I have unusual powers?" I asked.

"Of course not, Jess. Dad and I will always support you, regardless of what you are or who you are. It's our job as parents. You should feel lucky that you have us around when others out there have very neglectful parents, or even no parents at all. And no matter how unusual you feel you are, no matter how much trouble you go through, you're still our bundle of sunshine. And we'll be by your side for every second of your ongoing recovery."

"Thanks, Mom. I'm way too lucky to have you and Dad as my guides through the trials and tribulations of life."

"No problem, sweetie. We're happy we still have you around after Larson left for college."

We leaned into each other for a big hug. Then I declared, "I have superpowers. I'm damn proud to have them. And nobody can change that."

"That's what I'm talking about, Jess," Mom said with a look of gratitude on her face. After we unwrapped from our hug, she then asked, "By the way, would you like more treatment for your burns? I heard they were still hurting and irritating you during dance practice."

Melissa Snyder came to mind when Mom asked me this question. "Thanks, Mom, but I'm good," I answered. "I know someone at school who can instantly heal others' wounds and injuries with a single touch."

"Oh, there are other students at your school with superpowers? Not just you?"

"Yes. Plenty of them, in fact. Even Garrett Lowe, the Manzanita shooter, developed the ability to control fire through his own anger—it's how he managed to break out of prison and resist the police along the way. Did you ever find out the latest on him?"

"Not as far as I know. I haven't seen him on the news much as of late. But perhaps that's for the better; the media has already given enough notoriety to these mass shooters anyway."

"You have a good point there. Thanks again for the talk, Mom." I gave her a quick kiss on the cheek before heading back to my room, going back to working on the geometry homework that I needed to finish in two days.

While I found it relieving that Garrett Lowe's whereabouts remained a mystery to me, uncomfortable thoughts about him did lurk in my mind over the evening, including during my sleep.

What could Garrett be up to now? Was he planning another mass murder? Or did he have something even more sinister in mind? I didn't even want to think about how much deadlier he might now be with his flame powers as opposed to being a delinquent armed with a Glock 34 pistol.

I wished I could have more time to seek Garrett and put a stop to him. I wished I could dedicate myself more to playing the role of our town's local superheroine. But I was still a teenager. I had a lot of school crap to deal with in the meantime. Projects, upcoming finals, my dance show at the end of the year, the immaturity of some of my classmates . . .

Trying to get good grades while the recently escaped mass shooter who took your best friend's life continued to haunt my mind. Not the first scenario I would ever have imagined myself in.

—⁂—

As our first full week of school after the shooting dawned, I arrived on campus earlier than usual so that I could dodge the long lines that were inevitable as Manzanita students continued to deal with the lingering trauma of May 23. This was the strategy I devised for today in order to ensure I was the first person to arrive at the office of our school therapist, Dr. Domínguez-Salas. My plan worked. And while I could've just waited to schedule an appointment, I was too desperate to see her at that moment. Some people out there didn't find therapy useful at all, but I wasn't one of those people. Receiving help from the school therapist could go a long way toward speeding up that process for me, and I was going to take advantage of this resource I was grateful to have at my school. She'd been one busy woman over the past few weeks, so any time that one managed to find with her was a stroke of luck.

"Hello, *señorita*," Dr. Domínguez-Salas greeted me. "And what might your name be?"

"Jessica," I answered. "Jessica Summer."

"Hello, Ms. Summer. Didn't you speak at the memorial last Saturday? You made an amazing speech there."

"Yes, that was me," I answered. "And thank you for the compliment, Dr. Domínguez-Salas. Very much appreciated."

"Oh, my pleasure. How come you have so many bandages all over you, by the way?"

"Long story, Dr. Domínguez-Salas. Basically, the guy who shot our school gained flame powers and broke out of prison two weekends ago. I tried to stop him, but he got away and burned me in several spots. But that's just the tip of the iceberg with all the crap I've been dealing with, as much as I hate to say that. Everything has been overwhelming me so much lately, so I was desperate to have a non-scheduled meeting with you."

"I perfectly understand, *chica*. Come have a seat." As I took my seat, she asked, "So, how have you been doing since the shooting overall?"

"I haven't been much better than I was on the day of the shooting and the day after," I explained. "I know that everyone has had a difficult time dealing with this recent tragedy, but I've been shaken in particular because my best friend Lizzy was shot dead, and I had to see it happen in front of my eyes. As of now, the trauma still lingers, still hurts. But at least I have so many people to look to for support. My parents, my friends Orlando and Charlotte, and you, too, I'm hoping."

Offering her best condolences, the school therapist told me, "Aw, I'm so sorry to hear about the death of your best friend. Makes me glad that you reached out to me before we could even schedule an appointment together. That said, I'll try my best to help you out. And I truly look forward to working with you. You seem like a wonderful girl. Let's continue on; any new developments going on in your life?"

"More than I would like," I stated half-sarcastically. "I hope this doesn't result in any trouble, but now I can do some very unusual things."

I sat straight up, using my powers to create a sense of weightlessness within the room. My body and that of Dr. Domínguez-Salas slowly started to lift off our respective chairs, and the other objects in the therapist's office followed our lead not long after.

"I hope you're not freaking out," I told Dr. Domínguez-Salas as we floated around in the air. "This must be a weird experience for you to have."

"I'm not," she said. "I don't even know what to think right now. This feels like being in space."

Maintaining a state of calm in my head like I had before whenever using my powers, I returned the gravity in the room to normal, landing us and all the objects in the room safely and slowly on the ground. My anxiety crept in a bit as I had a brief worry about causing objects in the room to fall too fast and shatter. But overall, I was able to return everything in the room to normal with relative ease. Dr. Domínguez-Salas looked like she was about to gasp.

"*Ay caramba*," she reacted. "I honestly think that's amazing what you can do, Jessica. I would've never imagined, growing up in El Salvador, that the comics I read as a kid would end up becoming real life."

"Yep, I'm a comic book character now. And that's not my only power, either," I said. "I can fire bright balls of energy from my hands, fly through the air, and probably a whole lot of other things. When I wished to have superpowers, I didn't think once about the complications that the presence of superpowers at our school would create. More anxiety to my daily life that I don't need with all the high school craziness I already have to deal with."

"That doesn't sound like the comic books I read growing up," Dr. Domínguez-Salas snarked, leading us both to laugh. I was happy she could lighten the mood and speak in support of my comic book powers.

"So you don't think that I might pose a threat because I can do unusual things that humans aren't supposed to do?" I asked for clarification.

"Oh no, of course not. I always try to respect everyone, no matter what quirks they might have, as long as they don't intend to harm others in any way. And it's no different with superheroes like you, *chica*." Dr. Domínguez-Salas said the word "superheroes" like it was a title of honor.

"Thank you for understanding, Dr. Domínguez-Salas. In fact, you've just got me thinking: After a talk I had with my mom last night, I've decided that I don't need to keep these powers secret. I'm proud of what I have. No matter how others view me because of them. No matter how much suspicion some staff members at our school have thrown at beings like me. I'm not afraid to show those around me that I'm extraordinary. It's just what I am, and I hope more people in my life start to respect that."

The school therapist gave me a round of applause. "Another wonderful speech, Ms. Summer," she said. "You should seriously consider being a speech writer or public speaker."

"Thanks, but no thanks," I said with a giggle. "I have many other priorities for my future, to be honest. But I do appreciate the flattery you gave me there."

"Whatever makes you most happy, I will support every step of the way. Anyway, thank you for our time today, Jessica. I look forward to working with you more in the future. Get better soon, *muchacha*."

There was still a long way for me to go before I could fully get over my post-shooting turmoil, but developing a sturdier rapport with Dr. Domínguez-Salas was a terrific start. She had a lot of work cut out for her in the days since the shooting, but the job she'd done so far left quite an impression on me. I was glad I found another helpful ally amid this unusual period of my time at Manzanita High School.

CHAPTER

9

I may have saved Melissa Snyder a little more than a week prior, but that didn't mean I now admired her like countless others on campus—especially numerous male students—did. She, Darren, and the rest of their posse still remained the bane of my existence at Manzanita. So when I walked up to their table in the cafeteria after finishing my lunch, I started to second-guess my decision to do so. It was like making an attempt to befriend the Plastics from *Mean Girls*. Except for the fact that today was Wednesday and none of them were wearing pink.

As if everything else about Melissa Snyder wasn't enough to make me cringe, so did the name of her group of friends: MINK. The acronym stood for the first initials of their names: Melissa, Irene, Natasha, and Katie. So creative of them.

"Oh, look. The hot nerd wants to make friends with us," Melissa said to her fellow MINK girls as I walked up to their side of the popular kids' table. With a smirk on her face, she then took a sip from her chocolate milk carton, as if trying to imitate Kermit the Frog in his famous "none of my business" Internet meme. I didn't know if I should feel flattered that Melissa Snyder just called me a "hot nerd," or if I should be offended.

"Hello, loser," said Irene. "Finally looking to make your way up the Manzanita social pyramid? We can help you with that."

"Good one, Irene. But that's not what I'm here for," I replied. "There was an important matter that I wanted to talk to Melissa about."

"Oh? And what's in it for me, Jessica Summer?" Melissa asked.

"Melissa, I'm not trying to make one of those outrageous teen movie bets with you. I just want to ask you for a favor."

"A favor, huh?" Melissa leaned back on her side of the table and crossed her legs, her pose true to her status as class princess. "Carry on."

I displayed to Melissa the white bandages left over on my feet and arms. "So, I know that you girls are probably looking at me weird because of these bandages still on my body," I said. "I still have them because of the many burns that I got from fighting Rage, the new firebending alter ego of the same kid who shot up our school and tried to kill you after he got his powers. They're bad enough that they haven't come close to healing yet. I have my big show with the dance troupe coming up in two weeks, and it's been so difficult for me to participate in practices and put in sufficient preparation for the show because these burns have been causing me too much pain to be able to go through each of my individual dance moves. So I was hoping that you could use your powers to cure my pain."

"Oh yeah, I remember you asking me about that the other day, nerd . . ." Of course Melissa Snyder would resort to sarcasm in this situation. "If I'm being honest, though, that's a rather selfish favor of you to ask for. And people accuse me and my friends here of being selfish . . ."

Irritation began to rise up inside me in response to Melissa playing coy. "Look, I saved you from getting burnt to a crisp by the Manzanita shooter last week. Would it kill you to pay me back the favor?"

Melissa locked her gaze onto me. "You know what, I think that's fair," she said. "I can be a bitch sometimes, but I'm not that much of a bitch." Hey, at least she admitted it.

I took a seat at the popular kids' table right next to Melissa. I took off my flip-flops to allow her to heal the burns on my feet first. Melissa slid off her own white block heel sandals as well, placing her own feet onto mine in what I assumed was a game of footsie that she wanted to play with me for some weird reason. I could've asked Melissa what the hell she was doing out of instinctual skepticism, but for some reason, I actually liked the sensation.

"Don't move your feet just yet," Melissa told me. "This will only take a few seconds."

The sensation I was feeling only got better when a sparkling pink glow emanated out of Melissa's feet. In those few seconds, my own feet were bathed in the most therapeutic substance in the universe. My eyes began to close, and a soft smile traced my face as the soothing sensation continued. When Melissa moved her feet off of mine, my own feet looked completely clear, as well-polished as I tried to make them every morning. As I slipped my flip-flops back on, I didn't feel any sharp sting on my feet at all.

"Wow," I reacted. "Just like magic."

"Pretty much," Melissa said. "So, now that you see that I'm not that bad after all, are you now willing to negotiate a peace treaty between you nerds and us campus royalty?"

"How about . . . no. No amount of magical therapy is going to make me start to admire you or your little buddies, Melissa Snyder. But feel free to go on. Your work's not done yet."

"I see. So where else are you still feeling pain?"

I removed the bandage on my right forearm, as well as a couple of other ones circling my midriff, revealing the other parts of my body where Garrett burned me.

One by one, Melissa placed her hands where my lingering wounds were, returning me to the most soothing sensation in the universe as her healing auras emanated once more. I knew that the sight of Melissa placing her hands and feet on certain parts of my skin might look strange to others in the cafeteria, but that didn't stop me from continuing to like it. As much as I was enjoying Melissa's magical therapy, however, I started to feel a little guilty about resorting to it rather than sticking with Nurse Morris's more conventional methods of medicine. I promised her that I still had my trust in her, after all.

Still, on the bright side, the most irritating girl in my class undid the damage that Garrett did to me. Her power wouldn't bring back Lizzy or any of the other nine slain students (unless she also had some kind of resurrection ability that I hadn't seen yet), but it was great to witness the positive forces of the universe cancel out the harmful ones.

As I looked for where my scars were, well, they weren't there anymore. I no longer felt a thing in those areas of my body that Garrett scorched. When I turned my head up, I noticed that almost everyone in the cafeteria had been watching us the whole time. Some looked at us in amazement, while others just tilted their heads away as if there wasn't anything out of the ordinary going on in the cafeteria. Even a few school staff members passing by took a glance at me and Melissa. As for Melissa herself, it was difficult for me to tell if she disliked all the attention, or if she was enjoying the spotlight like she usually did.

"Thank you for that, Melissa," I said. "Glad you decided to show your hidden nice side for once."

"You're very much welcome, Jessica," Melissa said. "You should feel lucky that I agreed to help you out. I'm rather stingy when it comes to using these powers."

Although Melissa's magic-powered physical therapy only lasted a few seconds, I wished it would've taken much longer than that, because I enjoyed it that much. I could sense why Nurse Morris was afraid of her job being in jeopardy. And once more, it disheartened me to think about how she'd react to hearing about how my burns and bruises healed so fast.

Now that Melissa finished healing me, I walked back to my secret spot where I spent lunch periods with Orlando and Charlotte. I worried for a bit that the two of them already left because of how long I was away, but luckily, they were still sitting on the beach and gazing at the crashing waves of the Pacific Ocean.

"Where were you?" Orlando asked. "You were away for quite a while."

"Oh, just stopped by the cafeteria for a quick chat with . . . Melissa Snyder." I hesitated to say her name because the mention of it made me nauseous, even if she decided to be kind and helpful to me for once. Plus, it was too damn hard to admit to my best friends that I wanted to see her for a brief moment. Geeks and popular chicks mixed like oil and water; we weren't supposed to show any sign of amicability toward one another.

"Melissa Snyder? What did you go see her for? She tends to forget that so-called 'losers' like us exist."

"Take a look at my feet and arms, and you'll see why." I had Charlotte and Orlando gaze at those parts of my body; it didn't take long for them to notice that there was something different about them.

"Your burns are all gone," Charlotte noted.

"That's what I went to Melissa for. One touch from her, and any injury or wound you suffer disappears like magic."

"Melissa Snyder got a superpower, of all people? What kind of world have we come to . . ." Charlotte continued.

"Both her *and* Darren Owens. Of course, Darren had to get supersonic speed, and now he's claiming that girls will be even more into him now, as if they weren't already flocking to him so pathetically . . ."

"Oh boy. Manzanita High School's definitely not the same anymore. Hell, the whole world in general isn't the same."

"Well, what else would you have expected when people at our school gain mysterious superpowers out of nowhere?"

"True that." The three of us then laughed in unison.

"I have to give it up to you, Jessica," Orlando said. "You were willing to put up with the MINK girls' bullshit, all to convince Melissa Snyder to use her magical power on you. You've got guts, girl. More than I imagined you did."

"I sure as hell didn't want to go up to those fools. But I think it'll have been worth it in the end. No more having to dance through the pain."

"I can't believe I'm saying that I have confidence about the prospects of our upcoming show again because of Melissa Snyder," Charlotte said. "But dance practice sure wasn't the same with you on the sidelines. Glad you can hit the dance floor in full force again, Jess."

"I got so tired of having to sit out practices because of my burns. Happy that Garrett can't take away the enjoyment I have for dancing like he did those ten innocent lives. Shall we do a bit of practice, C. C.?"

"With pleasure. It's about time you once again start . . . getting into a rhythm."

"Okay now, I can't even call that an attempt at a pun."

Before lunchtime ends, Charlotte and I got up, slipped off our flip-flops and began rehearsing parts of the piece that I was leading for our upcoming show. Quickly putting aside my usual cringy reaction to Charlotte's attempts at clever wordplay, I was more stoked than ever to practice my choreography with her. With every stretch I made and every spin I performed, I no longer felt any unbearable sting anywhere in my body. I felt like I was dancing at 100 percent health again. Somehow, in spite of all those practices I had to sit out, my choreography and chemistry with Charlotte hadn't missed a beat.

—∞—

Before fourth period started, I made my way to the dance room with my confidence intact, ready to lead the dance troupe again. It didn't take long for my teammates to notice that I didn't have bandages on me anymore, and that my skin was completely clear and smooth, as if nothing even happened to me in the first place.

"All your burns are gone," said my red-haired teammate Rachel Lowry, whom I considered my closest friend on the dance troupe aside from Charlotte. "They looked very bad a day ago. How did they heal so fast?"

I got close to Rachel's ear, preferring to keep the answer to that question to myself. "I have a friend here who has magical healing powers," I mumbled in her ear. "Well, maybe not exactly a friend, but yeah, she used her instant healing powers on me so that I can dance without any issue again. I got really tired of sitting out practices."

"Hmm . . . not sure if I can take your word for it," Rachel told me, mumbling like I did. "But we sure missed having you at practice. Regardless of how your burns got better, we're glad to have you back."

"Thanks, Rach," I said, speaking out loud again. Waving my arms up, I said to all my teammates, "What are we waiting for; let's get going again!" A few hollers saturated the room.

As all of us stood up and got in formation, the first face to catch my eye was that of Kayla Hidalgo, our dance troupe's co-captain alongside Megan Miller. The smile on her face was conspicuous to me, and I was glad I left another great impression on her knowing that she'd be my co-captain for the 2024–2025 school year.

Although I sat out practices for only a couple of days, I sported a rejuvenated vibe with every move I performed during Wednesday's class, more stoked than ever to get into a rhythm again. From the very first call of "five, six, seven, eight" that I made, a burst of empowerment echoed among my teammates now that I could lead them without issue again. I may not have had the title of dance troupe co-captain yet, but it was an encouraging sign when the rest of the team looked up to me as if I did.

CHAPTER

10

The Manzanita Comic Book Club, of which I had been co-president since the beginning of the school year, was one of my favorite outlets to escape from my adolescent troubles. Since I joined the club on my very first day of high school, it had been a welcoming space for me and numerous other Manzanita students who felt like outcasts in a school where athletic guys and snobby popular girls ruled the roost. For me and countless other nerds throughout campus, it was our go-to getaway spot during after-school hours, a place where we could discuss comics and pop culture without facing mockery for being "loser geeks." This time around, however, the meeting was bitter and nerve-wracking knowing that it was my first ever Comic Book Club meeting without Lizzy.

As Lizzy's best friend, I had the obligation to start the meeting with a speech dedicated to her memory. I'd already done this twice before—once at the public memorial held at our school's football stadium, and once at Lizzy's private funeral. But my experience in making such speeches didn't do anything to get rid of the butterflies in my stomach that I had the first two times I delivered a speech in her honor. Standing in the very front of room 303, Manzanita's room for astronomy classes, the lights on the ceiling were like a giant spotlight shining down on me.

"Good afternoon, ladies and gentlemen," I said to start my announcement. "Before we begin discussing our final comic of the year and start making plans to watch *The Vigilante: Beginnings* in theaters together, I would like to start off by dedicating this meeting to the memory of a devoted member of our club who tragically lost her life in the mass shooting that rocked our beautiful campus almost two weeks ago."

Before I started succumbing to my emotions again, I cleared my throat twice. "As you may know, Lizzy Manchester was an unapologetic geek. She lived and breathed pop culture, and integrated her Comic Book Club membership into her campus identity. Comics, books, and movies served as a key inspiration for the advocacy for which she gained recognition among those who knew her on campus during her two years as a Manzanita Marauder. So, even if you didn't know Lizzy well, at least try to recognize this important lesson that she's taught us: Pop culture isn't just silly, pointless entertainment intended to distract us from real-world issues. It can play a significant role in shaping society and teaching the world what equality, justice, and harmony should look like. What society has the potential to be. What we should know about these aforementioned real-world issues. In these uncertain times, as book bans skyrocket throughout the country and libraries face more scrutiny than ever, never is this lesson more important and more relevant than it is today."

Enthusiastic applause filled the room, with some in the classroom shedding tears. Even members who didn't know Lizzy well—some of them relatively new members, others who didn't spend much time around her because of their shyness or other factors—were able to recognize the massive void that her death left in our club.

"That was a beautiful speech, Jessica," said Kenzie Holiday, who shed a few tears. "I'm not sure I know anyone else in my life who could've made a dedication that touching. If there is, I haven't met them yet." It was an honor of the highest order for me to hear that coming from *the* biggest comic book and pop culture geek on campus—bigger than even me.

"Thank you for your kind words, Kenzie," I said. "Now, let's have a moment of silence in memory of Lizzy Manchester and everyone else who lost their life in the tragic shooting or suffered serious injuries from it." For all of ten seconds, not a single sound came out within the classroom. Heads bowed, and everyone in the room tried to contain their emotions. Then I broke the silence with, "Thank you. Now, let's get to more positive topics, please."

After a somewhat awkward laugh, I continued speaking to the seven other club members seated behind me and Kenzie. "So, as you may all know, a lot of people at our school have recently become, in essence, our favorite comic book characters. Not to brag or anything, but you may have heard somewhere that I've now become one of those characters." I stuck my right palm out, flashing a photon ball from it for everyone in the classroom to see. Expressions of awe filled the room, but none more so than that of Kenzie.

"Hell yeah! My co-president is a superhero now!" she said.

I shut off the photon ball generated from my palm and put my hand down. "Anyone else have cool new powers that they want to demonstrate?" Before anyone in the classroom had a chance to start their own demonstration, a short, pudgy girl opened the door and walks in. It was my good friend from the special needs program, Lorelyn Ash.

"Hey-o!" Lorelyn said with peppy enthusiasm. "Sorry I arrived a little late. This is the very first time I've ever attended one of your club's meetings, so I had some trouble finding the classroom. Did I miss anything?"

"Well, you didn't get to hear Jessica's incredible speech in tribute to Lizzy, our fellow geek who lost her life in the shooting," Kenzie replied.

"Oh yeah, I heard about that . . ." Lorelyn said in a lower tone. "I like Jessica Summer; she's a good friend of mine. And Lizzy was very cool; I liked her too. So I'm very sad about what happened to her." Lorelyn walked up to me and gives me a hug, a move I reciprocated in a split second. Our hug filled the room with a heartwarming aura.

"It looks like we have a new member of the Manzanita Comic Book Club," Kenzie said. She turned her attention to Lorelyn after she left our hug and said to her, "Welcome to our club, miss. My name is Kenzie Holiday; I'm the co-president of this club alongside Jessica, whom you already seem to know. Here at the Comic Book Club, we live and breathe all things pop culture, share our favorite comics with each other, have movie nights together, and participate in various other superhero-related activities. All that said, can I get your name, please?"

"Elseven." Oh. I didn't know that she had an alias now.

"We're happy to have you here . . . Elseven." Kenzie said, making a brief pause because of how strange she found the name "Elseven" to be. "Out of curiosity, have you attended any meetings of ours in the past?"

"No, I have not," Lorelyn—I mean, Elseven—answered. "This is my very first meeting. You people all seem very cool, though. I now kind of wish I had joined you guys earlier . . ."

"Hey, better late than never, Elseven. You have a very interesting name, by the way. Is that really your name, or just a cool nickname?"

"Well, my real name is Lorelyn, but after getting these cool powers, that name is too lame for me now. So now I go by Elseven."

The girl who now called herself Elseven turned her attention to everyone in the class, injecting a more dramatic tone into her voice. "A few days ago," she narrated, "I watched *Frozen* for the billionth time. And as I watched the movie, something peculiar happened to me: I could now generate beautiful ice magic like Elsa herself! Curious to know why I ended up gaining a fictional character's ability, I watched an episode of *Stranger Things* right after finishing up the movie. Afterward, I gained Eleven's psychic powers just like I did with Elsa's ice powers! Hence how I got my new name: Elseven. Elsa plus Eleven. I'm still trying to figure out how my power works, but the basic gist is that I just watch a character in a movie, show, or comic book use their special ability, and then, after one such occasion, boom! I can now use it in the same exact fashion that they do. So I wanted to join your Comic Book Club because it feels like the perfect environment for me to take advantage of my new ability with all the comics and movies you folks read and watch."

"Well, you've come to the right place, Lorel—Elseven," I said. "Here at the Comic Book Club, we have all the comics in the world to offer you so you can find more new powers to obtain." I flashed the biggest smile that I'd made thus far today; Elseven tended to bring that out in me, no matter what the circumstances.

I offered Elseven the most recent comic book that I read: the final issue of Wonder's iconic massive crossover event, *Skirmish through Spacetime*, which launched Wonder into official comic book superstardom during its twelve-issue run in 2003 and 2004. "I feel this comic would be the perfect start for you. It contains just about every single Wonder character and superhero team you're familiar with: the Protectors, the Soul Triad, the Xenos, Captain Wonder, etc. Plenty of new powers for you to find and gain from this book."

Instead of just grabbing the comic from my hand, however, Elseven put her right hand behind the comic from a distance of about two feet. Her facial expression indicated that she was putting a laser focus into . . . whatever it was that she was trying to do. She also looked like she was starting to tremble.

"What are you doing, Elseven?" I asked.

"You'll see," she replied. "It'll take a few seconds; I'm still trying to learn how to use this power."

The comic floated away from my hand and into hers, wrapping against her fingers like a magnet to iron. Everyone in the class oohed and aahed at Elseven, while Kenzie clapped her hands at hyper-speed with an enormous grin on her face. When the comic reached Elseven's hand, red liquid started to flow out of her right nostril.

"Did you ever think to realize that copying Eleven's telekinesis would lead to a higher frequency of nosebleeds for you?" I asked Elseven with a smirk on my face.

"Oh, no worries, Jessica. I prepared for that." Elseven took a pack of tissues out of her pocket, grabbed a tissue, and cleared off the nosebleed with it. She then put the used tissue in her pocket and said, "I bring them with me everywhere I go. Just in case." She elicited a giggle from me, and my smirk widened into a full grin.

"You're the best, Elseven," I said. "Enjoy gathering new powers from your new comic. Just don't forget to give it back to me when you're done with it."

"I won't." Her new comic book in hand—or rather, floating in hand—Elseven did a few skips around the room, let out a few gentle puffs of her new Elsa-derived ice magic, and said, "Friends don't let it go!" I could tell where she got that catchphrase from, as weird as it probably sounded to the others in the room.

"So, we have Jessica's cool cosmic abilities, and Elseven has her own unique twist on the ability to copy others' powers," Kenzie said to everyone in the class. "Anyone else want to share their cool power that they now have?"

"Ooh, me, me," a blond-haired boy, Aaron Joseph, demanded, jerking his raised hand up and down.

"Okay. Go ahead, Aaron."

Aaron ran to the left edge of the room and then melted into a glimmering, silver liquid form. When he assumed this form, he morphed into a puddle, then navigated through the classroom door like an electric current through a wire and then melted straight through it. As reactions of "whoa" scattered through the room, Aaron phased back through the door the other way around and popped out of there, then reverted to his physical form.

"Cool, you're like those kids on the Capri-Sun commercials now, Aaron!" Kenzie said.

"Or Alex Mack," Aaron added, nodding his head and grinning. "Or the T-1000."

"Who else in this room got cool powers?" I asked the class. "Raise your hand."

Two more hands went up: that of a slim Asian kid named Corbin Wong, our club's resident anime and manga geek, and Paige Reading, who'd been spending the entire meeting writing across two sheets of paper with laser-focused intensity after our moment of silence for Lizzy, not even having uttered a single word.

"I'll have Paige go first, and then Corbin next," Kenzie said, pointing to them each when she announced their names. "You've been strangely silent this whole time, Paige. What does your power look like?"

"I'll let my pencil do the talking," Paige said in her typical soft, relatively deep voice. "I was rather busy writing; that's why I was keeping quiet."

She continued to write down more words, and then after a few seconds, a trio of bug-sized fairies and a baby dragon popped out of her pile of papers, slowly gaining color as they came out of the page. The rest of the classroom gazed in awe as the creatures sprang into the real world.

"Don't mind baby Chelwyn here," Paige said. "He doesn't bite at all. He's a very gentle creature." Most of the rest of us came to Chelwyn and pet him like he was a rabbit at an animal shelter. I spent the most time among us petting and snuggling him.

"Looks like you've got a best-selling author career in the making, Paige," I said, with reminders of Lizzy floating in my mind; she was halfway done with her first non-fanfic novel before her untimely passing. I always saw a bit of Lizzy in Paige, to be frank.

"Corbin, your turn," Kenzie said. "Show us what you've got."

"For sure," Corbin said as he got out of his seat. "Just a warning, though, I wouldn't say that I have the best handle on my new power yet."

With each step Corbin took to the front of the class, we felt the ground underneath us shake a bit. We brushed it off as no big deal, however, having seen enough extraordinary phenomena inside this room today. Once he was standing in front of us, Corbin generated an even greater shaking sensation from his body—enough to create visual distortions within his vicinity.

"Damn. Intense," said Terry Pratt, the sole freshman member present at today's meeting.

As Corbin continued to demonstrate his power, however, objects in the room shattered. Glass flew apart in two of the windows on the side of the classroom. The biggest damage done was to the powerful refractor telescope owned by our school's astronomy teacher, Mr. Rigel, with half of its top falling off its tripod. If you could've measured Corbin's nerves with a mercury-based meter, the mercury would've overflown and broken off the meter.

Terry shielded himself with his hands out of his concern over whatever was going on. "Dude," he said, "shut them off, Corbin."

"I'm trying," Corbin said. "But I don't know how."

"Try relaxing and finding your inner calm," I advised Corbin. "Think about something that calms you down, brings you peace. Like what you would do if you were a Harry Potter character trying to cast a Patronus."

"Okay," he said. Corbin closed his eyes as the shaking in the room continued. After a few worrisome seconds, the shaking stopped, leaving behind broken windows, desks split in half, and a damaged telescope. Fortunately, no one got hurt. But after what just happened with his comic book power, Corbin scanned his surroundings as he walked back to his seat.

"I'm really sorry about that," he said. "I told you I can't use my power well. Maybe it would've been better if I didn't even share it to start."

"Corbin, it's okay," I said. "A lot of people go through initial struggles with their powers when they tap into them for the first time. Beacon didn't master his light powers right away when he first discovered them. Neither did most of the Xenos with all their extraordinary abilities. With all the bullshit we go through as teenagers, you shouldn't feel any shame over your powers going haywire."

"You have a point there, Jessica. Thanks for the pep talk; you've made me feel better about my powers now."

"No problem, Corb. We're always here for you if you ever need support. And everyone here with superpowers will try to help you control your powers better."

"Thanks, Jess. I'd very much appreciate that."

Despite the much-needed words of encouragement that I gave to Corbin, I felt some concern in the back of my mind about his powers leading school staff to catch our club damaging property with our abilities. I knew for sure that Mr. Rigel would have something to say about it, considering the damage done to his valuable telescope.

Eh, don't worry about it too much, I think. *How are they going to find out that someone with comic book powers caused all this damage anyway?*

CHAPTER

11

On Friday, I had my first scheduled appointment with Dr. Domínguez-Salas during first period. Although I already had a walk-in appointment with her before, going into her office felt like lifting a five-ton boulder off my back. And I couldn't care less about missing a few minutes of geometry.

"This has been a long time coming, Dr. Domínguez-Salas," I said after taking my seat. "But here we are."

"And you made it, *chica*," the school therapist said, clapping her hands. "I knew you would."

"Thank you for your encouraging words."

"My pleasure. So how has your recovery been going so far, Ms. Summer?"

"I can't say it's been a hundred percent smooth sailing; if I did, I'd be lying. But overall, it's been going great. The trauma I've been feeling has been less than it was earlier in the week, and it's a blessing to have the type of support system that I've had in the circumstances I've needed to face. I know this is a rather nerdy thing to say, but being back at school is restoring some semblance of normalcy in my life after everything I've been going through. It's great seeing my friends again, going to dance practice again, holding Comic Book Club meetings again."

Dr. Domínguez-Salas took a brief pause to write down some notes before continuing. "I love hearing that from you, *muchacha*. And your powers? Have you had any issues with them?"

"I did create a minor fuss while playing around with a friend of mine who also has comic book powers . . . but that's only because there was a security guard in the area at the time. Otherwise, so far, I haven't had problems with my powers, or created any, or worsened anything because of them. Unless you want to count my battle with the Manzanita shooter last week, but that didn't take place on school grounds, and I had to fight him anyway to prevent him from taking any more lives after his escape from prison."

Dr. Domínguez-Salas jotted down a few more notes. "Your recovery has been impressive, Ms. Summer," she said after a few seconds of focused silence.

"Thank you. I don't know how I've been able to get through it all, but somehow, I have. I had to watch my best friend in the whole world die in front of my eyes and went through a lot of bullshit in the days that followed, and soon after, my life further changes forever after gaining all these fancy new powers from a shooting star wish I made. All while going through the typical trials and tribulations of teenage life, no less. But of course, that's a typical superhero origin story there . . ."

"You couldn't have said it any better, Ms. Summer. And you're the first person that I've witnessed go through a superhero origin phase."

"I'm guessing that I won't be the last. Heck, I'm certain I'm not the only one at this school who's gone through such a phase." I laughed and then continued. "Superpowers are here to stay, whether we like it or not. Of course, I'm part of the 'like it' side, in case you can't tell . . ." I laughed again, but this time with Dr. Domínguez-Salas laughing in unison with me.

"And since you brought him up, how have you been feeling about the shooter fleeing prison?"

"It's been tough news for me, of course. To hear that my best friend's murderer fled prison and gained his own deadly powers, I can't describe in words how disheartening that's been for me." I ignited my golden-yellow glow and flashed yellow energy balls from each of my hands. "But with the powers I now have, I no longer have to feel helpless against him. I can now put him in his place, just like my favorite superheroes would."

Dr. Domínguez-Salas gave me a round of applause. "It thrills me to hear that from you, Ms. Summer. And how have your experiences been with your powers so far? More positive, more negative . . .?"

"Well, as a longtime fan of comic books and superheroes, I thought it would be a dream come true to gain superpowers and get to be a superhero and save people from massacres and tragedies and all that stuff. But now it feels like certain members of school staff—I'm not going to name names—are becoming suspicious of me and other students with cool powers like ours. It's as if people have found another excuse to bully those who aren't like them, just because of a judgmental perception that we might be dangerous people. Having learned over the years about the effects that racism, sexism, homophobia, and all those things have on the demographics they target . . . it's an uncomfortable thing to think about."

"Hmm . . . I see. Well, I'm an immigrant to this country, having come here about fifteen years ago and having to start from scratch after leaving my family and loved ones for a brand-new life. Of course, that came with all sorts of troubles. I had difficulty speaking English, and I can recall a good few people saying nasty things to me like 'Go back to where you came from.' But I persisted through it all, settled into American culture, and now I just look back at the positives. I know what it feels like to be judged and come face-to-face with major adversity, Ms. Summer. So know that, if you ever feel like others are bullying you because of your special powers, I'm always here to support you."

I got out of my seat for a bit to give my school therapist a big hug. "Thank you, Dr. Domínguez-Salas," I said. "That means a lot to hear from you."

"Oh, *de nada*, Ms. Summer. I always do what I can to make this office a welcoming environment for all." When I returned to my seat, Dr. Domínguez-Salas asked, "So, anything else you'd like to discuss today?"

"Nope, that's about it. If anything comes up, I'll let you know."

"No problem. My office is always here if you ever encounter anything unforeseen."

"And I'm grateful for that office and, as always, for all your work. See you again soon, Dr. Domínguez-Salas."

It took a full two weeks for me to finally hold my first scheduled appointment with Dr. Domínguez-Salas, but it was a wait very much worth going through. As I walked out of her office and back to my geometry class, I started to see clear light at the end of the tunnel for the first time in a long time. The unique stresses I was dealing with weren't going away any time soon, and I had to continue coping with them to some degree. But with the end of the first full week back, it meant more time for us to move further from the shooting's aftermath.

—∞—

After taking the time I needed to grieve and overcome the difficulties of the past few weeks, I had my first performance with my band, Flowchella, since the shooting. A chance for my life to further return to normal.

Our late afternoon show, taking place some two hours or so before sunset, marked our last one of the school year. Being our first show since the shooting, it was a bitter one for me, just as much as my first Comic Book Club meeting since our return to school. We had to delay our show by a week to give ourselves more time to deal with the shooting's aftermath, which at least placed our final performance at a time after Melissa healed my burns and bruises, making sure that playing that afternoon wouldn't be such a drag for me physically.

I was the guitarist and part-time singer for Flowchella, and my bandmates—keyboard player and singer-songwriter Rudy Gillick and drummer Braxton White—shared a brotherly bond with me that went beyond our association as a school band. In fact, I considered them my closest guy friends aside from Orlando. So of course, when we met up onstage, they each welcomed me with some of the biggest hugs and condolences I'd gotten since we returned to school after the shooting—much bigger hugs, even, than the first time we met at school after the shooting. The crowd at our show, which consisted primarily of Manzanita students but included a few students from other high schools in the area, gave us an incredible round of applause when they watched our group hug. We followed our group hug by asking for a moment of silence from the crowd in honor of the Manzanita shooting victims before starting our show. I already went through a moment of silence a few days ago to start the week's Comic Book Club meeting, so as eerie as starting a performance in such a somber manner was, it wasn't anything new for me.

I had only had a week to practice the chords for Dua Lipa's song "Break My Heart"—or, to be technical, Rudy's latest parody song "Break Apart"—due to my focuses shifting elsewhere for most of the past couple of weeks, so I was nervous about how my guitar playing would be. I showed minimal rust, however, and hearing those chords come out of my guitar, which I had named "Jaehwa" after the real name of K-pop superstar Baby Diva (Jae-Hwa Bae), was the most satisfying sensation in the world for me. Our first song of the afternoon wasn't just another performance; it was a crucial accomplishment for me in trying times.

"Thank you, Manzanita! That was my latest tune, 'Break Apart,' a parody of Dua Lipa's 'Break My Heart,'" Rudy said to the crowd. While the people in the crowd hollered and clapped, they turned most of their attention to Rudy, but also gave some of it to me as well, more so than usual. Rudy and Braxton didn't tell me yet if they lost any close friends in the shooting, so I couldn't speak for them, but many knew from my speech at the public memorial that I lost my best friend in the shooting, so it meant a lot to see the crowd give me such humbling sympathies. It helped that those inside our concert's beachside venue could spot me onstage easily, not just because of my blond hair and being the only girl member of Flowchella, but also due to the fact that I was barefoot. Yes, I performed barefoot onstage, thank you; on occasions, my peers would refer to me as the "barefoot rocker" or "barefoot guitarist."

Although my band's specialty was parody songs—courtesy of Rudy, who wrote parodies of hit songs both as a hobby and sometimes for school assignments—we also performed covers of popular songs from various eras, primarily rock songs. The next song we played was "Face Down" by The Red Jumpsuit Apparatus. I did okay through most of the song, focusing on nothing but my guitar playing until we got to the first mention of the line "I've finally had enough."

At that point, a figure that looked like Garrett Lowe popped up in front of my eyes somewhere within the crowd, provoking me to freeze up. My guitar tune ceased, even as Rudy continued singing and Braxton continued drumming for a few seconds after. The crowd stopped jumping and came to a standstill. It wasn't long after that Rudy and Braxton ceased their own music while I bobbed my head down in response to the unpleasant emotions engulfing me. My body began to shake a bit while I knelt on one knee and glowed golden-yellow again. My glow was brighter and more intense than it was the first time that I demonstrated it to my parents; perhaps it had to do with the fact that the sun was shining down directly at the venue where we're playing, and it wasn't just my emotions acting up.

"Jessica, are you okay?" Braxton asked.

A split second after Braxton's question, a powerful explosion of bright white light burst out of my body, something similar to the solar flares that I used to read about in space books and on space websites growing up. The students in the crowd stumbled backward, and many of them shielded their eyes; just about all of them had a hard time opening them up. Fortunately for Rudy and Braxton, they threw their hands in front of their eyes in time, protecting them from the exceptionally bright light that I just ejected.

"Sorry, sorry, I'm so sorry about that!" I yelped to the students in attendance, waving my arms in front of me. None of them reacted, appearing too busy to deal with suddenly being blinded. I was oddly thankful for the lack of reaction, though.

Rudy took his microphone out of its stand to make an announcement. "Hello, can I have everyone's attention, please?" he said. "We are very sorry about what just happened. We hope you can understand that our guitarist, Jessica, has been going through a very difficult time the past few weeks. We are certain that she was not intending to do that at all. We're going to take care of her for the time being, so for now, we're going to pause the concert until further notice. We hope to resume playing, and we will give an update as soon as we're ready again. Thank you."

As the crowd cleared, I looked for Garrett on the floor behind the stage, but he wasn't anywhere. In fact, he seemed to have disappeared just before I accidentally blinded the students who attended our concert. That was the only sense of relief I had at the moment. Otherwise, I was both frozen and regretful. It was even worse that Orlando and Charlotte were among those that I blinded with the bright burst of light I let out, as I saw them at the front of the crowd, and they told me earlier that they would be attending this concert.

"I'm so sorry about that," I said to Rudy and Braxton, who walked close to me in support. "My emotions got the better of me . . . I knew I was pushing myself. But I swore that playing with you guys again would return me to normalcy. Too bad nothing is normal anymore . . ."

"Jessica, it's okay," Braxton said. "I don't blame you for pushing yourself too hard."

"We promise we're not mad at you, man," Rudy said. "I can't speak for you folks at school who now have fancy powers, but things happen."

"We're rock stars at our school. Rock stars tend to go through major issues, just like you are. So you're not the only one, Jess. It's just standard rock star stuff, I suppose." Braxton giggled, trying to make light of a tough situation. I giggled back at him, though a bit awkwardly.

After our little talk, I stood back up and walked over to where my flip-flops were to slip them back on. "I could use some relaxation time right now," I announced. "I'll let you know when I'm ready to get back onstage. Let's stay in here, though. I'd love to relax at the beach, but I don't want to run into anyone who could get upset at me for what I just did."

"Sounds like a plan," Rudy said. "Better safe than sorry."

Some time after sitting around, we decided to cancel the rest of the concert and end it early to give me more time to take care of my mental well-being. Rudy promptly made the announcement to the crowd as they filtered back into the venue before we went back home. I met up with Orlando and Charlotte as the crowd emptied out, recognizing Orlando right away by his blue-and-yellow soccer jersey, which he wore at least once every week. Rudy and Braxton departed together while I checked up on my best friends.

"Hey, glad you two could come to our show," I greeted them. "Sorry that I blinded you two. And that my antics got the show canceled early."

"Hey, no worries, man," Orlando said. "We knew that burst of light you fired out was going to be very intense, so we covered our eyes on time and didn't get affected. I have to admit that was pretty cool of you, what you did."

"Thanks . . . I guess. Are you okay too, C. C.?"

"Never better, Jess, I promise," Charlotte replied; I believed what she said. "Let's go home."

Despite the encouraging words that my bandmates gave me, and the fact that Orlando and Charlotte were able to avoid the worst of my flash like Rudy and Braxton did, I was still regretful about ending our last concert of the year after two songs because one of my powers went out of control. And I was so stoked to cover "Face Down" on my guitar, too. The only bright spot that I took from our performance, other than the incredible support I received from both attendees and my bandmates, was that Rudy, Braxton, and I were able to take our annual end-of-the-year band photos at the nearby beach. But overall, this wasn't how I wanted Flowchella's final show of the year to go. I was imagining much more than a performance cut short by one of my comic book powers.

As much as I craved a return to normalcy, nothing was normal in this post–Manzanita shooting world, nor would it ever be again with the presence of people with comic book powers. The concert was another unpleasant reminder of that. Thanks a lot, Garrett Lowe, aka Rage.

I'd been taking yoga classes at East Beach on Saturday mornings since the start of springtime, and no yoga class was a welcome breath of fresh air for me as much as this one. Because of its proximity to where the shooting took place, our last two classes were cancelled, so this was my first Saturday morning yoga class since the shooting. Between my therapy appointment the day before and beach yoga with an abruptly cancelled concert coming in between, I couldn't have asked for a better sequence of mental health relief.

My yoga class was a short ten-minute walk away from where I lived, and it was a very relaxing walk for me the whole way there. The fresh air coming in, the beach and the Pacific Ocean in front of me, the slapping sounds of my flip-flops—all these noises, sights, and more combined to give me my own live ASMR display. There were worse places in which to attempt to overcome lingering mental anguish than sunny Santa Barbara, California. And for that, I couldn't be any more grateful. A big shout-out to my parents for choosing the perfect place to live and raise a family.

The first thing I did when I got to the park where I took my yoga classes was wait for one of my classmates, Haruka. A short Japanese American woman around my parents' age, her daughter Ellen, a high school junior, was one of the ten students who lost their lives in the shooting. Haruka was the tenth of around fifteen students of varying ages to arrive at today's class; when she got there, we made sure to give each other the biggest hug of our lives. Tears emerged from my eyes as we embraced.

"I'm so sorry for your loss," I said. "I didn't know Ellen very well, but I had algebra class with her as a freshman and was impressed by how bright she was."

"Oh, thank you, Jessica," Haruka said, also crying. "It was an honor to hear you dedicate your memory to Ellen at the public memorial a week ago. That takes so much selflessness for you to do that."

"Thank you, Haruka. It's such a shame that your daughter lost her life that Thursday. She seemed to have a bright future ahead of her."

With a loud sniffle, Haruka said, "Ellen died trying to save her best friends from succumbing to the shooter's rampage. They might not have made it out alive without her courageous efforts that day. At least she ensured that everyone who knew her will remember her for years to come, even in spite of passing away too soon."

"That's so brave of her. I wish I could've done the same, without the dying part, of course."

"That reminds me, how have you been dealing with the loss of your friend? What was her name again?"

"Lizzy. Lizzy Manchester. To be frank, I don't think I'll ever get over her death completely. That's a hole in my life I can't imagine being able to replace. But I'm taking things day by day. And I'm lending my support to Lizzy's parents whenever I can. I talked to them the other day and they said that the famous comic book writer Scott Lowe offered to help them out in a joint collaboration to help put a stop to American gun violence. Scott Lowe is my idol, so that really made my night when they told me that."

"That's fantastic. I'm so glad that you mentioned that, Jessica, because Mr. Lowe got in contact with me and all the other parents who lost their kids in the shooting regarding that same project. I'm not as familiar with his work as you are, but to know that he's decided to do something about gun violence in response to what his son committed warms my heart so much."

Haruka caught her breath before continuing. "That said, I hope we can do something about the issue soon. It's festered on for too long, even hitting our own peaceful beachside community. I lost my daughter to gun violence, and I can't let another parent lose their child or children to it, either. Fortunately, Mr. Lowe's ongoing efforts have made me more optimistic about the situation."

"That's a subject to save for another day, Mrs. Sugiyama. I'll do what I can to play my part in resolving the issue, but it's an issue I personally don't feel comfortable talking about, especially not here. It brightens my day to hear that Scott Lowe spoke with you, too. I'm glad you've gotten a taste of how wonderful of a man he is."

Okay, enough time for tears. Time to put my energy into this yoga class. No better way to let my sorrow and trauma melt away for the day, after all.

Each beach yoga class that I took lasted a full hour. Around halfway through that hour, as I entered my next warrior pose, my bright yellow glow reemerged. It wasn't nasty and intense—more like I entered some type of nirvana. I could sense everyone in my class looking at me puzzled, including our yoga instructor, Ms. Anders. But that didn't matter to me. I was in my own little world, and in this world, my powers were a gift, not something to arouse suspicion.

The end of yoga class should've gone down like the end of any other day. I wrapped my yoga mat, slipped on my Rainbow flip-flops, and prepared to walk back home. But at that moment, every other participant's eyes were on me as if I just beat a puppy to death. The attention was somewhat unsettling, but that hour of yoga left me relaxed enough that I was able to not let it bother me too much. Whether I liked it or not, I was going to stand out in a crowd by virtue of having abilities that no human being was supposed to have. And I just had to deal with that; it's just life.

As people started to depart class, Ms. Anders walked up to me and asked, "What was that going on with you today? Your . . . bright, glowy thing?" Ah yes, of all the people to ask, she had to be the one.

"Oh yeah, you see, I have all these fancy powers now," I answered.

"Ah. I see you're one of those people who benefited from the Great Bestowal."

"The Great Bestowal? What's that supposed to be?"

"Oh, you didn't hear? Millions of people throughout the world gained all types of superpowers like the ones in comic books and movies about a week ago. No one knows how they got them, or what caused them to gain such powers, but scientists, government officials, and many other people are working to solve this mystery. Some are welcoming our new superhumans with open arms, while others are claiming that they need to be cured."

My shooting star wish. That must have caused this Great Bestowal. As absurd of a claim as that would sound to others, it was the only way that I could explain this new world of superpowers that we were in. At least from my perspective.

It was true that people elsewhere in the world gained comic book powers, after all. Of course they wouldn't only be present in Santa Barbara, or only in America. That wasn't how superhero tales and franchises worked, after all. Why else would superheroes have to save the world all the time, as opposed to merely "saving the city?"

CHAPTER

12

The new school week—the second-to-last week of school before finals week (and my dance show the Sunday night before we start finals week)—was more of a return to normalcy compared to the week that preceded it. Campus safety was still a concern due to both the shooting and the shooter's recent escape from prison, as well as numerous students on campus still learning to harness their new comic book powers; as such, school security was still much more stringent than it was before the shooting. However, now that we had time to allow our grief and trauma to subside a bit, this week felt more like a regular school week. Students on campus were projecting a livelier atmosphere than they did a week ago, a difference that was night and day for me. No tears and emotional hugs to be found, either.

Because Manzanita was only a ten-minute walk from my house, I tended to be one of the first people to arrive at my homeroom class every day. My homeroom buddy, Shelby Roy, typically arrived somewhere between five and ten minutes after I did. Shelby was one of the few popular kids on campus that I could tolerate, perhaps because she hung out with a different group from the MINK girls and Darren's posse (though some of them weren't much better than Darren and Melissa's gang either). She was also nice enough to be amicable with their clique—as irritating as Melissa, Darren, and co. could often be, including to some of the guys and girls in her own clique.

"How's my favorite nerd?" Shelby greeted me. She called me "nerd" and "geek" in a kinder manner than the MINK girls did.

"Better than I was last week, that's for sure," I replied as Shelby took her seat next to me.

"That's fantastic to know. Has your mental health been starting to improve?"

"I'd say so, yeah. Bit by bit. It's helping, getting back into the rhythm of school activities again. Things will never feel the same without Lizzy, obviously. But I'd say I'm starting to get over my trauma somewhat."

"That's wonderful to hear, Jessica," Shelby said. "I'm happy for you. Hope things continue to look up for you."

"Thanks, Belb." That was my affectionate nickname for Shelby. "How have you been doing yourself?"

"Well, just like you and everyone else, I've had a difficult past couple of weeks, Jess. Especially knowing that the shooter might have been targeting me in his massacre because of the girls I hang out with. So therapy has been a real godsend for me."

"Do you meet with Dr. Domínguez-Salas? She's the best."

"Oh, yes. She's so wonderful and understanding. I also discovered a few weeks ago that I now have a cool new magical power. It's given me brand new confidence in life and, best of all, has helped me with overcoming the trauma that I've felt from the shooting."

"You have a comic book power? How come you didn't tell me earlier, Shelby?"

"I was a little hesitant to tell you at first, and I admit it wasn't a good time coming back to school for the first time since the shooting. But after thinking about it for a bit, I now feel comfortable showing you the cool new ability I now have. Come with me to the hallway; I want to show you my cool power there so that we don't distract anyone in homeroom."

"Good plan, Belb." Shelby and I departed our seats and walked through the door. Our homeroom teacher hadn't arrived yet, so we didn't have to worry about the possibility of getting in trouble with him.

I folded my arms and leaned back on the locker closest to our homeroom class, while Shelby stood next to me and faced me. "Show me what you got, Belb," I said with a smirk.

As she stood in place, Shelby's body started to glow, but in a different way from the aura of bright yellow energy that surrounded me when I utilized my powers. Her entire body became encased in the colors of the rainbow as multicolored energy flowed through every corner of it. Then, she pointed her right index finger outward, emitting a magnificent ray of multicolored energy from it. A couple of students who walked by us turned their heads back and glued their eyes to Shelby's rainbow beam the whole time that we saw them. After a few seconds, the beam disappeared, and Shelby put her arm back down as her multicolored glow faded away and the features of her clothing and body became visible again.

"You have the same power as Gleam? That's so awesome!" I said to Shelby.

"I thought the exact same thing when I tapped into my power for the first time," Shelby said. "Gleam is my bae. I even own a copy of the album from her movie."

"Oh, that album is my jam. Her and anything by Baby Diva. I don't care either that Gleam is a fictional pop star."

Shelby ceased our conversation to pull out her phone and take a peek at it. "Ooh, we better get back inside," she told me. "Homeroom starts in two minutes."

Shelby and I were able to walk back into our classroom before Mr. Thompson arrived. In his right hand were a large pile of papers. My mind pondered what those papers could be for, as he was holding enough sheets to give to every student in the room.

Around three minutes after Mr. Thompson entered the classroom, Principal Warden made his daily public announcement to the school. But it wasn't the usual announcement regarding the latest events happening on campus or those occurring in the near future.

"Hello, Marauders. Principal Joel Warden here," our principal said over the school speakers. "For safety reasons, we have decided that it would be best to institute a set of rules that will regulate the use of superpowers at our school."

Those first few words already made me want to fall off my seat. I didn't blame Manzanita for wanting to establish new rules to keep the student populace safe. People with superpowers were a relative novelty, after all, and we did need some regulation regarding the potentially dangerous powers that some of us possessed. But based on the recent behaviors and attitudes that I'd seen from certain staff members on campus such as Nurse Morris, I got the feeling that the rules Principal Warden was going to announce were not going to be pleasant for us superpowered folks.

"Starting today, students who have superpowers are forbidden from using their powers on campus in any manner. Even if one's powers go off by accident, they will still face punishment from the staff for triggering their powers. If you ever observe any students using their powers in any manner, we encourage you to report that student, or those students, to the front office immediately and describe what happened as best you can."

Even if our powers went off by accident. That's how I knew that our school had chosen to single out students with comic book powers and paint us as a grave danger to everyone around us These rules weren't about safety; they were about marginalizing students who possessed extraordinary abilities. In all likelihood, some of those on our school staff had been fans of characters like Heroman and Beacon over the years. Would they force them to not be their super-selves if they were Manzanita students?

Continuing with the announcements of the new school rules, Principal Warden added, "In addition, any student who uses their powers in sporting competitions will face severe punishments, including suspension from competition or even a complete, permanent ban from athletic activities."

After the principal concluded his announcement, I gazed at Shelby, who was as still as a statue. It was difficult for me to decipher her emotional state after she showed me her power just minutes before the official announcement of the powers ban. But whatever her emotions were, they definitely weren't pleasant ones.

In the meantime, Mr. Thompson was going around the classroom to hand a sheet of paper to every student in the room. The sheet of paper contained the full list of rules that the school now applied to people with comic book powers and the use of said powers on school grounds or during school-related activities.

Using your powers to sneak a peek at neighboring students' answers and cheat on tests in other ways; okay, I got that rule. But no using your powers even in private settings? Not being allowed to use your powers to help out others with tasks they were having difficulty with? I wasn't one to utilize my powers to make certain everyday tasks easier, but I considered many of these rules a violation of freedom of expression.

"This is ridiculous," I said to Shelby. "It's just like how certain people try to suppress others for being gay or black or autistic or any other group they perceive to be a threat to society."

"Here's my favorite one: No using any powers to create works of art," Shelby said, pointing to where the rule was listed on the sheet of paper in her hand. I had the feeling that Paige Reading wouldn't like that rule.

"Now that's how you know these rules violate our freedom of expression. We have a *literal* violation of freedom of expression here. Lizzy would snap at this list of rules, man."

"You have to give credit to the school for coming up with every possible scenario they can think of in which to forbid students from using their powers, though. That must have taken a lot of thinking and imagination."

And then there was the punishment system the school created for anyone who used their powers on school grounds or during school activities:

First offense of rules: One-week suspension
Second offense: One-month suspension
Third offense: Suspension for a full semester
Fourth offense: Complete expulsion from school

That was already quite a start when any use of powers during school hours would result in a one-week suspension from classes. I was now curious to know if any other schools in Santa Barbara instituted similar rules against using powers. If that wasn't the case, then I might've had to consider transferring to another school where students with powers would be allowed to use them on campus grounds.

As I walked out of homeroom on my way to my first period geometry class, I took a quick look at Shelby as she headed to her own first period class. It was disheartening to think that seeing her rainbow powers for the first time in person might be the very last time that I got to see someone with comic book powers show off their abilities on campus. What was an awesome moment to witness was now a bitter one around half an hour later.

I thought that things would be returning to a relative normal in our third week of school following the resumption of classes. I thought that my therapy appointment the previous Friday would set the foundation for restored stability in my daily life. But nope, my school just had to throw everything off balance by instituting a massive crackdown on students with comic book powers.

Walking out of my second period English class, I may not have been paralyzed physically, but I had been paralyzed mentally since the announcements made during homeroom. Even when my teachers and classmates cracked occasional jokes today, my facial muscles didn't have it in them to curve my mouth into a smile. All that my face could communicate was the same still, worried look, along with occasional shivers within my body despite the trademark Southern California 70-degree midday temperatures.

Before I met up with Orlando and Charlotte, Victor Ullman crossed paths and made eye contact with me. He was quick to note the expression of uncertainty on my face that contrasted with the beam of hope he emanated. Given what the school just announced with their rules singling out students with superhuman abilities, Victor's enthusiasm was one heck of a sight to behold. The only other student with comic book powers that I could even picture being like this today was Elseven.

"Yo, Jessica, what's good?" Victor greeted me. Interesting how, of all the distraught superpowered students at our school, he turned his attention to me first. Quite the honor.

I tried to utter a word from my mouth in response to Victor's greeting. But I had difficulty doing so, as if the muscles in my vocal cords weakened enough to make forming words a challenge for me.

"It's not about the new rules the school passed today, is it?" Oh, I didn't know he gained the ability to sense people's feelings through their body language as another superpower.

"Well . . . yes, I guess. I think I'd say so." Although many at Manzanita would be quick to call me a "nerdy outcast," I usually wasn't this shy and quiet in conversations. But this time around, it was a chore for me to provide a solid answer.

"If I were you, Jessica, I wouldn't let them get to you. I know the announcements this morning were rough for our kind. But we'll find a way around them. I'm sure of it. Groups like black people and the LGBT community have had to put up with so much more bullshit than what we've been facing so far. But that's never stopped them from fighting. Because every such group in history never stops fighting for more freedom and more respect in society. Why can't we do the same? Because we're going to, no matter how much others want to spit on us for who we are."

"Yeah . . . I guess you're right. What's the point of being hopeless, anyway?"

"That's the spirit, Jessica." Victor proceeded to grab me in his arms and squeeze me using every single pound per square inch of his newfound strength. For a few seconds, my breaths were shorter and fainter. It was like an enormous boa constrictor was wrapping itself around me, but at least it was a friendly boa constrictor.

After Victor let go of me, I needed to take some time to find proper feeling in my skin and nerves again. The magnitude of his strength was to the point that, whenever he squeezed me, he made me feel like a shapeshifting being trying to readjust to their standard body.

"I appreciate the kind gestures. But just out of curiosity, what did you want to talk to me for?" I asked. "You caught me by surprise a bit, Victor."

"Oh, just looking to spread the love in these hard times, man. And you were the first person with powers I saw who wasn't . . . looking so great. So I thought, *Why not make her day better? I might as well.*"

"In that case, you keep making others' days better, Victor. All of us could use it." I flashed a smile and a thumbs-up in the football player's direction as we parted ways before I met up with Orlando and Charlotte to head to our secret lunch spot.

I tried to maintain Victor's pep talk in my head as I settled back into the harsh reality of the new normal for students with comic book powers at Manzanita. The same discomfort that I felt a week ago still maintained itself inside me as I made my way to my usual beachside lunch spot with Orlando and Charlotte. I could only imagine how much more awkward lunchtime today would be if I didn't have a pair of muggles for best friends. On the bright side, at least I'd no longer have to watch Darren make a fool of himself showing off his super speed at school.

While Orlando and Charlotte were chatting with each other about their expectations for the Wonder Cinematic Universe's latest phase of films, the Temporal Saga, I remained quiet just about the entire time so far. I was experiencing the same statue-like feeling that Shelby had during homeroom. That I wasn't in the mood to participate in Orlando and Charlotte's current conversation about the WCU, a subject I would normally ramble on about for minutes or even hours, said everything. Heck, I couldn't even focus on the ocean and blue sky in front of me as a means of mental relaxation.

"Are you okay, Jess?" Orlando asked. "I haven't seen you like this since Lizzy's funeral." Ah yes, he had to bring that up.

". . . not really," I replied. "I could say, 'I'm fine,' and move on from there. But I'd be lying my ass off if I did."

"Is it because of the new rules that the school announced today?" Charlotte said.

I heaved a huge sigh and replied, "Yes. I feel like those rules are telling me to be ashamed of having powers. I'm scared that they might be the beginning of an even greater crackdown on students who have superhuman abilities. I'm not just worried about myself, but for everyone else I know who has comic book powers. And I know plenty of such people."

"I know you feel distressed about these new rules. But the school's implementing them to keep students safe. Those powers you guys and girls have are amazing, but you know they can be potentially dangerous. And it's fair for the school to create rules that forbid the use of powers on school grounds considering that they haven't yet figured out how to effectively deal with students who have superpowers. It's a very new thing for them that they never had to deal with before."

"I can understand that, C. C. And of course, I agree with creating rules to keep students safe. But so many of those rules go way overboard. And they're very unfriendly to students who are still learning to use their powers properly. A kid in the Comic Book Club is having trouble keeping his powers in check. What if they go off without his intention during school hours? He'll be suspended for something he didn't mean to do."

"I don't want to sound insensitive to your situation, but you might be making too big of a deal about this, Jessica," Orlando said. "You appear to be panicking too much about these new rules when they were just announced today. We haven't even seen them in action yet. Maybe they won't have as much of an effect as you're assuming they will."

"It feels a bit silly that you two are the ones to explain," I rebutted. "I don't mean to criticize you two . . . but neither of you have powers. You don't know what it feels like to be viewed like a foreigner because of them. I swear the school has something against my right to be me. Our right to be ourselves. And if the suspicion I've been seeing toward students with superpowers is any indication . . . I fear that these new rules will become permanent."

"Maybe it'll be a temporary thing; you never know," Charlotte said. "Like how we were required to stay home every second of the day during COVID until scientists were able to figure out how the virus operates. Maybe these new rules will remain in place until teachers and faculty figure out effective ways to allow students with powers to utilize their abilities in a safe manner."

"We can only hope. As much as I'd like to be optimistic, it's hard for me to be. Society always has to find a new group to marginalize. And those of us with comic book powers are becoming an easy target."

—∞—

On an otherwise uneventful walk from our beachside lunch spot back to the main campus, Orlando, Charlotte, and I witnessed a kid storming out of the boys' bathroom a few minutes before the lunchtime bell was supposed to ring. He was dressed in a silky purple costume as if it was Halloween, and his backpack was hanging by one strap on his right shoulder, waving like a flag on a very windy day. The way he was acting aroused suspicion in me due to the skepticism I had of everything going on around me as a result of the school's new rules against superpowers. So I started to rush after him, even if it made me look like as much of a fool as him.

"Jessica, what are you doing?" Charlotte asked me, provoking me to halt myself for a few seconds.

"I need to know what he's up to," I answered. Just before the kid in the purple costume disappeared into the distance, I took off in pursuit of him. Even though he was well ahead of me, I still tried to close the gap as best I can. This would've been the perfect time to activate my flying ability if school staff weren't such jackasses.

"Smart of you to run after someone in flip-flops," Orlando said from across the hall.

"You know me, Orlando," I said back to him. "Flip-flops are the only shoes I wear this time of year. And every day except during the winter."

When I caught up to the kid in the purple costume, I encountered him at the campus entrance. He stood upright and placed his hands on his hips, an air of confidence painting his face.

"Looks like I've found my origin story at long last," I heard him mumble to himself. "Just as his high school announces a ban on superpowers, teenager Greg Nathan finds a prime opportunity to prove himself as a superhero. And so he becomes . . . Plasma Kid! The Defender of Santa Barbara!" After speaking in a barely audible tone, he shouted out his new alias in stark contrast to his previous mumbling.

The boy who now called himself Plasma Kid raised his arms up in the air, converting the air around him into sparkling electrical bolts of white and purple hues. The bolts then flowed into his body, giving him the appearance of a human plasma globe. The electrical bolts above Plasma Kid's head fizzled away as three campus security guards stormed in from behind and tackled him onto the concrete below. They pulled him back by tugging on various sections of his costume, preventing him from escaping their grasp.

"Greg Nathan," one of the security guards said; it was the same one who called Victor out a week ago when he and I demonstrated our powers to each other. "Did you hear the rules that the principal announced earlier? No using superpowers on school grounds?"

"You've got the wrong person!" Plasma Kid pleaded. "I'm not Greg Nathan, man; I'm Plasma Kid! Teenage superhero in the making! The Defender of Santa Barbara!"

"We know better than to trust any of you Exceptionals in the slightest," another one of the security guards said. "Quit it with your massive delusions."

Exceptionals. That's the first time I ever heard the term. The way the security guard said it, he was using it as if it was a label for one to be ashamed of.

The three guards escalated their aggression toward Plasma Kid as they began to slam their fists onto the back side of his body, including on the head. After a few seconds, his body flopped to the ground. But that didn't stop the guards from continuing to use excessive force on him. All I could do was stand back, my entire body frozen in place and unsure how to react to what I just saw.

Although I'd seen clips of police misconduct on the Internet, I'd never witnessed it firsthand in my life before. My legs and feet turned into Jell-O as I walked away from what just happened in front of me. Regret over my reaction started to pour all over my body with every step I took when I started to realize that I found a prime chance to be a superhero, only to opt for ill-timed inaction.

I didn't notice her at first, but Maryam Asghari, whom I recognized by the face that I saw on her YouTube channel as well as the vivid red hair underneath her hijab, was standing on the side across from where the security guards continued to brutalize Plasma Kid. She ceased her steps and cupped her mouth with her left hand, her yelps audible from her side of the campus entrance as tears soaked and reddened her face. As shivers surged down my spine, I walked over to Maryam's side of the entrance and watched campus security drag away Plasma Kid's limp body.

As much as I would've liked to tell Maryam how much I loved her YouTube content and ask her if she remembered me from our biology class last year, it was clear that I didn't have time for that. As her tearful howls continued, I wrapped my arms around her, hoping it was enough to comfort her.

"I'm so sorry that you just saw that," I told her. "Let's report what just happened to campus staff and the police right away." Maryam didn't say a word as she hugged me back. While the two of us were nothing more than acquaintances, and I mainly knew her through her YouTube channel, the condolences we showed to each other were as if we had been best friends our whole lives.

Because he was the one who announced Manzanita's new rules forbidding the use of comic book powers on campus, I wasn't comfortable with talking to Principal Warden; I was afraid that he wouldn't trust me if I discussed the incident with him. So instead, I reported the horrific incident I just witnessed to my academic counselor, Mrs. Ether, with Maryam by my side, still choked up.

"Hello, Jessica," Mrs. Ether greeted me. "What can I do for you today?"

"Hello, Mrs. Ether. I know that you're not the best person to be discussing this with, but me and my friend here just witnessed a horrific beating of another student by campus security for violating the new rules against superpowers. I wanted to bring up the incident to someone I can trust before reporting it to the police, so I thought you were the best person to talk to about it."

"I'm grateful that you have your trust in me as your counselor, Jessica. I will let Principal Warden know when I have the time. In the meantime, the nearest phone is over there, right next to the door on that side." Mrs. Ether pointed to a black landline standing across her office.

"Thank you, Mrs. Ether." I turned my body in the direction of the landline, with Maryam following my lead shortly after.

Maryam couldn't walk at a normal pace at the moment, so I got to the phone slower than I should, matching my walking pace with hers and finding it better that way anyway. Although her sobs weren't as loud as they were earlier, they were still audible, and tears were still dripping from her eyelids. Still shaking and shivering, I picked up the phone and dialed 911. An operator answered after two beeps.

"911, what's your emergency?" asked a female voice.

"Hi, my friend and I would like to report a police brutality incident we just witnessed," I said. "The two of us are currently sophomores at Manzanita High School. While we were on our way to our third period classes, we saw three security guards at our school beat up a boy around our age for using his superpowers. They punched and kicked him repeatedly until he became unconscious. Earlier today, our school officially implemented a set of rules banning people with superpowers from using their powers on school grounds, and the guards we saw were using unnecessary force on a minor for breaking new school rules. We were not involved with the incident in some way; we happened to be bystanders to it, and now we're very shaken after what we just saw."

The operator waited a few seconds before answering again; although I assumed she was taking notes, the wait felt longer than it actually was because of the discomfort that Maryam and I were feeling. "Thank you for your report, ma'am," she said. "Is it okay if I speak to your friend, too, please?"

"Sure thing." I handed the phone over to Maryam. She was in such shock that even mouthing words to the operator on the phone was a chore for her. All she could respond with was constant sobbing. So she handed the phone back to me.

"I'm sorry about that; my friend doesn't appear to be able to speak coherently at the moment," I said to the operator.

"It's okay. Can I get your names, please?"

"Sure. My name is Jessica Summer. And my friend's name is Maryam Asghari." I spelled out Maryam's name to the officer in case she hadn't seen it before.

The operator paused for another brief moment before proceeding. "Thank you, Ms. Summer," she said. "Are there any more details you can give us about the incident?"

"The incident we witnessed today was at the entrance to the campus of Manzanita High School. I can't say for sure what the boy's whereabouts are, but I believe that he's unconscious at the moment. The boy's name is Greg Nathan; he's my neighbor and around the same age as me, and he now possesses superpowers over electricity."

"Thank you again, Ms. Summer," the operator said after another brief pause. "We will let the Santa Barbara Police Department know about the incident, and we'll take care of things from there."

"Thank you, ma'am. I appreciate the good work you're doing."

"No problem. You have a good rest of your day, Ms. Summer."

"You too, ma'am." As I hung up the phone, I thought, *Yeah, there's no way I'm going to have a good rest of my day after what I just watched. It was already bad enough to begin with, anyway.*

Maryam and I made our way to our respective third period classes, still walking slower than usual. We were going to be late for our classes, but I didn't think that mattered. An endless silence hung over us as we strolled down the hallway, and I waved goodbye to Maryam as we parted ways, both of us still not saying a word and maintaining a frozen expression on our faces.

When I entered my French class and took my seat, the only sounds coming out of me were the slip-slap sounds of my flip-flops. I didn't bother to say a peep about what I just saw at the entrance to campus; I thought it was better that students and teachers found out about it themselves later on.

In spite of what I saw at the campus entrance a few moments before, I still had the guts to go on with the rest of my school day. Even then, the shivers in my body still remained, my throat was so dry that it needed several jugs of water, and I was much quieter than usual, even in a French class that required a high degree of vocality for the sake of grasping a foreign language. Meanwhile, I had no idea where Maryam went. But given her reaction to Greg's beating, I assumed that she went home early to cope with the trauma that she was going through.

CHAPTER

13

On Tuesday after school, the first thing I did when I got home was open up Maryam's YouTube channel. The turmoil I saw her in after witnessing Greg Nathan's beating Monday afternoon didn't discourage me from anticipating her latest YouTube video, but I did expect to see something different from her usual content with more things on her mind than the latest outfits she wanted to showcase.

Before I clicked on the thumbnail for her latest video, I first read its title: "Exceptionals, I stand with you." Exceptionals. There was that word again. Perhaps she also first heard the term from the security guard who called Greg by that word before beating him to a pulp.

From the very first second of the video, it was apparent that Maryam emanated a much different vibe from that of her normal fashion content. Donning a green headscarf that allowed her newly scarlet red hair to stand out from beneath, her tone was more educative than leisurely.

"*Dorood*, my friends. I'm Maryam Asghari," she said, her typical introduction to her videos. After she was too choked up to speak the last time I saw her, it was comforting to hear Maryam able to form proper words again.

"Today, there's a very important topic that I wanted to discuss, and that's the emerging issue of superism." Superism—there was another term I hadn't seen before. As positive as the word sounded, I didn't have a pleasant feeling about what it could be.

"By now, you should be familiar with racism, sexism, anti-Semitism, and—as we Muslims know too well—Islamophobia. Ever since the Great Bestowal, the mysterious global event in which certain people throughout the world gained extraordinary abilities such as flight and superhuman strength, those of us with superhuman abilities, now known as Exceptionals, are confronting a new form of bigotry: superism."

So not only were there people with comic book powers elsewhere in the world and not just here in Santa Barbara, but society also applied a brand-new label to them with the term "Exceptionals." Although it sounded like a compliment toward people with superpowers, it appeared to be more of a label used to justify another kind of prejudice.

"Now, I know that you folks are looking to watch me showcase the latest trends in hijabi fashion, as well as my own personal twists on it," Maryam continued. "But for today, I wanted to put that aside so that I can bring up a matter that's very personal to me, and might be personal to some of you folks, too."

The video cut at that point to the next frame before Maryam then said, "So, as you might know from the video that I posted two videos before this one, I'm an Exceptional now. As in, I have incredible magical powers that no human being is supposed to be capable of. 'Superpowers,' as you comic and movie enthusiasts would call them." I blushed for a second when I heard that comment.

When the video skipped to the following frame, it displayed Maryam next to her collection of hijabs; my eyes couldn't believe they were seeing them for the first time. She tilted her head in the direction of her hijab collection, and her right hand glowed the same scarlet red color as her hair, which also gave off an intense glow. One second, Maryam's hijabs were pulled out of place by some kind of mysterious telekinetic force; the next second, they were all back in their spots in her closet, in the same order and arrangement as at the beginning of this video frame. When Maryam arranged her hijabs back in order, she generated a different glow from her hand: a vivid green you would find only on emeralds. Even her hair changed into that same emerald-green color as she rearranged her hijabs. I found it quite fascinating that her abilities came with the added effect of changing her hair color.

"And that's not all I can do," Maryam said as she looked back to the camera and her hair reverted to the red tint that it had before, the same shade that became her apparent new hair color after she gained her powers. "As far as I know, I can shift event probabilities as well as interact with the spiritual consciousness of others. But that's not why I'm making this video. There are far more important issues for me to bring up than the demonstration of what my powers are and how they work."

The next frame returned to Maryam's living room, where she filmed most of her videos showcasing fashion content. "As a proud Muslim American, I condemn violence of all kinds. Our religious book, the Holy Qur'an, states that when someone kills a fellow human being, it is as if they killed all of humanity. I believe as well that when someone assaults a fellow human, it is as if they assaulted all of humanity. And what I witnessed this past Monday was horrifying to me beyond belief." Maryam proceeded to describe Greg Nathan/Plasma Kid's egregious beating by Manzanita school security guards, something I'd prefer not to go over again. We're better off not reliving the moment, okay?

"When I discovered my powers, I didn't know what to think at first. I didn't want to believe they were real, and that whatever I was doing had to be the sole work of Allah—*subhanahu wa ta'ala*. But once I came to accept them, I thought, *Imagine what I could do with these incredible abilities. It'll make it much easier for me to find specific jobs when I'm older, for one thing . . .*" she continued. "But watching my classmate beaten to the point of becoming unconscious opened my eyes to the reality of Exceptionals' place in society. From there, I've made a commitment to educating myself. And I hope to make you folks aware, too, whether you're an Exceptional or not. I've provided you some links in the video description so that you can check them out and learn about the rising effects of superism on Exceptionals."

I paused the video so that I could click on the three links under Maryam's video description. Three new tabs popped up, and the brief glance I gave to the titles of the links indicated that the pages were a news story, an article about the effects of superism worldwide, and a guide to confronting superism.

When I resumed the video, Maryam continued. "I know that all of this is likely difficult for you to process, especially if you're an

Exceptional like me. I prefer to be lighthearted with what I post here. But I felt this was so important to bring up that I couldn't put it off for any amount of time." She came close to tearing up, but didn't do so.

"There's more potential with us than you want to admit," she continued. "If you could see that potential in us and avoid judging us, it'll be much easier for us to make the world a better place, the way we want to. I work with the special needs class at my school as a teacher's assistant. One of my favorite students there, perhaps my favorite of all, is a girl with Down syndrome named Lorelyn. Well, she chooses to go by Elseven now, but that's beside the point. As a TA for a special education class, I don't judge my classmates because of their disabilities. I respect them for the students that they are, rather than identifying them only by their disabilities. Because of that, Elseven is able to live up to her potential without any unjustifiable restrictions on her education, and she's grown into an incredible student and wonderful girl. On top of that, Elseven is also an Exceptional who can copy the abilities of fictional characters. So she faces two kinds of discrimination: ableism and superism." Color-coded definitions of the terms "ableism" and "superism"— the former in red, the latter in blue—flashed on the YouTube video window for a few seconds. "With the new rules at our school, I worry for her safety now. And that breaks my heart so much."

Somehow, Maryam was able to hold back tears during this part of the recording. I was, too, but I did wish I could be shedding real tears; I just wasn't able to for some reason. Bringing up the perils that Elseven faced and could face did that to me.

Maryam concluded, "Two years ago, in my ancestral homeland of Iran, women throughout the country took to the streets in protest of their country's so-called 'morality laws' after one of their own, Mahsa Amini, was murdered by religious police for allegedly wearing her headscarf the wrong way. She was not the first to face such an ordeal from Iranian authorities, and it was an honor to watch my countrywomen speak their minds in the face of decades of adversity. Like my fellow Iranian women, I am not going to stay silent in the face of injustice, and I will use my platform to speak out against any kind of prejudice that society throws at us Exceptionals. If you're an Exceptional yourself, whether you've encountered superism or not, I advise you not to stay silent, either.

An attack on one Exceptional is an attack on us all. May the grace of Allah be with us for the foreseeable future." The video ended with Maryam folding to the ground in the traditional stance that Muslims take when performing one of their daily prayers.

Knowing what she went through yesterday, it impressed me that Maryam responded with the utmost bravery. When she was alive, Lizzy would often inspire me to speak up for the little guys in society; Maryam was having that same effect on me after watching her latest video. She may not be going out and fighting against bad guys using her powers—something that, as a pacifist, she seemed to prefer avoiding—but she became a superhero in my mind.

After I finished watching Maryam's video, I turned my attention to the links that she provided in her video description. The link to the news story detailed Plasma Kid's violent beating yesterday, so I didn't bother to read it. The pages that grabbed my attention were the guide to fighting superism, and the article about how the world's newest form of prejudice was affecting Exceptionals.

The same jolt of inspiration I had following the George Floyd protests and the Women's March flowed through my body while reading about how to respond to superism in my life and in society. Just like Lizzy would've taught me in this scenario: Amplify Exceptional voices. Educate yourself. Don't stay silent.

I was confident about my ability to play a major role in making life better for the entirety of Exceptionalkind. (Did I just become the first person in history to come up with that term, by the way?) But as much as I wanted to have a hopeful attitude after reading the anti-superism guide, the human nature of letting the negative and shocking resonate in my mind above all got to me.

The article describing the daily effects of superism, which was fittingly written on a social justice website, focused on the effects that anti-Exceptional prejudice had on Exceptionals' mental health since the event that society now dubbed the Great Bestowal. It detailed a couple of examples of superist incidents that occurred here in the U.S.: one of them a middle-aged man's tantrum against a girl with superhuman leaping abilities, the other a more violent one which resulted in the death of a victim who gained the power to see through walls. Then there were the posters and works of art that portrayed humans with superpowers as a violent menace. The most egregious one to me was a poster of a guy with glowing red laser eyes underneath an exaggerated scowl beaming a threatening look toward a young blond woman who looked much like me while also touching her in a suggestive fashion. Meanwhile, the skirt-clad woman had an expression of horror scrawling her face as the young man glared at her; the image in its entirety wouldn't look out of place as the poster for a scary movie. Stamped on top of the menacing poster was the question: "Would You Like a Freak to Date Your Daughter?"

These posters and billboards aren't much different from the propaganda posters against black people in the 1800s and anti-communist advertisements during the Cold War, I thought.

Upon finishing the article, I was motivated to find out more about superism throughout the world and how Exceptionals were responding to it, as difficult of an experience as I knew it was going to be. Knowing that it was accelerating into full force at my school, I considered it a duty to learn more about it.

For what must have been the first time in recent memory, I was willing to go on the CNN website, hoping to find more answers about Exceptionals' new place in the world. Sure enough, the story on CNN's front page was enough to satisfy my simmering curiosity. Of course, it was through another one of those incredibly harsh news stories.

"Is a brand-new demographic of people who now possess mysterious, extraordinary abilities becoming the latest marginalized group in society?" the anchor on the screen asked to start the video posted on their front-page news story regarding Exceptionals. The question he asked was even paraphrased on the headline to the side of him on the screen: "Exceptionals: Victims of a newfound societal prejudice."

"A question many are now wondering as individuals throughout the world, known as Exceptionals, confront major prejudice from society, including in India, where a young girl with the incredible ability to replenish the natural landscape around her has started to face suspicion from many of her countrymen in spite of her potentially world-altering abilities. Not helping matters is the Indian government's harsh attitude toward individuals like her who have gained superhuman capabilities out of nowhere."

As much as I started to notice discriminatory attitudes toward Exceptionals at my school, this news story made me feel lucky about my current living circumstances. That there were worse places to live when you had powers that human beings weren't supposed to have. CNN wasn't shy about painting India as a frightening hellhole for those who ended up gaining comic book powers. I couldn't speak for the experiences of those who lived in India, let alone their Exceptional population, but given my own experiences with what society now called "superism," I was able to get some sense of what the circumstances of Exceptionals in India must have felt like.

The last words I heard from the reporter on screen before I turned my online attention elsewhere were, "As superism rises, how can Unexceptionals—those who were not lucky enough to gain strange powers in the Great Bestowal—learn to better understand Exceptionals?" Upon hearing that commentary, I said out loud to the screen, "What a good question. I think you Unexceptionals can try to figure that out yourselves."

Because of how hard the news was for me to handle, I decided to tune out of the CNN story at that point, as intriguing and important as their ongoing news piece was. Instead, I looked to websites that weren't controlled by massive corporations in search of what I was hoping was less biased and more optimistic information. Alas, scouting these more independent news sites still brought me several more unpleasant stories:

> Boy with mysterious metal-corroding abilities harassed on NYC subway
>
> 30-year-old Colorado man fired from job after revelation of psychic powers
>
> In south of France, primary school student possessing x-ray vision called "alien," told to "go back to (her) planet"

Fears of magically empowered beings abound throughout Colombia

As I browsed these news articles online, I noticed that the prejudices that people with comic book powers were facing over the past few days bore a striking resemblance to the fear and loathing experienced by the titular race in Xenos, one of Wonder's most iconic franchises.

In the Xenos comics, the Xenos were a demographic among a race of human-like beings inhabiting the fictional life-bearing moon Hera. Unlike other characters with powers in the Wonder Universe, the Xenos were despised and dreaded by their home society for their immense powers, rather than being hailed as heroes. Countries like India very much felt like real-life versions of Hera, and those of us lucky enough—or, perhaps, unlucky enough—to gain comic book powers were starting to become the Xenos among Herans.

Despite the fear and suspicion that Exceptionals had been facing from the rest of society, and the anxiety that such prejudice was igniting in me as the potential originator of the recent emergence of such individuals, it was comforting to know from the website I was browsing that there were also numerous humans worldwide who were standing up for the place of these newly marginalized folks in society. Such people were common in a lot of the countries and areas you'd expect: Sweden, the Netherlands, Germany, my home state of California, and other places where liberal activism was commonplace. But there were also several surprising countries that weren't thought of as synonymous with social justice, such as Iran, where many were clamoring for the rights of Exceptionals. That was something I know Maryam would be proud of, and it was heartwarming for me to know that we were receiving such support worldwide in the midst of the newfound suspicion we were facing.

I thought we were getting better as a society. We were supposed to learn how to treat disadvantaged groups with more respect and sympathy after the day George Floyd's murder was caught on tape. But we didn't learn our lessons at all, not even after the pandemic years that put the inequality in our society out there for the world to see. Instead, we came up with another excuse to harbor nasty prejudice toward others. I hoped that our powers wouldn't become a reason for humanity to lower our standing in society and launch a crusade against our kind. The last thing we needed was a Jim Crow-style system against

Exceptionals. Or more schools and workplaces forbidding the use of superpowers within their crowds like Manzanita High School has.

Heck, why did society need to stop there? How about entire countries imposing laws banning Exceptionals from using their powers under any circumstances—even accidental ones—within their borders? Luckily, no matter how things ended up going down for society, Exceptionals could look to people like me and Maryam who were ready to keep fighting and speaking up. I took pride in knowing I could be that beacon of hope for Exceptionalkind.

CHAPTER

14

Wednesday, June 12 marked our final Comic Book Club meeting of the year. In spite of the events earlier that week, I maintained my anticipation to discuss our last chosen comic book for the school year—the fifth and final issue of Wonder's limited crossover series *Beacon and Gleam: Sunshine and Rainbows*—as well as the Vigilante movie we watched together this past Saturday. My excitement for our meeting evaporated, however, because of the low turnout. In fact, no one was in the astronomy classroom except me and Kenzie, and we were supposed to be two minutes into our meeting.

"Still no arrivals yet," I said to Kenzie, sighing afterward.

"Be patient, Jessica," she said. "People should start to arrive soon."

"You don't think that no one's come today because of—"

"Maybe everyone's too busy preparing for finals to come over," Kenzie said.

"Good point. I wouldn't blame them for that."

Before we could go over the agenda for our meeting, a plump girl of about five feet tall came through the door, our meeting's first attendee aside from the two of us. It was Elseven.

"Hey girls!" Elseven greeted us. "Sorry for being a little late. Still learning how to find this classroom . . ."

"Welcome back, Elseven," Kenzie said. "Happy you could join us again today."

"Thank you for showing up today," I told Elseven, her new name still somewhat odd for me to hear or say. "You're the first person to arrive for our final meeting of the year. Two minutes after we were supposed to start, even."

"I wasn't going to let everything going on keep me from coming here," Elseven said. "I'm not one to stay silent in the face of adversity. Believe me, I've been through plenty of hardships myself."

"You can never let us down, Elseven." A smile emerged on my face, and I said, "Friends don't let it go."

Kenzie smiled as well when she heard me say Elseven's new catchphrase. "I see that Elseven's rubbed off on you," she said.

"I've known her since eighth grade," I said. "She's rubbed off on me for a while."

Elseven took a comic book out of her backpack. "Oh, and before I forget, here's your comic back, Jessica," she said. It was the same comic I let her borrow at our last meeting.

"Thanks. Hope you found plenty of fun powers to gain from *Skirmish through Spacetime*."

"I sure did; it was a blast doing so!" Elseven giggled.

"So, which characters' powers did you copy?" I asked Elseven.

"Who's that character from the Xenos who can turn invisible?"

"I believe you're talking about Transparent."

"Yeah, that's it. I copied his ability to turn invisible because I thought it would be really cool to pull off sneak attacks with my telekinetic powers. Pew! Boom! Didn't see that coming? That's because I can go invisible now!" Elseven giggled and continued. "Of course, I had to copy the powers of that Continuum guy, too. He looks really powerful."

"Of course; he's able to alter reality with a touch of his fingers—essentially the greatest power one can have. Just be careful using that power; such an ability could have some serious consequences if not used correctly."

"I'm not planning to use it very often, Jessica. My mom told me to be careful with my Elsa ice powers after she saw them for the first time because of how they function when Elsa isn't in the best mood. So I already know a thing or two about having to be responsible with my new abilities. Learning how they work, how to handle them properly, stuff like that."

My mouth rounded into a smile. "Glad there's one Exceptional who understands that those with power must not be reckless. It's an important lesson we need to keep in mind with recent events at our school."

"Jessica just quoted the most famous line from the Beacon comics, Elseven," Kenzie said. "It's from his very first comic in 1996 after he gains his powers and goes a little too wild when he uses them for the first time, causing a lot of unintentional destruction in his hometown that forces him to spend some time in jail—a sentence that ends up being excessive as a result of him being black." It was so like Kenzie to have Beacon's origin story memorized by heart. I swore she kept a binder of every single superhero's origin story somewhere in her room. Both Wonder *and* Spectacle heroes.

Even with only three of us present in the room, Elseven's presence lifted up our moods for the rest of the meeting. We brought up how the themes of the *Beacon and Gleam* series mirrored our adolescent life experiences and current events, its fun juxtaposition of the titular duo, and debated whether Gleam would be a bigger pop star than Baby Diva if she were a real person. We also reflected back on our movie night the previous Saturday, the three of us all agreeing that the latest *Vigilante* movie was a promising foundation for the upcoming reboot of the Spectacle Expanded Universe after its previous incarnation was a spectacular multiyear flop. The limited turnout at least allowed us to have more personal and genuine conversations with one another than we would be able to with our usual attendance. So we didn't let it get to us one bit.

The final Manzanita Comic Book Club meeting of the year didn't go the way I would've liked it to, but I was glad that, with the help of Kenzie and Elseven, I was able to find a way to make the most of it and make it a memorable final meeting. With just the three of us in the classroom, the close-knit vibe of the meeting made it feel like our own little impromptu sleepover, only taking place in the afternoon rather than the evening.

After finishing my dinner—I was able to chow down my entire vegan schnitzel this time—I headed out to the beach again, just in time for the sunset. With the summer solstice arriving in a few weeks, I was able to catch the sunset at a relatively late time, somewhere around eight. But I wasn't there just to watch the sunset. With all the stresses I'd been going through, I desired to watch the night sky in all its glory progress from sunset to twilight to the start of evening.

As twilight set in and I strolled along the sand, I saw Garrett for a brief moment, provoking me to flinch at the sight of him. At least, I thought I saw him. But it turned out that he wasn't there at all. My mind just decided to play a trick on me.

Come on, don't be silly, Jess. Who else is going to be out here aside from you? You've got guts to be outside by yourself at this hour a few weeks after you went through a horrific school shooting. Do you really need to worry about Garrett too much? I know he has a creepy crush on you, but he probably doesn't have time to stalk you again. Most likely, he's too busy planning his next killing spree, like any murderous freak who just broke out of prison would.

In spite of the brief and unnecessary freakout I just had, I found a spot at the beach to sit on, alone and trying to get over said freakout. Even if I needed to return home by 11, I felt at peace with hardly a soul within my vicinity. The sky was a little lighter than it was the first time I sat on the beach by myself to gaze at the night sky, so at least I didn't look like a total fool sitting on the beach alone after sunset. But it was still dark enough that I could see the brightest stars in the night sky.

As I looked toward the dimming twilight in front of me, I heard the slapping sounds of someone's flip-flops and the jingle of a dog's leash. Before continuing my stargazing, I peered to my left to see who was passing by. It was Melissa Snyder, who was dressed in atypical Melissa Snyder fashion: a gray T-shirt paired with red gym shorts. By her side was a large Labrador retriever with dark brown fur.

"What a pleasant surprise to see you here," I said to Melissa as she walked by.

"What, I don't have the right to take my dog on an evening walk?" Melissa snarked. "Oreo here needs a workout every once in a while."

"Okay, fair. At least your dog is adorable, I'll give you that." I snuggled my face onto Oreo's as if she were my own. Even though I hadn't met Melissa's dog before, I already liked her more than I liked Melissa herself.

"I thought you don't hang out with losers like me," I said to Melissa as I finished snuggling with Oreo and lifted my gaze over to her hazel eyes. "That being around me would 'ruin your cred.'"

"Okay, so I admit that I've never been the nicest person to you," Melissa said. "But I've been doing a lot of reflecting lately, and I've realized . . . I can now see what it's like to be at a disadvantage in society."

"What do you mean by that? You're the last person who could possibly understand such things."

"Well, yes, I've never really understood what it's like to be a marginalized individual. White, blond, pretty, middle class, most popular girl at her high school . . . how can I possibly understand the type of shit that black and Hispanic people go through? Even after George Floyd's murder, I still can't truly understand what it's like to be one of them—and perhaps I never will. But I think I now get what it's like to be a marginalized group like them. Because somehow, the fact that people like you and me can do things that no human being is supposed to do equates to being a demographic that one must fear and put down."

"Are you talking about being an Exceptional, Melissa?"

"Yes. That's what I mean. And when I healed you that afternoon during lunchtime . . . I can't help but think that that's what convinced school staff to ban Exceptionals from using their powers on school grounds. That day, I spotted Nurse Morris out of her office and at the cafeteria for a moment, giving me a look of suspicion after I healed you—I think she might have caught me doing so. I've been uncomfortable on Manzanita school grounds ever since. So if you think you haven't been seeing me as much as usual . . . that's why. I've been trying to isolate myself because I've been so upset at how things have been going in my life. And now there's the added trouble of feeling marginalized because I can perform literal magic tricks. That incident with Plasma Kid yesterday has made me even more scared to go to campus."

Awkward as it was at first, I leaned toward Melissa and saturated her with my empathy through an embrace. For some reason, it felt quite nice. "I know what you're talking about, Melissa," I said. "I saw it unfold with my own eyes."

"You were there? Then why didn't you try to save him?"

"I was too scared. The security guards seemed to have something against Exceptionals, so if I tried to intervene, I was sure they would beat me to a pulp, too. Now that I think about it, even though it may have been the right decision to stay out . . . I should've done something. I should've stepped up for my fellow Exceptional. But instead, I just stood there. And a kid's in the hospital because of my boneheaded decision." I sank my face into my hands, replaying the incident in my mind. I was even imagining Maryam behind me, trauma soaking her face and hijab.

"That doesn't sound to me like the geek who's obsessed with superheroes," Melissa said.

"I guess it's a growing process being one. Every superhero I love has gone through their own challenges and difficulties. They don't save the day a hundred percent of the time."

"Like how Techno-Man and Brawn got into a nasty spat with each other in *Inner Feud*, throwing the future of the Protectors into question?" Somehow, Melissa explained the plot of the 2016 WCU movie as if she knew it like the back of her hand.

"You watch Wonder movies, Melissa?"

"I have to at times if I want to stay in touch with what's cool with the crowd. Besides, it's hard to find someone who's never watched a single Wonder movie. Somehow, Hollywood's decided that all the geeky stuff you losers crave is the hot thing in society nowadays." Melissa giggled and cringed at the same time.

"Melissa Snyder stooping down to my level. I thought I'd never see the day," I teased.

"Shut up." Melissa smiled and gave me a playful tug on my shoulder. "That reminds me—there's something I wanted to confess to you."

"What's that?"

"Lately, I've been getting the notion that you've thought of me as having the most perfect life because I'm the most popular girl at

Manzanita. I don't know if that's out of some sense of envy or something. But the perception you have of me is not at all the reality."

"What do you mean? Everyone at school loves you, Melissa. You never have to worry about being teased for your place in the social hierarchy. And you've got the best fashion sense of anyone I know."

"It's not easy being as popular as I am, Jessica. You may think that my life is all fun and having a good time at parties. But it's too much pressure to maintain the popularity that I have. To maintain a glittering reputation like mine. You probably look at all the hot guys around me and think, 'Wow, what a dude magnet Melissa Snyder is. She's so lucky.' But it's not fun being a dude magnet. I do love the guys I hang around. But it's so tiring receiving dirty comments from other guys left and right. Comments that are too inappropriate for me to mention here."

Ah. Now I could see the legitimacy in Melissa's words. I knew for sure that Lizzy would have something to say about that if she was here beside us.

"If you wanted to know why I hesitated to heal your burns . . . that's why. It's so damn tiresome having to deal with people who desire to use me for my superpower. Plenty of guys I know, many of them I've never met before, have injured their legs or other body parts on purpose. Just so they can fulfill their horny fantasies about me."

"Seriously? That's really stupid," I said, laughing. "Sorry about the laughing; I don't mean to be insensitive to what you go through at school every day. I sure as hell shouldn't be when I'm writing my semester paper for English about Sarah Everard's murder in the United Kingdom. I would be a terrible feminist otherwise."

"That's funny, I wrote about that same topic for English last semester. And that was before our school fell victim to a misogynistic madman's shooting spree. It really opened up my mind more to the treatment I've gotten from guys our age. And the treatment that our gender receives worldwide, really."

"We chose the same topic for our English paper? I never thought I would be saying that. I guess we have a lot more in common than I give us credit for." I giggled again, but this time, in a well-timed fashion.

"Oh yeah. You don't see my sensitive side often because I've been so nasty to you. But at heart, I want to be like Lizzy. I feel I don't do enough to be the feminist champion she was. There are too many distractions holding me back in my life to do that."

"I never knew you looked up to Lizzy. You barely knew her or ever talked to her."

"I heard a lot about her women's rights aspirations, though. Her commitment to the cause was something I always admired about her, regardless of what group of people she hung out with." Melissa leaned her body forward onto Oreo's side, resting her head on her body and glancing at me. Oreo loved every second of it.

"Look, I may appear smug and arrogant on the outside. But deep inside, I'm hurting a lot. Much like you've been since Lizzy's death, Jessica. As if being immensely popular at school wasn't enough, it led me to become a direct target of the Manzanita shooter. Yes, my bitchy attitude goes hand-in-hand with being popular. But I've also been acting that way to mask the mental scars I've had from being Garrett Lowe's top target. Almost murdered by him, even. Nowadays, I'm very scared that I might meet the same fate as Lizzy. I'm everything that Garrett abhors: hot, female, blond, popular. And now that he's an Exceptional himself, he's even more dangerous than he was on the day of the shooting. Heck, what am I doing here walking my dog alone at night when Garrett could come out of nowhere and attack me at any moment?" Melissa laughed nervously. "Of course, that's not worth thinking about every single second. I gotta overcome my fears somehow. Walking Oreo across the beach by myself allows me to do that. Not to mention the therapeutic feeling I get by doing so."

"To be honest, I had the feeling he was going for people like you and Darren in particular. Especially after I watched his 'Reckoning' video. It's why I saved you two from him that other day; I couldn't let him murder you two after he took Lizzy's life."

"Thanks, Jessica. I appreciate that. I'm not willing to live my life scared every day, even after everything he's put us through. We can't live like that just because our school experienced an unexpected tragedy. Of course we need to be vigilant. But we also must try to be brave. Just like your favorite fictional superheroes. We can't let our trauma get the better of us. If those superheroes you love so much can overcome their personal problems, we can too, Jessica."

Naturally, I was quick to agree with Melissa's words. "Well said. If Garrett ever tries to do something to you, I promise I'll look out for you. I've got your back, Melissa." My left hand grasped her right, and they squeezed ever so tight.

"You got it, Jessica. Maybe you don't realize it, but you're starting to become every bit like the superheroes you geek out over. And I'm not saying that in a rude manner. You seem to be doing a good job of trying to be like your favorite comic book characters."

"Thanks. That means a lot to hear that from you, MelSny." Melissa blushed upon hearing me call her by her nickname for the first time. "Is it okay if I call you MelSny? Or is that something only your posse is allowed to do?"

Melissa laughed. "I'm cool with it," she said. "Maybe it's best you don't call me that in front of my girls, though."

"Fair enough." I sent a light smile to Melissa. Then Oreo got up and let out several energetic barks.

"Hey, it was nice talking with you, Jessica. But I better get going; Oreo wants to get back to her walk," said Melissa. "It's getting dark, anyway. Don't want to get my parents too worried about me and Oreo."

"You go do that, Melissa," I said. Before saying goodbye to Melissa and her dog, I stood up and rubbed both sides of Oreo's face one more time while giving her a few playful smooches. Yeah, my affection for her was still higher than it was toward Melissa, even though my view of her had changed after our conversation.

While Melissa returned to her evening dog walk, I stuck around my spot at the beach a little longer. I lived close enough to the beach anyway, and I already had dinner; my parents didn't mind me sitting or taking walks on the beach by myself at night as long as I was back in the house by 11 p.m. The night that I made my shooting star wish was an exception, but that was because I snuck out of the house at the time; Mom and Dad weren't aware that I was taking a walk on the beach that night. I made sure not to confess it to them, either.

Speaking of shooting stars, I peered at the horizon ahead, and for the second time in a three-week span, I spotted one lighting up the evening sky. Just like the one that I saw the night after the shooting, this shooting star was much brighter than the others in the night sky—bright enough to rival the planets in our solar system. Unlike your typical shooting star, this one emitted a gorgeous rainbow glow; the one that I wished on sent out a rainbow glow, too.

As I focused my eyes on the shooting star, I felt some kind of magical energy flowing through me. It was a subtle sensation, but I experienced this mysterious surge in my body nonetheless. Whatever it was, it was empowering me from the inside. I didn't know if it was coming from the shooting star itself, or I just had an interesting history with spotting shooting stars. Either way, it was as if all the confidence and optimism that I had before the day of the shooting returned to me.

After the shooting star faded away from the evening sky, my body glowed again. It was a silvery white one this time—one that complemented the colors of the moon, and the very same one I remembered generating at Lizzy's funeral when I got into a group hug with Mr. and Mrs. Manchester. The sensation I was experiencing became stronger and nicer. With curiosity soaking me, I decided to put my hands out in front of me while relaxing myself. In doing so, each of my hands projected glittering beams sporting the same color as the silvery white aura that I was emitting. Like a little kid, my mouth opened in amazement at the sight of testing out one of my powers that I didn't use much before. I was starting to think that there was something about shooting stars that clicked with me. That they were my good luck charm or something.

As the time approached 10:30, I walked back to my house with the opposite feelings of what I had on that first night I saw a shooting star. My silvery white glow faded out, but the good vibes within me remained. I carried these good vibes with me as I crawled into bed and dozed off into the next day. Having *Beacon and Gleam: Sunshine and Rainbows* issue #5, which I read again before relaxing on the beach and chatting with Melissa, helped to sweeten the good night's sleep I was about to have. It helped that the comic expressed my current mood so well with its theme of balancing high school life and life with superpowers together, and the unique pressures that came with having powers, whether you were an ordinary teenager like Beacon or a world-famous pop star like Gleam.

CHAPTER

15

My eyes opened, and I found myself floating on my back in the middle of a very strange area. Looking around me, it was clear that I was no longer in Santa Barbara. Heck, I was no longer even on Earth.

The sky above me was an endless rainbow with brilliant white auroras glimmering here and there. The ground below me? There was none. All that was underneath me was that same endless rainbow. That's all I saw around me. I didn't see anyone or anything else. Just all the colors of the rainbow blending together anywhere I looked.

Was this a dream? It had to be.

Still dressed in the same Mistress Mystic pajamas I was wearing when I went to bed, my body floated about in a lying position. It was like relaxing in the Dead Sea, only surrounded by rainbow hues all around instead of a body of water saltier than the ocean. I didn't see anything else until an unusual figure appeared in front of me.

Whatever this being was, he looked nothing like any being one would find on Earth, nor did he even look like any of the artistic depictions of alien life that I'd seen before. To me, his form resembled a white dress. No lower limbs to be found, just a pair of arms linked to the upper part of his body, with nothing resembling hands at the ends of his limbs. All that he had for a face were a pair of hollow, transparent eyes—and they weren't located on his upper body like they were for the Earth creatures that I was familiar with, instead situated on the bottom part of his figure. This figure resembled a ghost, but I wouldn't call him one, either.

In spite of the being's otherworldly appearance, I avoided assuming that he meant any harm. He didn't scare me, either, as I'd seen plenty of bizarre-looking beings from Wonder and Spectacle comics and movies. In those universes, a being with his appearance would be par for the course.

"Where am I?" I asked. "Can you get me down from here? I don't want to fall to my death; I'm too young to die . . ."

"Relax, Jessica," the strange being said to me, his reverberating voice possessing an ethereal vibe. "You're not going to fall to your death; you can walk like you'd be able to in your world. It may look odd to you, but you won't see anything resembling solid ground in this dimension."

"Wait, how do you know my name?" I focused on his eyes, still finding it weird that they were located on his lower body rather than his upper one. While I was still in a lying position, I further noticed how unusual this being's overall body structure was.

"I've been watching you from afar. Ever since you first discovered your powers a few days after the massacre that occurred at your school."

"You've . . . been watching me? So I'm not in a dream then, right?"

"You're not in a dream, Jessica," the figure said. "This is reality. You're in a different dimension from your homeworld. Or, to be precise, your consciousness is. Your physical body is still present on your home planet, deep asleep. I only transferred your spiritual consciousness to this realm. So it may feel like a dream to you, but I promise you, this is a real place."

"So you live in an endless rainbow? Sounds awesome, but also rather boring if this is all your world is."

"Oh, I promise you that there's more to this realm than the rainbow expanse of space that you see around you. Welcome to the Aurora Dimension, Jessica Summer."

Curious to find out what the rest of this place looked like, I descended from my floating position in the same way that a swimmer doing a backstroke would return to an upright position in a swimming pool. Despite the lack of anything concrete to stand on, my bare feet experienced the sensation of standing on a soft, cozy floor. The touch on my soles brought out every positive emotion in my body, the same sensation I got from walking on grass without footwear.

"Feels nice to be standing up again," I said. "And what might your name be, floating white dress?"

"You can call me Ids," the being answered.

"Ids?" In spite of how simple it was, his name was peculiar to me. "Does everyone in this dimension have short names like you?"

"I actually have one of the less complicated names in this world. Most of us have longer names that would be a chore for the beings from your world to pronounce. Our language and writing system are quite complex even in comparison to the most difficult languages in your world."

"I'll take your word for it then, Ids. In the meantime, how about I take some time to familiarize myself with my new surroundings here?"

"One step ahead of me, Jessica. I'll be happy to make you feel more at home here."

While I couldn't consider it a walk by Earth standards since there wasn't anything to walk on (in spite of somehow being able to walk here like I would on Earth), and even though Ids was a floating creature, I took a "walk" with him in order to find out more about this Aurora Dimension. Growing up, I never imagined that I would find myself in one of those magical realms that Mistress Mystic explored on a regular basis—how fitting that I was wearing a Mistress Mystic shirt while I was here. But now that I was living a superhero story arc starting from the origin story phase of watching Lizzy die in front of my eyes, it was natural for me to be exploring alternate dimensions. I was just glad I didn't find myself on a hostile planet or in an eerie dimension to start; this Aurora Dimension appeared to be a pleasant place.

"So, can you explain to me how you found out about me?" I asked Ids as we strolled around his home dimension. "And how we gained this connection in the first place? I hope you haven't been stalking me this whole time or anything; I unfortunately know what it's like to be stalked."

"The shooting star that you wished on created a gateway between our worlds after I initiated the Great Bestowal in your world," Ids explained. "That allowed your consciousness to enter this dimension while you were sleeping. I sent that shooting star into your home universe so that your consciousness could gain access to the Aurora Dimension."

"Wait, hold up. You're the one responsible for the Great Bestowal?"

"Yes, that was me, Jessica. I'm the one who brought superpowers to your world."

"That was you who granted my wish? Oh, thank you, thank you!" I could kiss Ids . . . except he didn't have a mouth. Or a concrete physical body that would let him feel my kiss.

"That was not a wish that created the world of superheroes and supervillains that you now live in," Ids said. "It was all my doing. The shooting star wasn't a real shooting star, but a figment of my power. I sent it from my dimension to your planet, and it saturated the entirety of your Earth with its magic, imbuing certain people like you with superhuman abilities. Not everyone, though, because I didn't want to make your world too chaotic by giving all its inhabitants superpowers."

"Hmm . . . deciding to recreate an entire planet but keep it in balance. I like it. Not going to lie, it would've been cool to live in a world where everyone has superpowers. But if I've learned anything from Wonder's Earth Supreme comics series back in my universe, it's that a world where everyone has superpowers isn't as awesome as one would expect."

While I couldn't read any facial expressions from him due to his lack of a conventional face, Ids's body language made it clear to me that he didn't understand a word I was saying. Apparently the beings of his world weren't into comic books like I was.

"Whoops, sorry about all that geeking out from me. It's a rather bad habit of mine. But on to the important question: What inspired you to make superpowers become real in my world?"

"In my dimension, *vshqi*—that's the term we use in the same manner that you use 'people' in your world; the singular form is *vashq*—always looked at me as a joke. They would ridicule me every chance they got. I wanted to prove myself to them; show them my true worth and potential. Show them I could make an immense impact on others. So I embarked on a search through many different universes, discovered yours, and then converted it into a superhero universe like one from those . . . collections of pictures that your people read for entertainment. What are they called?"

"Comic books."

"Yeah, those. To make another planet in another dimension better and more colorful by turning it into a world containing extraordinary beings . . . that was the ultimate way I could prove to my kind that I can be more special than they ever thought I could be. With my species' ability to peek into events going on in other dimensions and universes, I saw that you were hurting after you watched your best friend's murder. I sensed your desperation. So I wanted to offer you my help. I anticipated that you would make a wish on a shooting star . . . so I sent a fragment of my power to your world, one that resembles what your people would call a 'shooting star,' that would turn some of your kind into beings with superpowers."

Since I couldn't give Ids a kiss, I instead chose to show my gratitude to him for bringing my wish to life by giving him a hug. But he decided to pass on one, apparently puzzled by my gesture.

"Your forms of showing affection are . . . rather odd," Ids said. "Anyway, if you were curious to know what I brought you here for, Jessica, it's because I've seen that you've been in major trouble as of late. I had anticipated that turning some of your kind into superhuman beings would come with certain complications unprecedented in your world's history. And I know that you have a grudge against the madman who shot your best friend dead that you've been dying to satisfy. So I was hoping I could help you out. Train you to help you get the most out of your powers."

"Ooh, a cinematic training montage," I reacted. "Yes, I could use something like that to gain more confidence for my eventual fight to stop Garrett Lowe."

"A cine-what?"

"Like in our movies, where characters train for a big, upcoming fight. Movies are this form of entertainment that we create where we tell stories through a series of moving pictures. I assume there's no such thing in your world?"

"We don't have the tools that are used to create those things. Even if we did, we wouldn't be interested in them. We'd find your movie and television creations to be a pointless waste of time. The beings of the Aurora Dimension place more of a value on reading and writing, myself included. I think there's a reason that your people say reading is good for the mind, while television is bad for it."

"Hey now, I recognize the value of reading. My best friend was a writer. I'm part of a book club at my school. I'd love to share the literature of my world with you one day if I ever get the chance."

"You seem like a very intelligent girl, Jessica. Consider that a fantastic start to our upcoming training."

"They do call me a nerd in my world; it's a title I take pride in. So many thanks for the compliment, Ids."

To walk through space without any semblance of solid ground below me was still strange to me, but at the same time, awesome in an otherworldly manner. This Aurora Dimension, whatever it was, really was something I'd only find in a fantasy novel.

As Ids and I continued walking, I saw a brief flash of someone who appeared to be Garrett Lowe. At first, I brushed it off like it was nothing, and continued walking to wherever Ids wanted to take me. Then the Garrett flashes became more frequent, first appearing in the same spot, then from all different directions. Soon after, voices started to surround me too. They were short bursts of sound, but wherever they popped up, they accompanied the image of Garrett in my eyes.

"Hello, Jess—" Garrett said before flashing away in a split second. Regardless of how briefly he appeared, his voice sounded so real.

"No—how are you—how did you—" I stumbled and landed on my rear, fearing I was about to fall until I realized that the Aurora Dimension had some sort of invisible ground acting like a solid surface.

"Jessica, are you okay?" Ids asked.

"Never better, Ids," I answered. "Just . . ." I paused for around two seconds. ". . . a little overexcited for this training. And a bit nervous. Both, really. Don't know what to expect. But that's the excitement of it, you know?"

"Ah, I understand. Be patient, Jessica. We'll reach our destination soon."

Soon enough, Garrett appeared again, this time from behind, very close to me. And not in the form of a flash, either. He attempted to grab me, but before he could, I ran off, drifting far away from Ids in the process. Then Garrett appeared in front of me again. Did he get the ability to teleport from the Great Bestowal to go along with his flame powers?

"Don't try to run away from me, Jessica Summer," he said. "You can't avoid me forever. We're inevitable."

I swung a punch at Garrett's face, only for him to disappear. Then he appeared behind me again, standing in the same upright position that he was before. I flung a photon ball at his chest, but then he disappeared again. With this apparent new teleportation ability of his, I had no chance of landing a hit on him. Any hit. Energy balls, punches, kicks . . . he was just going to find a way to dodge anything I threw at him at the last second. Knowing this, I decided to stop trying to attack him, fearing the next appearance he might make.

Remember what Melissa told you tonight, I thought while trying to anticipate where he'd appear next. *Be brave. Face your fears. Just like your favorite Wonder heroes would. Melissa didn't mind walking her dog at night in spite of Garrett endangering her life. Why should he intimidate you, too?*

Soon enough, there was Garrett in front of me, pointing a pistol at my head. I let out an enormous shriek, my mind trying to confirm that the gun in his hand was the same one that Garrett used during his mass shooting. All I could do was stand still as he prepared to take my life. Garrett cackled with sinister delight . . . and then, he was no longer there.

"Jessica! What's wrong?" Ids asked.

"It's Garrett—the guy who shot my school—he's here—I don't know how he got here," I blabbered in a panicky manner. "Run away, Ids! He might shoot! Or burn you to death!"

"Huh? I don't see anything," Ids said to me. "And even if this Garrett was here, I'm sure I wouldn't have to worry about being burned or shot by him with this body. I'm sure I'd kick his ass, anyway."

It started to settle in my head that I was not in this place; my consciousness was. I was never in any danger, and I was going to be okay.

I bobbed my head around, looking for that head of smooth black hair and that well-kempt but undoubtedly sociopathic face. It was no longer in sight. To my relief, Garrett's random appearances ceased. The fact that he showed up here, however, left me—or rather, my consciousness—with a massive mental scar spanning my entire body. It turned out that the Aurora Dimension was no longer the pleasant paradise that I assumed it to be at first.

"I don't know what's going on with you, Jessica. But whatever it is, it's just a mental thing," Ids said. "If you want to prove yourself as a superhero, you need to get the mental aspect down along with the physical challenges. My hope is that our training session will help you so that you can reach the full potential of your powers with more ease."

A few drops of sweat rolled out of my forehead, and I paused for a few seconds. "In that case, I'm ready for our training," I said. "I'm dying to get through it now."

"Happy to see that kind of enthusiasm from you, Ms. Summer. I believe in you. You've got this, Jessica."

After a few minutes of walking following my brief freakout, Ids opened up a portal. Inside the portal was an area of space that looked very different from the part of the Aurora Dimension that I'd already seen: instead of a glittering expanse of rainbow, the space inside the portal was an eerie blood red.

"Come on in, Jessica," said Ids. "No need to fret; you won't be in any danger here."

I passed through the boundary of space between the part of the Aurora Dimension that I'd familiarized myself with and the area inside the portal that Ids opened up. After I entered, Ids closed up the portal door, and now the only space surrounding me was this expanse of deep red. Aside from the color of the space around me, it didn't feel much different in here. I was still experiencing the same sensation of being able to stand and walk without any tangible ground touching my feet.

"This, my Earth friend, is the pocket of space where our *vshqi* train and fight with each other," said Ids. "It's our equivalent of what I believe your kind refers to as a training ground. In your language—you can ask me later how we can speak English despite coming from an entirely different dimension—we call it the Battle Zone. A rather generic name, but our native name for it is a lot more elaborate and creative."

"Gnarly," I said, my eyes zigzagging around the expanse of blood red that I now found myself in. "We didn't enter another dimension or universe, did we?"

"You're still in the Aurora Dimension, Jessica. This is a different section of it. Not every pocket of space in our realm looks the same."

"Ah, okay. Couldn't you have just opened the portal to this place right away from where we were standing before, by the way?"

"In our world, you can't access certain areas until you physically reach them; everything would just come to us easy otherwise. A special sensation in our minds alerts us to when we've reached specific spots to open portals to." The way he described this power of theirs, it must have acted like a GPS, a mental navigator of sorts.

"All right. I have yet to see how your powers work, but you look like a decent, formidable enough opponent, Ids. Bring it." I settled my feet in, locking my arms and legs into my best combat pose. Since I'd never fought in this place, however, I might've been acting a tad bit overconfident.

Before I could make the first move, Ids summoned an empty circle in the middle of the red expanse we were in. The circle started to grow in size at a gradual pace, and as it did, it brought with it winds that must have been far stronger than the most powerful winds ever recorded on Earth. Soon, it tore open a larger, expanding emptiness, making a distinctive mark in the middle of the red expanse, distorting the immediate area around it. The force of this pitch-black void started to reach me, preventing me from walking any faster than a snail's pace. After who knows how the hell long, Ids closed off the empty circle, and its influence faded away. My eyes wanted to go nowhere but to Ids.

"Whoa . . . did you just . . ." I said to him.

"Yes," Ids said. "Those entities that are powerful enough to ensure that even light can't get out? That was it."

"You can summon . . . *those* things?" I pointed to where the relentlessly hungry void was, my amazement too strong to allow me to mouth out the words "black holes" instead of "those things." "The strongest objects in my universe?"

"Yes, Jessica. Them. And that's just the tip of the iceberg with what I can do. I can gaze into other worlds, create new universes, even warp reality however I like if I wanted to."

"Damn . . . and I thought my powers were awesome. Even if I've only scratched the surface of their potential so far."

"Actually, in this world, I'm a rather unimpressive being. Everyone in our dimension possesses such abilities from birth. So what your kind perceive as incredible, we just view as nothing out of the ordinary. Hence why I feel like a joke among my *vshqi*."

"Dude . . . why couldn't I have been born in your dimension? You had to alter my world in order for beings like you to become real there. Heck, why didn't you take me here before? This place feels like a nice escape from my reality."

"I didn't want to freak you out. It wasn't a valid choice at the time, knowing what you had been going through. Best to start off slow, you know."

"Okay, fair." Ids rushed at me, but I whooshed upward in order to dodge his attack. The quickness of his combat caught me by surprise, as he barreled toward me two seconds before I could counterattack, knocking me back several feet. Despite being nothing more than an intangible entity, his ram somehow stung a lot more than I expected. It didn't take long for me to get back on my feet, however, and I answered back by firing several photon blasts at Ids, aiming for his eyes because I assumed that's where I'd deal the most damage on him. Alas, not a single scratch on him.

"Oh, I didn't tell you, Jessica, I'm quite resilient," Ids said. "And pack much more physical strength than my frail appearance would have you think."

Ah. So he was one of those fighters. I was too used to assuming that beings like him were as glassy as they were potent.

"Not all of your kind are this surprisingly brawny, are they?" I asked.

"Our strength and durability vary by individual. But yes, it is well beyond your species' norm, despite how frail we appear. Plus, we can resist plenty of attacks on account of being energy beings."

Shaking off the tingling I felt, I sprung upward and sailed toward Ids, projecting my right fist outward. Just when I thought I was about to get him that time, I ended up elsewhere in much less than a split second, nowhere close to where he stood. He didn't even pummel me either.

"The f—" Ids warped himself to the new spot to which he sent me, then flung his right limb at me. Taking a cue from my dance classes, I performed a chaîné turn to dodge his attack. I jumped up and attempt to plant my right foot between his eyes. Then he warped several feet backward, and I touched nothing but the imaginary ground.

I sprung forward and propelled myself into the fastest aerial speed I could manage. Ids stopped me mid-flight, keeping me hovering without allowing me to break free. He swung me in the other direction, slamming me down into where the ground would be. My body tingled again.

"Come on, Jessica. You can do better than that, girl," he said.

The way Ids said this, I didn't take kindly to it. Without intention, he ended up sparking something in me. Second by second, it built up until my ire hit a tipping point.

Some kind of cosmic matter erupted from my body, blowing Ids away before he could react. It left behind the brightest glow possible, one that would be visible for billions of lightyears in my home universe.

After taking a bit of time to settle down from what I just did, I was a brand-new girl. My reflexes picked up speed, allowing me to land direct hits on Ids before he could retaliate. Despite his resilience, he could feel the force from my blows this time. My photon balls were more intense, my dance steps swifter. Even when Ids fired a few of his own energy projectiles at me, I neutralized them all with my force bubble. Instead of Ids being a step ahead of me, I was several steps ahead of him.

Nothing could stop me, and I didn't want to stop, either.

Ids didn't go down easy, however, and he was prepared to fight back. But rather than unleash another flurry of attacks at him, I chose to conserve my energy. Something sizzled in me, not as intense as the explosive force that I unleashed earlier, but still quite the surge.

As my nerves crackled from the ongoing buildup, I began to envision my fight against Rage. Instead of seeing Ids's featureless white figure, I imagined a flaming madman in front of me, taunting me and tossing misogynistic banter and perverted remarks in my direction.

While facing off against a being as powerful as Ids for the first time was never going to be easy, I admitted that my focus wasn't where it needed to be. I had major worries that Rage was going to show up during this training and torment me further—worries that turned out to be for nothing when his form didn't show up after all. This time around, however, I brushed off those concerns like they were never there, and my focus was at its max. As such, imagining Rage in front of my eyes played a beneficial role for me rather than acting as a hindrance, empowering me and driving me to be the best Exceptional that I could be.

Photon energy piled up in my hands, particle by particle. As it did, I pushed my arms outward with my hands in a cupped position. And as Ids sprung forward to land another blow on me, I soaked him in an enormous beam of light, one bigger than I'd ever fired out before; one that provoked me to use up every bit of power in my vocal cords.

Ids was okay; all that happened to him was that he fell backward a few feet. Since he didn't have a mouth, I couldn't read anything on him resembling a full facial expression. But it was safe to say that I impressed him. Whatever just came to me, I wanted it to flow through me again the next time I encountered Rage, dammit.

"Impressive job, young lady," Ids said as he pulled himself back up.

"Nothing personal, Ids," I said. "You said you wanted to train me. I just made the most of it." A confident smirk painted my face as Ids opened up a portal, revealing the rainbow expanse I saw around me when I arrived in the Aurora Dimension for the first time.

"I think it's a good time to wrap up our training now," Ids said. "The improvement you made as a fighter during our session is remarkable."

"Eh, it was nothing," I said, shrugging. "My job isn't done yet. I'm just getting started."

"And that's precisely the position I wanted you to find yourself in. It's an honor to assist you in your growth as an Exceptional."

"The feeling is mutual, Ids. Thanks for your help."

"My pleasure." Ids stepped through the portal back into the rainbow expanse of the Aurora Dimension, and I followed behind him before he closed the portal. An endless rainbow surrounded the two of us once again.

"You're starting to realize your full potential, Jessica. I'm proud to see such progress from you in a short amount of time."

"It helps having you as my personal Master Yoda, Ids. Aka a guru figure who helps me tap into my abilities. I know that our training took place only with my consciousness, but I will for sure carry what I've learned from you into the real world."

"I imbued you with incredible powers knowing that they would be a formidable defense against whatever threats came your way. You just needed to find a way to tap into them in the most effective way possible."

"Sometimes, these powers have felt like a curse for me with the fear and prejudice that so-called Exceptionals have started to face from the rest of society. But now I'm more at peace with having these special gifts. You've been a great help in that regard, Ids."

"Mind not what others think of you, Jessica. Let your negative emotions and experiences help you improve yourself instead of hindering you. If you keep those things in mind, you can play a huge role in improving your society and helping your kind find their place in it. And you'll have an easier time taking on Rage when that time comes, too."

I nodded my head once while looking down at Ids's eyes. "I will try, Ids. Those tasks are easier said than done when you're going through the roller-coaster ride that is high school, though." I giggled and then continued. "But if that's what it'll take for me to defeat Rage and send him back to prison, I'm all for doing so."

Ids put his right arm up, as if to give me a salute. "Good luck, Jessica Summer. I believe in you."

"Thanks. So, how do I leave this place?"

"It's not too hard, Jessica. Just close your eyes, relax yourself, and you'll slowly feel yourself fade back into sleep. Same thing you'd do if you were preparing to go to sleep."

"Ah, okay. Sounds simple enough—unless you're an insomniac, of course. Anyway, how can I come back here in the future?"

"As far as I know, you can only access my dimension after seeing the shooting star that connects us and while asleep. So now you can come here on your own will, provided you satisfy those two circumstances."

"I'm assuming that the shooting star that will lead me into this dimension emits a rainbow glow. As far as I know, I don't see other shooting stars do that."

"Yes, that is correct, Jessica. The shooting star with the rainbow glow—that's the one that gave you your powers and created a connection between our spirits and dimensions."

"Well, I hope to see it again soon. I already want to explore more of your world and meet some of its inhabitants aside from you."

"Based on what you've told me, it sounds like you're going to love this place."

I nodded to Ids and smiled. Then we parted ways and I waved farewell to him. "May we meet again one day, Ids."

"The feeling is mutual, Jessica Summer."

After Ids and I parted, I took a short walk through the Aurora Dimension, soaking in the fantasy realm one more time before I was ready to go back to sleep.

To lull my soul back into the real world, I floated onto my back again into the same position that I was in when I first found myself here. I turned to my side and laid my arms next to my face as if I was getting ready to sleep. Then I closed my eyes, and after an indeterminate amount of time, my consciousness faded out of the Aurora Dimension. I found my physical state again, and I was back on Earth, returning to sleep in the comforts of my bed.

CHAPTER

16

Some who gained superpowers from the Great Bestowal weren't so lucky in terms of the power they gained. They could've gained the ability to alter the chemistry of substances and solid matter, they might have gained the ability to travel through time . . . or their fate could've been more like my English classmate Connor Harris, whose Exceptional ability caused others to instantly get sick just by coughing or sneezing at them, or even speaking to them.

As you could imagine, such an ability hadn't exactly been a cakewalk for Connor since he discovered it. He first activated it when he participated in a speaking assignment for his Spanish class on the first day after school resumed. The student that he did the speaking assignment with ended up catching a severe flu that he didn't recover from until the very last week of the school year. Ever since, everyone at school had nicknamed Connor "Super COVID" because of his power, and people had to practice strict social distancing at all times around him to avoid getting sick from him.

To help Connor feel better, I decided to take the seat closest to him for Thursday's class. I had the need to keep him company so that he wouldn't be further distraught by the power he had in the wake of the Plasma Kid incident from four days ago.

"Hey, Connor," I greeted him. Connor had been quite shy since he gained his power, so I caught him by surprise when I attempted to strike up a conversation with him, especially since I didn't talk to him that often.

"Oh, hey . . . Jessica," he answered. "You're . . . quite peppy today."

"Well, summer vacation is approaching, and the school year's almost over. Why can't I be peppy?" Despite my energy, I still couldn't avoid the social consequences of sitting near Connor.

"You're sitting next to Super COVID?" Manzanita lacrosse star Edmundo Diaz said to me. "Have fun sitting out the dance troupe show this weekend because you decided to take the stupidest risk in the world."

"Edmundo, don't," I chastised him. "He's had a hard time lately, as have all of us Exceptionals. Don't make things worse for him." Edmundo's only reaction was a sideways nod and a blank frown.

With our essays due the next day, our teacher, Mr. Bradley, was kind enough to give us the last thirty minutes of second period to work on the final drafts of our English papers. I focused as hard as possible on finishing because of the passion I had for my chosen topic: how Sarah Everard's murder in the UK sparked my desire to speak up more for women's rights like Lizzy often did. Recent events surrounding Exceptionals, as well as the rejuvenation I felt from the previous night's dream—if you want to call it that—only further amplified the energy I was putting into my essay.

In spite of the enthusiasm I put into writing in class, I took time to converse with Connor every once in a while, even from afar. I made sure to watch out for his well-being after the rude remark that Edmundo made about him.

"Thanks for having my back, Jessica," Connor said.

"Hey, no problem," I answered. "It's been a tumultuous time for folks like us, and with all the teasing you've experienced, I thought it would be nice to look out for you. Sorry that I was hesitant about it at first; I didn't want to get sick from you like everyone else. But at the same time, I didn't want you to feel alienated by everyone." Though we had to speak up somewhat because of the distance between our desks, the two of us did make sure to keep our voices down so as to avoid distracting the rest of the class.

"It's a nice change of pace that someone's willing to tolerate my power. Wish I could've gotten something like what you have."

"You never know if your power could end up being useful for anything, Connor. I know it isn't fun to have, but have you ever thought about how you could put villains and criminals out of commission just by breathing in their faces?"

Connor let out a laugh loud enough to reverberate through most of the classroom. Lowering his voice back down, he continued, "That would be such a brilliant thing to do. Just imagine if I foiled a madman's plot to take over the world just because I got him sick . . ."

Connor's laugh was audible enough to catch the teacher's attention. "Quiet, Connor," Mr. Bradley said, covering his face with one hand as he walked by Connor's seat. "Your classmates are busy writing a very important essay."

"Oops, sorry, Mr. Bradley." Connor brought his attention back to me, his voice low enough to stop being a distraction. "So what are you writing your essay about, Jessica?"

"You remember when a woman named Sarah Everard went missing in London and was eventually found murdered by a local police officer? And how that was a shock to women throughout the world? I still remember my best friend being so upset about it that I came over to her house to comfort her. And this was back when we were still social distancing because of the pandemic. It was so good to see her in person when we were still a few days away from getting our first vaccines. Crazy thing is, Everard's death was confirmed only a few days after my thirteenth birthday on International Women's Day three years ago. So that just made it hit harder for me."

"That was just sad," Connor said. "First we celebrated the impact that women and girls have made on our society, and then a few days later, a young woman is found dead. And women can't go out on their own without feeling safe as a result of things like that. I had trouble believing it at first, but after everything we've been through over the past several years, anyone would be nuts to deny the problem."

"I'm glad someone gets it, Connor. I wish more guys and men would understand the unique obstacles that women face in society. Your gender needs to speak up more for us women and girls instead of ignoring our problems because you don't know what our experiences are like. Humanity isn't going anywhere until that changes."

Replace "guys and men" with "Unexceptionals" and "women" with "Exceptionals," and you pretty much had the same sentence.

—∞—

Right after school, I decided to spend the afternoon chilling at my dad's surf store with Charlotte and Orlando. Summer Sea Shack wasn't just the surf shop that my dad owned, it was also the primary hangout for students who attended Manzanita High School (as was the beachside mall which Summer Sea Shack was part of). As a result, plenty of kids at my school knew me as the daughter of the guy who ran Summer Sea Shack—including, sadly, Darren Goddamn Owens, whose posse were regulars there. With the official start of summer approaching, plenty of Manzanita students were present at Summer Sea Shack and the adjacent mall, including a few hanging out near us at the patio where we were sitting. To my chagrin, among those people were Darren and his boys: running back Wendell Bath, quarterback Jimmy Baker, and (backup) cornerback Shane Crawford.

"Ayyy, look who's here!" said Shane, a tall, lanky kid with straight brown hair. "Sitting in front of Daddy's store, too." And let the cringing begin.

"What's up, Blondie?" Darren greeted me, glancing at my feet before shifting his eyes to my face. "Cute shirt, by the way."

"Thanks," I said with reluctance. It sounded like Darren had a taste for Abercrombie & Fitch clothing, something I'd be happy to keep in mind from now on.

"Yo, Jessica, how about you strip down to your bikini for us?" said Wendell, the lone black guy in Darren's group of friends. "Perfect time for it with the beach next to us. We got some nice music for you to show off your body to, too."

"Wendell . . . not in front of my dad's shop," I replied. "He works here, you know. I'm not even wearing a bikini, anyway."

"Ooh, Jessica Summer in her lingerie? Even better . . ."

Wendell lit up a fuse in me, provoking me to toss a photon ball at him. Then he pulled up his shirt, revealing a set of well-built abs. When my photon ball hit his abs, it bounced straight off of them, ricocheting across the sand in front of us and flying off into the horizon without hitting a single object or person. Thank goodness there wasn't anyone in the direct vicinity to get a deflected photon blast to the face.

"Oh . . . I didn't know you could do that now," I said.

"Mmm, yeah, the power of these chocolate abs," Wendell said.

Chocolate abs, really? Why couldn't he have given them a name like how certain people name their signature weapons? Then again, it was *so* like Wendell Bath to give his abs such a cringy label.

"Jessica, just try to ignore them," Charlotte said. "Any chance they try to be nice to us, they'll inevitably . . . fumble it." Charlotte giggled and then continued, "Get it? Because they're football players . . ."

Ah, right. I was not into sports at all, so it took me a while for me to realize the punchline there. At least that made the pun less painful to my ears than most of the other ones I'd heard from her, though.

The only way I could react to Charlotte's advice was with a half-smile. Ugh, those assholes just had to interfere with what was supposed to be a relaxing Friday afternoon. I may have become cool with Melissa Snyder, but I never saw myself being cool with Darren or any of his friends. And that was despite the fact that I saved Darren's life a few weeks ago.

To avoid seeing the faces of Darren and his pals, I switched seats with Orlando so that those four wouldn't be as much of a distraction for me. It didn't stop them from giving me weird looks—my long blond hair stood out too much to them—but at least it helped me keep my cool better. I didn't want my negative emotions to manifest themselves again with the immense abilities I had, knowing that superpowers and anger or anxiety could make a bad combination.

While Orlando now had to directly look at the faces of those four as we were chatting, the next subject he brought up helped him stay engaged in our conversation. Good thing he didn't have to worry about getting crude looks and odd fantasies about him from those four imbeciles.

"Dude, did you hear that the school suspended the security guards who beat up Greg Nathan unconscious only until next Tuesday?" he said. "Only a week-long suspension. Meanwhile, Manzanita's also suspended Greg from classes until the start of October for using his powers at school . . . even after they announced that first-time offenders of the new rules would start with a one-week suspension. Poor kid's not going to be able to take his finals and advance to eleventh grade next year after he got beaten unconscious by a pair of security guards who deserve a way harsher punishment. Can you believe how ridiculous all of that is?"

Shock surged into me upon hearing this news. At the same time, however, it somehow didn't surprise me that my school would do something like that. Still, hearing about the massive degree of difference between the sentences handed out to Greg and to the security guards who beat him to a pulp almost caused my powers to act out of anger-fueled impulse again.

"As the lone Exceptional among us, oh yeah, I do," I said. "I'm betting that if those security guards were Exceptionals and Greg wasn't, they would've been canned right away. Luckily for them, they've reaped the benefits of Unexceptional privileges. It's like how the police bring out tanks during Black Lives Matter protests yet seem to be chill with letting a bunch of white rednecks barge into the Capitol in an attempt to overturn an election they claim their guy was robbed of."

"Look at that, Orlando, our girl telling it as it is," Charlotte said, clapping her hands. "We understand how distressing this news is for you, Jess. We'll support you every step of the way in the midst of such injustices."

"Thanks, C. C.," I said.

"I've been thinking . . . I'm not an Exceptional myself, so I'll never really know what it's like to be at a disadvantage in society as a result of having cool powers," Orlando said. "But with all the things that your people have been going through since the Great Bestowal happened, I need to start speaking out for Exceptionals more. I've spent so much time speaking up for women and girls despite not being one myself. And that was before Sarah Everard happened, before our Supreme Court overturned *Roe v. Wade*. So why can't I be a voice for Exceptionals, too? That's what Lizzy would want."

I reached my arms over the table we were sitting at to give a group hug to both Charlotte and Orlando. "I love you guys," I told them. Then I saw Orlando's eyes peer elsewhere.

"Who's that jabroni standing over there?" he asked, focusing his eyes on the parking lot to our side.

Arriving in front of the Summer Sea Shack patio was another one of those shady journalists; I could tell from the microphone in his right hand and the white news van parked in the distance. The news reporter was a tall, lean man, sporting jet black hair and a distinctive black mustache over his mouth, one not dissimilar to that of Luigi from the Mario games. Smoother, gray facial hair dotted the lower part of his face below his mustache, and underneath his suit, he was wearing a conspicuous red tie that echoed the one SpongeBob always wore. He turned his head to the side so that he could make eye contact with me.

"Based on the look he's giving me, I think he wants to talk to me," I told Orlando and Charlotte. "I don't think he'd find either of you two as interesting since you don't have powers."

"Hey now, I take offense to that claim," Orlando said. "I can offer those media goons an Unexceptional perspective. We have important things to say, too."

"Just saying . . ." I said with a nervous smirk. "Anyway, I'll be right back. Let me just talk to this guy first." I left my seat and walked to where the man in the suit was standing in the parking lot.

I didn't know how this man knew where to find me. I didn't know how he got to our side of the beach, either. It would be incredibly creepy if he knew where I was going to be beforehand. But then again, was privacy really a thing these days?

"Excuse me, are you Jessica Summer, miss?" the journalist asked me.

"Yes, I am," I responded. Before I could say anything more, he was quick to pester me with questions.

"Hello, Ms. Summer. Or should I just call you Jessica?"

"I dunno, it doesn't really matter, frankly. I don't know why you want to make a big deal out of that . . ."

"No problem then, Jessica." Weird how he requested to call me by just my first name when he didn't even know me personally . . . "Anyway, my name is Dick Jackson, and I'm a reporter for the national news network USNC." Someone tell me how a guy with that name managed to get a gig with a national news channel . . .

"I've been covering a multitude of news stories with regards to Exceptionals ever since their mysterious emergence approximately three weeks ago, and my news channel was hoping to get your own thoughts on the phenomenon," Mr. Jackson said. I wonder if this man was even aware that there were at least two other Exceptionals hanging out here too, one of whom just deflected my own power.

"And you wanted to seek my opinions in particular because . . .?"

"Why wouldn't I want to speak with the girl who almost took down Rage, the Manzanita High School shooter? No better figure to interview on the matter than Santa Barbara's aspiring superhero." He sounded a little too eager to interview me.

"You seem to be forgetting to put an emphasis on *almost*, Mr. Jackson. Or shall I say, *Dick*." That was very satisfying, choosing to call Mr. Jackson by his given name. "I wasn't even able to defeat Rage. I let him get away. Not exactly the look of a good superhero. Besides, I have too many personal matters in my life to even have time to be a superhero."

"Don't doubt yourself so much, Jessica. You Exceptionals are a wonder to behold, more so than any other marvel that humans have ever seen in history. And you are no exception, Jessica. Look at how awesome your powers are. The ability to generate light energy, the power of flight, altering surrounding gravitational fields . . . With such abilities and more, I've already come up with a nickname for you: the Cosmic Girl."

"Oh, I have a nickname now? Cute. Feel free to go now, Di—Mr. Jackson." I was about to call him by his first name again, but then I decided not to out of respect—at least what little respect I had for this fool. "I've dealt enough with stalkers lately, thank you." As irritating as he was being, at least Mr. Jackson had the audacity to show a fascination with Exceptionals. It was a breath of fresh air amidst the superism that I'd been witnessing and the overload of negative stories I'd seen about Exceptionals on the news.

Preferring to avoid flying away from him for obvious reasons, I tried to walk as fast as my Rainbow flip-flops could take me to whatever corner of the beach I could find where Mr. Jackson would stand out too much clad in a suit on the sand around beachgoers. Then boom, he showed up again, out of nowhere, right in front of me. His sudden appearance prompted a split-second panic attack from me before he returned to being a mere inconvenient nuisance.

"Wait! How did you—"

"Ah yes, I forgot to tell you," Mr. Jackson said. "I'm an Exceptional myself."

Aw great, this guy could teleport, too? So convenient for a journalist who was trying to seek the details of my life like he was attempting to make a reality show out of it.

As much as I wanted to get away from Mr. Jackson, he wouldn't stop chasing me. I continued to power walk away from him and back to the Summer Sea Shack patio. But because of Mr. Jackson's teleportation abilities, it was far too easy for him to catch up to me. Every single time. As if it wasn't enough having to deal with Darren and co. again, this guy had to come into the picture, too.

"I'm sorry to keep disturbing you, Jessica," Mr. Jackson said, "but before you leave, I wanted to get your opinion on this movie that a Hollywood studio is making that's inspired by your life story."

Hearing that irked and confused me at the same time. "What? Someone wants to make a movie based on my life? What are you talking about? There isn't even any reason to make a movie out of my boring-ass life aside from the fact that I happen to have extraordinary powers."

"Yes, Ms. Summer. As strange as that may sound, it's true. An independent movie studio known as Bright Flash Studios has begun the process of creating a movie based on the Manzanita High School shooting from last month. They found your life story particularly interesting because they find the idea of a movie that plays out like a real-life superhero origin story very enticing. So they were looking to interview you to get some important details that they're seeking for their movie."

Wow. Talk about an insensitive way to score a quick buck. My high school had been grieving from the trauma of the sickening mass murder of ten young students, and now Hollywood was already looking to profit off both our grief and my powers? I couldn't help but imagine, too, that Bright Flash Studios wanted to focus on me as the inspiration for their protagonist because I lost my best friend in the shooting. Good luck finding a better superhero origin story than that.

As if Dick Jackson hadn't annoyed me enough, I had no words to give him, no answers for his questions about the proposed movie that he mentioned. The thought that a Hollywood studio would want to make a movie inspired by a shooting at my school managed to rub every single bone of negative energy in my body. And the movie had to focus on me—well, a fictionalized version of me—as the main character, too.

My golden-yellow glow came close to sparking, and my hands started to flash yellow too, but I tried to hold my powers back. I wanted to attack Mr. Jackson in a rage so badly, but I resisted the temptation to do so when, to my relief, a middle-aged man in a white polo shirt, gray shorts, and Rainbow flip-flops like mine came out of Summer Sea Shack, desiring to settle things with Mr. Jackson. It was my dad.

"Excuse me, who are you, and what are you doing here?" Dad interrogated Mr. Jackson.

"Dick Jackson with the USNC Network," Mr. Jackson replied, showing a bit of hesitance now. "And you are . . ."

"I'm Keith Summer. Jessica's father. You didn't happen to notice that you're standing by the same surf shop I've owned since the beginning of the century. And I saw you harassing my daughter from a distance, Mr. Jackson. I don't take kindly to that. For someone named Dick, you sure are able to live up to your name well." My father put on an air of intimidation that I'd never seen from him in my life.

"I suggest that you scram, Mr. Jackson," he continued, pointing and wagging his finger at the reporter as he spoke. "My daughter has been going through a very difficult time in her life, and she needs privacy right now. You news people have been nothing but trouble for our community since the tragic shooting at my daughter's high school, and we would appreciate it if you could just stay out of our lives and matters for once. Just a suggestion, Mr. Jackson."

After several minutes of bugging me, Dick Jackson finally walked back to his network's news truck. I gave my dad a hug and a quick kiss for stepping up for me at a fantastic time.

Dad and I walked back to the patio in front of Summer Sea Shack, specifically to where Orlando and Charlotte were sitting. Seeing the heads of Darren and his pals reminded me that they were there too, but like Charlotte advised, I just ignored them. No need to get in another fuss with them after what I just went through with Dick Jackson.

"Great save, Mr. Summer," Orlando said. "You should consider trying out for goalkeeper for the U.S. Men's National Team after that move."

"Not sure that I have the height and hand size for such a job," my dad joked. "But I do like the suggestion there, Orlando."

While it was relieving that Dad took a short break from work to get Mr. Jackson to stop pestering me, it didn't fail to escape me that I had more new stresses in my life to deal with on top of the ones I'd already been having. And this was just a few days before I began finals week the following Monday.

And then there was the fact that Garrett Lowe was still around, out of jail and armed with Exceptional abilities of his own, doing who knew what. Being an Exceptional at my school was becoming less and less of an ideal situation. And now, in the midst of all that, Manzanita was handed a Hollywood spotlight that it wouldn't want and didn't deserve. With a fictionalized version of me as its protagonist, and the plot for her story based on my own experience of watching Lizzy get shot in front of my eyes and the aftermath of it all. Just like Dad said, the people at my school were going to have something to say about the matter. Me being one of those people, of course.

CHAPTER

17

Some time after Dad and I arrived home, Larson came back home himself after wrapping up the end of his junior year at UCSB; he spent the entire afternoon moving all of his stuff out of his Isla Vista residence with Mom. Lucky for him, he returned just in time to hear the interesting story that happened with me and Dad earlier during dinnertime.

"Jessica told me about what happened with you and that national news reporter who was bothering her today," Larson said to Dad. "Very gnarly move on your part, Dad. I gotta admit that I'm jealous of Jessica and the way you stepped up for her. When do I get to receive that type of love from you and Mom?"

"Well, you know what they say about daddy's little girl and all," Dad joked.

"Oh, so are you saying that I should've been born with an extra X chromosome, Dad?"

"Larson . . . we girls go through so much shit worldwide on a daily basis," I countered. "Be glad that your sister got the long end of the courtesy stick today. Don't even think to brag about the male privilege you're lucky to be blessed with."

"Someone doesn't get a joke," Larson teased. "But then again, given what you've been going through, I should be more sensitive to the youngest lady in the house. It's what Lizzy would want, after all." He tipped his glass toward me for a toast.

"That's the spirit." I smiled at Larson and tipped my glass back to him before we sipped the Sprite in our respective glasses.

"I heard that a movie studio wants to make a film based on the events of the shooting. Such a stupid idea on their part. And of course, very appalling, too."

"Meh. The less said about it, the better. No way Hollywood is going to get away with allowing that movie to get the green light." I picked up my fork and took a bite of my tofu, making sure that my taste buds soaked in every wonderful sensation that the tofu brought me.

"I hope your finals went okay, Larson," Dad said. "Mom and I are so relieved you're still safe after that lockdown UCSB went into yesterday."

"Finals were not a problem for me," Larson said. "That lockdown situation did get scary, but luckily, it wasn't as worrying of a situation as we had feared."

"UCSB went into a lockdown?" I asked, sounding concerned. "What for?"

"We went into a brief lockdown yesterday after the Manzanita shooter came by and tried to murder a few sorority girls," Larson answered. Hearing the words "Manzanita shooter" come out of his mouth almost made me drop my fork.

"Wait . . . the Manzanita shooter? Garrett Lowe? Scott Lowe's son? Now known as Rage?"

"Yes, him. He stopped by Del Playa, looked for the first group of sorority girls he could find, and tried to murder them all with his flames . . . then some guy with all sorts of psychic powers flew to our campus and kicked his ass real good. Heard that Rage was no match for him, so he had no choice but to flee. So we were all fine in the end thanks to his efforts. All of the sorority girls that Rage went for were safe and sound, and nobody got hurt or killed. Well, except for one Alpha Phi girl's two German shepherds that Rage did manage to burn to death in cold blood . . ."

"Wait . . . Rage . . . what?" I didn't want to believe that Rage slaughtered a pair of dogs just for the hell of it, but it was impossible to deny it considering this was Rage we were talking about. I wished I hadn't turned off my news notifications after returning to school so that

I would've been able to catch that important news update and come to those poor dogs' rescue.

"He didn't kill a single person, but he killed a sorority girl's dogs. Enjoyed every single second of it, I heard. The kid with the psychic powers tried to save the dogs, but he couldn't. I heard that the poor girl who owned the dogs was so traumatized that she had to go to the hospital right away for emergency mental health treatment. Hope she's doing okay now . . ."

My agitation was already building up, then it hit a real apex. I screamed my lungs out, to the point of releasing a literal explosion of cosmic matter. Our dining table shattered, as did my chair and parts of the walls behind me. Mom, Dad, and Larson shielded themselves from the incoming bursts of impossibly bright cosmic matter with their arms, and my anger soon shifted to panic, knowing that I just landed in the very situation I'd been trying to avoid with my parents ever since discovering my powers.

". . . maybe it wasn't a good idea to bring that detail up," Larson said.

"Oh God, I . . . I . . ." Flustered, I cried out, "You hate me now, don't you, Mom and Dad? Knowing that you're raising a freak and an abomination who's rightfully feared by the rest of society?"

My parents' response was that they just . . . hugged me.

"Jess, it's okay, darling," Mom said softly. "Dad and I will always love you, regardless of the fact that you're an Exceptional. We'll defend you to the death if someone ever attempts to persecute you for being an Exceptional. But you do need to recognize that your powers are not a toy. They can pose a threat, just like driving a car or carrying a knife. So we hope you've been handling them with care and aren't using them irresponsibly."

"I saw a couple of kids at your school use their powers to pick on their friend for not being an Exceptional," Dad said. "They don't want to be friends with him anymore and view him as ruining their reputation. Funny what you observe when the students from your school tend to hang out at my surf shop after campus hours."

"Of course, we're not happy that you just made a massive mess of the dining room," Mom added. "But consider it a tough lesson regarding the role of your powers in your life. This is the rocky phase that your favorite superheroes go through when their powers end up causing unintentional problems."

"Yeah, you have a point there, Mom . . ." I said. "I was just afraid that you would end up treating me like dirt after something like this happened. It pays to be anti-Exceptional nowadays, you know."

"Jess, we've seen the mistreatment of other groups over the past few years," Dad said. "Both in our town and elsewhere in the world. And we've been doing as much as you have to try to understand their situations better. As a small business owner, I have a taste of what it's like to be the little guy. I'm not going to fall for the trap that society wants to set for me. Besides, that's what Lizzy would want."

"Awww, that's the spirit, Dad. Love you both. Always forever." I folded my arms over the shoulders of both of my parents, and Larson joined in himself.

"You can count on me to have your back, too, sis," Larson said. "I want to know how you were able to pull that off, anyway. I mean, it's not something I should just brush off, but still . . ."

"I'm not sure how exactly to put it, but . . . I learned it in a dream," I told Larson. "Kind of. It's hard to explain it properly, so I'll just say that I first pulled it off in a dream."

As I stepped back, the mess I ended up creating further settled into my mind. A broken dinner table. A shattered window and walls. Plates and pieces of our food scattered across the dining room floor. Guilt settled into my veins one second at a time, and I let out a deep sigh and dropped my face into my hand.

"I'm so sorry about this," I told my family. "Thankfully I know someone who has the power to rearrange things back into order, so I'll talk to her so she can fix everything that I unintentionally disassembled."

"Consider that a situation in which to be thankful that people with incredible powers now exist," Dad said. "This is why all of those people speaking out against you folks are horribly ignorant or misinformed."

"If I were able to create an explosion like you just did, I'm sure I would've reacted the same way to hearing about a delinquent boy who killed a pair of dogs," said Larson. "I can't fault you for responding to such news like that. Even though, you know, you did damage an entire section of our house that we now need to clean up. And you could've hurt one of us, too. Good thing we all dodged a bullet; consider yourself lucky, Jess."

—∾—

The stars couldn't have lined up for me better with my Saturday morning yoga class coming the day before my big dance show that weekend, and right after my incident at dinner the previous evening. While yoga wasn't the same thing as dancing, it made for the perfect practice with the same union of flexibility and rhythm that dancing had. I liked to consider it my warm-up for the show, as well as a prime opportunity to let out all the foul emotions that I'd felt from both the turmoil of this whole week and whatever trauma was still lingering in me from the shooting.

After my hour of yoga wrapped up, satisfaction flowed through me in a way that I hadn't felt from my previous yoga classes. I was already anticipating nothing but positive things for the rest of my day. At least until a group of adults—the majority of them white and male—appeared behind me moments after class ended.

The first sign that alerted me to them was how the park around me emptied out in a few seconds. The only people in my area were me and the protesters themselves. Whatever was going on didn't make sense to me one bit. Then again, what did make sense these days?

"There she is. The Cosmic Girl herself," one of the protesters said in an intense tone. Gosh, and they knew of me, too. Of course, this didn't come as that surprising to me; even when he wasn't there, Dick Jackson's influence must've found a way to hang over me.

I didn't know why these folks decided to show up at the same place as me, or how they figured out to show up where I was. To make matters worse, several of them were pointing rifles in my direction, creating an uncomfortable tingle that wanted to shatter me at the leg. To think that gun-toters could still be allowed to roam around unharmed after a mass shooting struck our community was preposterous beyond words. Where were the police when you needed them?

"You abominations must be ended," a man with a patriotic hat and a white mustache said. "Only God is allowed to have extraordinary powers like yours. And He will eliminate all of you anomalies in the end."

"We cannot let freaks like you threaten the very fabric of America," another man with a gun said. "You bastards are nothing but a destructive cancer to our country."

So began the flurry of gunshots, which freaked me out so much that I didn't react in time like I should have. After starting off dodging bullets and somehow not suffering a single scratch, I unleashed my force field to neutralize all the shots flying my way.

"You can't get away any longer, you alien scum!" shouted another one of the armed protesters, though I couldn't tell which one from inside my force field bubble. Still inside my protective bubble, I floated upward and unleashed a massive photon beam from the air against the hostile superists, blowing them apart in numerous directions and buying me time to fly back home with my yoga mat still in tow. If these people were going to lead a crusade against me for my powers, I might as well use those against them. Give them a taste of their own medicine; show them that we meant business. Plus, it was a good practice run for fighting against Rage. That didn't hurt, either.

Knowing that my family had my back, I thought about them on the whole flight back to my house, allowing me to subdue the stressful and negative emotions that were squeezing me when I encountered those gunmen. The fact that I had run into armed men for the first time since the shooting—and several of them, not just one—caused me shivers on my way back to the house. I was very certain it wasn't the thinner air up there at my flying altitude, too.

When I arrived back home safely—and thank goodness I did—there was one thing I had to do first before moving on with the rest of the day, as if I had any other choice: call the police. I couldn't believe this was the second time in six days that I was dialing 911 because of an emergency I suddenly found myself in the middle of. But such was the life of the lady that the public now called the "Cosmic Girl."

Because I did so five days prior, dialing the numbers 911 on my phone wasn't as strange of an experience for me as it was on Monday. But it was still every bit as spine-tingling, especially because this time, my life was on the line. And I had to encounter the menace of gunfire, too, not even a month since the mass shooting that shook my seaside high school to the core.

Once again, I heard an operator speak those six words, only through my smartphone this time rather than my school's landline. "911, what's your emergency?"

"Hello, operator. My name is Jessica Summer. I'm calling to report—" Before I could move on, I realized that the operator's voice sounded strangely familiar to me. "Wait, first off, didn't I speak to you a few days ago, ma'am?"

"I believe so," the operator responded. "You reported the brutal beating of an Exceptional at your school this past Monday, correct?"

"Yes, that was me. And unfortunately, I almost met my own deadly fate not too long ago. A group of protesters who are aware that I'm an Exceptional—the one known as the Cosmic Girl—tried to attack me with various types of rifles earlier this morning at the park on East Beach around 11 a.m., which is when my daily Saturday morning yoga class ends. They called me things like 'freak,' 'bastard,' and 'cancer.' One of them said that God would eliminate me one day. And while I can't describe what every single one of them looked like, I do remember that all but one or two of them were white, middle-aged men. Their clothing was full of red, white, and blue as well—hardcore patriots, apparently. As scary as they were, especially for someone like me who found herself in the middle of a school shooting a few weeks ago, I was able to deal with their gunfire thanks to my Exceptional powers. But while I'm physically okay, I'm mentally shaken." The angst in my voice went up when I concluded my call with, "I know you've spoken with me before, but I don't think you can imagine the magnitude of difficulty I've been going through these days. I really hope you're taking me and my words seriously; it's just not easy being an Exceptional in a world that fears and hates us."

The operator took a brief pause before she continued speaking with me. "I'm sorry for all your trouble, miss," she said. "But I promise you that I am listening to every single word you're saying to me. Thank you for reporting to me. I will let the Santa Barbara Police Department know as soon as possible so that we can resolve the issue and make sure that we can keep your town safe for your kind in these troubling times."

"Thank you so much, ma'am," I said. "I'm grateful for your courtesy over the past week, in both of the times you've spoken to me."

"No problem, Miss Summer. Is there anything else I can do for you?"

"No, thanks. I just need some relaxation time."

"I understand. Hope you do better for the rest of your day. Get some rest and take care."

"You too, ma'am." Thus ended my latest emergency phone call. I hoped against hope that justice didn't work against me like it did against Plasma Kid because of anti-Exceptional bias.

Any occasion in which I could spend time appreciating the beauty and wonder of Wonder media (no pun intended, I promise) was my personal version of heaven on earth. But after coming dangerously close to meeting the same fate as Lizzy this morning, I needed an escape into the Wonder Universe more than ever. So I directed as much of my focus as I could onto reading my most recent Wonder comic books, as well as catching up on the latest episode of *Jegina*, a series on Wonder's streaming platform WTV based on the titular Protectors member from Ethiopia (that luckily didn't include a single shot of gunfire), and of course, my big showcase at Manzanita's auditorium tomorrow. All the usual Jessica stuff.

As I watched *Jegina* on my laptop, my mom entered my room, and I paused the episode I was watching. "Jessica, is everything okay?" she asked. "I saw you on the news again."

"Oh yeah, things are fine," I answered, trying not to downplay what I went through this morning.

"Are you sure? I hope those gunmen didn't hurt you . . ."

When Mom passed through my door, she took a careful examination of me from head to toe and gave me a big hug. "You're okay . . ." she said after seeing that I didn't have a single wound on me. She was somewhere halfway between almost tearing up and actually tearing up.

"That's what these powers come in handy for," I told Mom. "To make sure that I don't end up like Lizzy. Or that ten-year-old boy in Minnesota who gained the power to see through walls and was beaten to death just because he could do so."

"We told you that your powers are nothing to be ashamed of. Consider them your ultimate blessing, sweetheart." Mom planted a kiss on my forehead, and I reacted with a simple smile.

"Those lunatics came out of nowhere," I said. "Like a character in a movie thrown in without any reason. I don't know why no one came to do anything against them. But somehow, I'm okay mentally. Still shaken, of course; having terrible flashbacks again at times. But still able to get through the rest of my day. I suppose it helps that I encountered those superist nuts right after yoga class."

"I'm glad to hear. You're figuring out how to overcome your negative experiences, Jess. I'm proud of you for that. You're becoming a stronger girl every day."

"I don't know how I'm doing it. But here I am." I glanced back at my laptop and the paused *Jegina* episode on my screen. "Is it cool if I go back to watching this episode, Mom? I'm really concentrated on it."

"You go ahead and do that. I wasn't going to disturb you for too long; I know how much you love your Wonder stuff. Hope you remain okay, sweetheart." Mom walked out of the room, and I resumed the episode.

While I couldn't fully brush off my experiences running into gunfire once again, I couldn't let uncomfortable thoughts intrude my brain too much. I was getting through all this. I was going to have a nice rest of my day. I was going to relax. I was going to be positive. And I was going to be all pumped up for my dance show the next day.

After all, it was what Lizzy would have wanted.

CHAPTER

18

Sunday, June 16. The night you've been preparing for all semester long. It's your time to shine now, Jessica Summer.

Not meaning to sound like Jessie Spano from *Saved by the Bell* here, but I was both a little bit excited and a little bit scared for this show. I was stoked to finally get the dance show over with and prove my worthiness of becoming a captain for the Manzanita Dance Troupe. Yet, at the same time, the scenarios of what might go wrong—particularly ones involving my powers—were bringing out my nerves. I may have had solid control of my powers and quickly learned to embrace them, but I was such a perfectionist about this night that I worried about even the slightest trigger of any of my abilities.

If my powers acted out, I might be kicked off the dance troupe completely. I'd never get a chance to become a dance troupe captain. And by inciting havoc with my powers at a public school show, I'd provide even more excuses for the superists to act out against Exceptionals at our school and beyond. Or worse, Garrett could show up there, freak me out, and cause me to trigger my powers at the worst time. Two Exceptionals in the same place, not just one, to help superists justify their prejudice.

Then again, maybe I was just overreacting. What was the need for me to worry as much as I was?

Before we began our show, all of us huddled together in a circle and focused on Ms. Newton. "Ladies, this is it," she said. "The big night we've all been waiting for. Good luck to all of you. And particular best wishes for any of you aiming to earn co-captaincy for the dance troupe next year." Hearing those words made me feel like the spotlight was shining solely on me, as if everyone else on the dance troupe wasn't even there and I was about to perform the entire show solo.

Next up to speak was Megan Miller. "Seniors, I can't believe this is our last show," the dance troupe co-captain said. "These last four years have been a wonderful ride, and it's sad to think it's now coming to an end. So let's make the most of it tonight. And to whoever is chosen to take my place as co-captain next year, I wish you the best of luck. I know you will do a fantastic job filling my spot."

After our quick team pep talk, I wanted to speak with Ms. Newton alone before the show began. The two of us went to an isolated corner backstage so that we could keep our conversation private.

"What's up, Jessica?" Ms. Newton asked. "Is everything okay?"

"Everything's fine," I answered. "It's just that . . . I want to be excited about this show. My ultimate audition to become dance troupe co-captain next year. But I just have so much pressure on me with everything going on . . ." I started to walk back and forth in the small space. "What if I fire off one of my powers without intention? And the show ends up ruined and overshadowed by any superism that comes about as a result? Will the others get mad at me for ruining the show if that happens?"

"Jessica, none of that is going to happen, I promise you. You're just having butterflies right now; that's understandable." Ms. Newton placed her hand on my shoulder. "Always remember that all of us have your back, no matter what. We accept everyone in our dance troupe, and that includes you Exceptionals. Even as superism has emerged in society, I've never had anything against Exceptionals. I've always kept my eye on them, watched out for their safety, observed how things have been developing for them. Especially because you're one of them, Jessica."

A smile emerged onto Ms. Newton's face. "Every time I hear about Exceptionals, I think about you. And you've been one of my favorite students since you first stepped into my dance room as a freshman. Your passion for our team is top-notch. And you always make our day better just by being present. If there's one reason you should take pride in the incredible powers you have, consider me one."

A smile spread onto my face as Ms. Newton placed her other hand on my right shoulder. "Don't let recent events get to your head, Jessica. You've got this. I'll be rooting for you all the way."

"Thank you for your kind words, Ms. Newton," I said. "I feel better now."

"Glad to hear. Enjoy the show, Jessica."

And with that, I walked out to the stage, siphoning all my focus into the first piece of our spring semester show.

Our first piece of the night was a simple contemporary number set to a gentle piano song. During that piece, I could somehow feel Ids in me. Even though I hadn't seen his shooting star again lately, it was possible his spirit continued to watch over me through some sort of fancy mental connection. Whatever I felt during that performance, it was harnessing a brand-new energy in me. Every step, spin, and turn that I took was smoother than I could ever recall them being throughout the many times that I practiced this piece in fourth period.

As I returned backstage, I could sense my anxiety starting to melt away. There was still a lot of it in my body, however, with two hours of the show still left. So I spent my downtime stretching out my body to keep it warm. I was in the mood for an extended hand-to-toe pose to keep my legs fresh before it was time for my next performance. Whatever nervous feelings I had earlier, I could feel them fading away through every bit of this stretch from thigh to knee to toe.

"Impressive," said Erin Logan, one of the two freshmen in the dance troupe. "Your flexibility seems to have improved since the start of the school year. Is that a result of your new superpowers?"

"Nope. Weekly Saturday morning yoga classes at the beach," I replied. "That's my secret. Look at how well yoga works out for the movie and TV stars." I transitioned from my extended hand-to-toe pose into a tree pose, then placed my hands in front of my chest to further let any unpleasant sensations evaporate. My teammates were happy to join me in stretching our bodies out as I continued with my yoga maneuvers, teaching them some of the poses I'd learned from my classes along the way. Call it our version of backstage antics for the night.

"After engaging in some yoga during a bit of downtime, Génesis Fernandez discovers her hidden super-stretchiness and becomes the superheroine Flex-Mex!" declared one of the dance troupe members in the same grade as me. "Watch out, Luffy and Elastigirl, you've got some competition!" All of us backstage shared a laugh together over the imaginary superhero origin story that Génesis thought up.

"So what's Flex-Mex's superhero gimmick, Génesis?" I asked.

"She hasn't thought about that yet. Beating up any racist who wants to drag society back decades is what I'm thinking."

"Ooh, I like that idea. Flex-Mex is already a role model of mine now."

"*¡Excelente!* She's already looking forward to the upcoming Flex-Mex and Cosmic Girl team-up." That sounded like it was going to be a very fun fan fiction.

"I don't think yoga is supposed to work this way," Jamie Warner, a short, blond-haired girl and one of the graduating seniors, said to me. "Aren't we supposed to be all calm and focused?"

"You can be whatever you feel like being here, girls. We're just doing this for fun, after all; style doesn't matter to me." I proceeded to fold my upper body into my left leg while pointing my right leg upward.

"Here's a new pose I learned from my class yesterday. It may already be one of my favorite poses." I got into the same standing split pose that I learned in yoga class the day before. My teammates attempted to imitate my maneuver, with mixed results.

"Ooh, I'm not sure that Flex-Mex has developed that level of flexibility yet," Génesis said. "Only in her regular identity, of course."

When Kayla and Megan came backstage following the conclusion of their piece, all of us were lined up in the same yoga pose.

"We return backstage planning to start playing a fun game with you guys, and then a wild yoga class appears," Kayla said. All of us laughed at Kayla's joke.

"Oh, my apologies for stealing your thunder, then," I teased.

"No worries, Jess," Megan said. "We love that you took charge of the team while the two of us were performing."

"Jessica's teaching us some poses she's learned from her Saturday yoga classes," Charlotte said. "It's been really fun."

"Ooh, sounds like we've been missing out on a lot then," said Kayla. She and Megan joined the rest of us in learning the standing split yoga pose while four of our dance troupe teammates walked up to the stage to start performing their next piece.

"Oh, you're getting this down better than I have," I told Kayla and Megan as they maintained their standing split poses.

"Well, we are dance troupe co-captains for a reason," Megan half-teased. "You've still got some work to do, kiddo."

"I can't disagree with you there, Megan."

As if to live up to the old adage "saving the best for last," the performance that I was leading had to come as the final act of the night's show. As a result, the wait for my performance, which went on for around two hours, was all the more agonizing for me. But then again, this was my ultimate audition for the title of Manzanita Dance Troupe 2024–2025 co-captain. I had to make the most of it.

Through each spin and turn, unpleasant memories of the past few weeks—from the day of the shooting to Plasma Kid's brutal beatdown—flashed in my mind. I feared that my distraction would cause a sudden stumble, a trip that would make my teammates fall with me. But I couldn't let these kinds of thoughts cause me to make the performance go haywire. I'd worked too hard all year for that. This was my moment, and I was not going to blow it.

Just tap into a sense of relaxation, Jessica. Use those techniques that you've been learning during your yoga classes. Channel Ids's spirit throughout you. Try thinking about your parents in the audience, too. Imagine how much of an amazing Father's Day gift nailing this performance would be for your dad.

Instead of firing out any of my powers on accident, I channeled the yogi in me as I made a stop into every pose, through each move of my performance. It helped that the poses I made during the performance were quite similar to yoga poses. From then on, my nerves calmed down, and each of my movements were more graceful.

And as we struck our final poses to wrap up the grand finale of our show, a big smile graced my face. I might not have officially earned the title of Manzanita Dance Troupe co-captain, but I was confident that I did enough to prove my worthiness of the title.

The curtain closed and then reopened after a few seconds to give us time to get in formation for the closing bows. The ceremony began with everyone who led a performance taking center stage to bow to the crowd; with my piece being the last one, I was the last dancer to go up before the three graduating seniors did the same with Megan in the middle. To wrap up the curtain call, all of us took a group bow, with the graduating seniors in the very center of the stage again in their final show for the Manzanita Dance Troupe.

Nothing notable happened during the closing ceremony except for our bows. None of my powers fired off like crazy, and no walls or ceilings got demolished and fell apart. Just the applause of the crowd, unanimous hollers, and no excuses for anyone to demonstrate signs of superism.

During the group bow, I caught a quick glimpse of Scott Lowe in the audience, amazement painting his iconic face. I had a difficult time confirming that it was indeed him, but I'd seen that face so many times that I was certain it couldn't be anybody but Scott Lowe.

Wow. THE Scott Lowe came over to catch my dance show. That was just . . . I didn't really have anything to say about that other than that it was awesome beyond words. And as an added bonus, he was sitting right next to Lizzy's parents. That was more than I could've ever asked for.

I wanted to rush off stage to Mr. Lowe's seat and say hi to him so badly. But I would've looked like such a dork if I did so. I doubt it would've looked good for my captaincy candidacy, either.

CHAPTER

19

After numerous emotional ups and downs over the past four weeks, Monday was the latest emotional jolt for me through this not-so-fun roller-coaster ride. One night after our successful performance at the spring semester show, Charlotte felt likewise. Sucked for us to snap back to reality after how much fun we had at the Manzanita auditorium around twelve hours earlier.

"I was expecting you to be a lot more upbeat today after you and Jess kicked ass at last night's show, Charlotte," Orlando said as we took our daily walk together to first period. "What's getting you down?"

Charlotte exhaled before speaking up. "I saw Garrett Lowe kidnap Darren Owens and Melissa Snyder this morning," she answered.

The news about Darren and Melissa didn't surprise me considering Garrett's views of them, but it was still difficult for me to believe at first. "Are you sure about that, C. C.?" I asked for the sake of clarification.

"Yes. I clearly remember seeing Garrett's face. The same one from his 'Reckoning' video. And I saw him stuffing Darren's and Melissa's bodies into the back of his car for a brief moment. They appeared to be unconscious, and also burned, I'm sure. I've already let Principal Warden know; since Garrett managed to get away, there's not much else he can do about it other than inform the school that he's on the loose again as well as contact Darren and Melissa's families."

"Where did you see them, Charlotte?" Orlando asked. "We could use more details."

"Darren and Melissa were chatting in Darren's car thirty minutes or so before homeroom. I saw them just outside the Starbucks in the shopping center by our school when I stopped there for a quick coffee before heading to homeroom. And then when I came out, that's when I saw Garrett jam Darren and Melissa into the trunk of his black BMW before he got in it and sped away. As I saw the BMW zip away, I realized, *Holy shit, that's the same car from Garrett Lowe's YouTube videos.*"

"You seriously watched Garrett's videos, too?" I asked.

"Yes, as much as I hate to admit it. But now I'm glad that I watched them because I might not have caught Garrett otherwise. The screech that his BMW made was so loud that it's still ringing in my head. Then I saw his face for a few seconds; it was the most nightmarish face I've ever seen in my life. I called the police to report what I had seen, but he had gotten away by the time they came."

"Do you have any idea where Garrett drove off to? Any reports about that?"

"I wish I knew, Jess, but no. I was just an unintentional bystander to Garrett's abductions; I know nothing about his whereabouts other than what I saw him do. I sure hope the police can give us more information soon."

It was common for us to pass by Melissa and Darren's circle of friends—Wendell, Shane, Jimmy, Irene, Natasha, and Katie—on our way to our classes. As much as I disliked those folks, it was too strange for me to see them so stoic and concerned instead of pompous and irritating like they usually were. The three of us only took brief glances at them, and none of us said a single word to each other. Melissa's and Darren's absences were impossible for us not to notice; it just wasn't the same when I walked by those people and Darren wasn't calling me "Blondie" or Melissa wasn't calling me a nerd, or both.

After we passed by Darren and Melissa's friends, I turned my head up to look at the sky above me. One second, the sun had its usual shine and the sky was mostly clear; the next second, a billow of smoke started to blot out the sun, dimming the light beaming down onto campus. That cloud of smoke wasn't there this morning.

"I think I know where Garrett may be," I told Charlotte and Orlando. And then, instead of heading to geometry class, I power walked my way to the front office of campus to talk to the front desk.

When I got to the door to the front office, I started pretending to hack, cough, and wheeze in an exaggerated fashion, all the while putting my mouth to my elbow. My fake coughs continued as I opened the door and make my way to our school's receptionist, Mrs. Zimmerman.

"Hey, sorry that this is a little last minute," I told Mrs. Zimmerman, letting out another fake cough. "But I'm starting to feel very sick, so I don't think I can be at school for the rest of the day. You know the drill: gotta stay home if I'm feeling sick. And I sure as hell can't afford to spread my illness to other students and make them miss their finals this week. Consider me doing a good deed for the rest of the school by taking the rest of the day off."

I let out another pretend cough before the receptionist answered my request. "I understand your situation, Ms. Summer," Mrs. Zimmerman said. "I'll record that in your attendance record, so you won't have to worry about anything else for the rest of the day."

"Thank you for that, Mrs. Zimmerman."

"No problem. Hope you're able to get over your illness soon, Jessica. I would hate for you to miss finals week."

"Thanks again, Mrs. Zimmerman." I was now sounding like I'd been underwater for three minutes straight. "I hate to miss school on the first day of finals week. But I need to do what I must. You won't have to worry about me missing finals week, because I promise I will be back soon. I'm sure this illness will only take a day or two to recover from." I cupped my mouth with my elbow again and fake coughed one more time before leaving the front office and departing campus, taking off into the sky in search of where Rage was holding Darren and Melissa captive.

As I flew to where the smoke plume was coming from, my initial suspicion was that Rage sparked a massive wildfire to satisfy his thirst for mass murder in a more widespread and efficient manner. As such,

I expected to fly to a location deep within the Santa Ynez Mountains, one of the areas where Santa Barbara–area wildfires would typically rage. However, I ended up making my way to an abandoned house somewhere along the edge of Santa Barbara city limits. It caught me off-guard. The space around me was mostly vegetation and shrubbery, but the area was clearly still a part of town, being a small neighborhood with only a few houses around.

The house that I ended up in was a freaky enough sight by itself, already rotting and dilapidated. The flames that blanketed it only added to the unsettling backdrop of the building, a drastic contrast to the rest of my sun-drenched seaside hometown. But that was child's play compared to what I encountered next.

The deeper I went into the abandoned house, the more flames surrounded me, the darker it got, and the harder it became to breathe. As I tried to dodge the flames, my patience shrunk in trying to find someone in there, to find out what was going on. When I encountered an enormous wall of fire blocking my way, I could make out a kid in a black shirt, the first person that I spotted inside the crumbling house. I leaped and floated above the wall of fire before it could get any bigger, and when my feet touched back down onto the floor, the kid turned around, revealing his face to me before I could make any steps toward him.

When my eyes caught sight of that face, I stopped in my tracks in an instant. The most haunting shivers stabbed my feet, cutting their way all throughout the rest of my body, the heat of the flames around me doing nothing to warm them away. A sinister but well-polished face topped by smooth, black hair—the vision of it was enough to trap me in a box of anguish that was too tight to escape. Even as he turned his head back around, each detail of his face continued to linger in my mind.

To Garrett's side were Darren and Melissa, marked by several burns on their skin and clothes and chained to a wall whose paint was fading and falling off. Darren struggled to unleash his arms from the cuffs binding his wrists, while Melissa stayed put, displaying heavier concern in contrast to Darren's typical unwavering arrogance.

"All these days I've spent formulating this plan, and now at long last, I can bring it into action," Rage said, cackling. "Today is going to be a glorious day."

"Did you forget who you decided to mess with?" Darren said. "Any moment now, I'll break free from these chains with ease. My speed and athleticism demand it." Garrett's only reaction was a bored, indifferent expression, having none of Darren's words.

"Be lucky that I didn't duct tape your stupid mouths, Darren Owens and Melissa Snyder," he said. "I was very tempted to do so. But then I decided it would be more pleasant to see the shocked looks on your faces before I scorch you two to death."

"You're insane to think you can get your way this time," Melissa said. "Someone's going to find us and rescue us. Someone's going to stop you like that Psion guy did. We're in a world where people with extraordinary powers can be real-life superheroes now, so do the math."

"You bitches really think that someone's going to come to your rescue and take me down? Nah. This is real life, you arrogant, bratty shits. In real life, tyrants take power. Wars erupt and ruin societies. The awfulness of the world trumps the good. Every. Single. Day." Garrett let out a deep laugh. "I may have not succeeded in slaughtering you assholes the first two tries, but rest assured, I *will* stand victorious this time around. And it will be *every* bit as enjoyable as when I roasted that Alpha Phi sorority chick's two annoying, pathetic dogs the other day."

My God. I knew my life was now a superhero comic book, but this guy was no comic book villain. He was a horror movie villain.

Ready to make his move, Garrett showed his right hand to Darren and Melissa and lit it on fire. Unfortunately for him, I was there to make my own moves, too. Rewrite his intended story the way it was supposed to go.

Trying to put all the negative emotions that he elicited in me to rest, I took a few steps toward where Garrett stood. My body was stiff, and I focused my vision solely on him, even if he didn't notice me right away.

"Garrett Lowe," I snarled. "I knew you were behind all this." I put my arms to my sides as both of my hands rolled into fists.

"Jessica Summer," Garrett said. "What a pleasure to see you here, my beauty. You've come just in time to witness the most beautiful moment of my tortured life. The most beautiful moment until you become mine, of course."

"Let those two go," I demanded. "They did nothing to ruin your life. No one ruined your life, especially not those girls that you think pushed you away. You just don't want to take responsibility for being the unpleasant, sexist douchebag that you are."

"The girl who I'm meant to be with talking trash about me? Bold of you, Jessica. Bold of you."

Rage set his entire body aflame and unleashed a torrent of fire in my direction. It was difficult to tell the flames he fired apart from the ones he already set, and the smoke and ash in the area stabbed my eyes as well. In a split second, I activated my force field bubble, which not only shielded me from Rage's incoming flames, but wiped away the aggravating sensations that were impeding my vision, too. Relief embraced me as the force field stopped Rage's fire in its tracks.

"Don't be so frightened of me, Jessica. I promise I don't want to hurt you," he said. "But you left me no choice there. Just be glad I won't leave you dead like the two other scumbags in this room."

"Like I'd allow you to do that," I said as I deactivated my force field.

"Really? I thought you don't like those two. You don't want me to end them? Think about how much our dislike of them unites us. Think about how much misery they've caused us at school. You should be happy for me when I eliminate those two scoundrels from the world."

"I may not be fond of those two, but that doesn't mean I approve of them being gone. After you took my best friend's life and murdered nine more of my fellow students, I won't let you take another life ever again."

"Oh, I murdered your best friend? I'm sorry; I was too busy trying to slay all the assholes who ruined my life to even notice!" Rage let out another terrifying laugh. "Man, that day sure was glorious. I may not have managed to murder all the people I wanted to, but I take pride in forever etching my name into the pantheon of American mass shooters. It feels so good to have taken every single one of those miserable lives. And that includes your precious—"

Before Rage could finish his sentence, I blasted a beam of photon energy at him out of a fit of my own rage. Rage lit his body on fire just in time, however, preventing him from receiving even the slightest scratch from my beam.

Now aflame, Rage leapt forward like a frog and attempted to land his fist on me. I managed to jump out of his path on time and countered by projecting a blinding flash of light into his face. Alas, it didn't faze him.

Rage's flaming body blended in so well with the rest of the fires in the abandoned house that it was hard for me to make him out amid all the chaos in the building. As if an invisible force was zipping around me, I remained on the defensive, looking in every direction.

I spotted a fireball hurling toward me, alerting me to Rage's approximate location. Before the fireball could hit me, I performed a spin-stop move from the piece I led at the end of the previous night's dance show to get out of harm's way. I continued to channel similar dance moves to dodge Rage's flames, kicks, and punches. None of his attacks came close to touching me, so much so that I could now relax myself as if nothing out of the ordinary was going on, so as long as I kept dancing about.

I waited for Rage's fire to go out before retaliating against him. When it did, I unleashed a miniature blue star at him, the first time I ever used this power; the combined brightness, heat, and potency of the blue star knocked him into a daze. Taking advantage of Rage's stunned state, I flew at him, punched and kicked his stupid face, and unleashed another photon beam that filled the entire building, all in quick succession.

My last attack sent him sailing to where the house's door used to stand, punching a hole in the crumbling wall to its side. Satisfaction hugged every fiber of my being; I landed several hits on him, and he never teleported out of the way to unleash a sneak attack at me from behind like I feared he would. Thank goodness his ability to teleport only existed in my freakout within a dreamlike period of my sleep.

With a clearer sight of him, I fluttered in Rage's direction, conserving my energy. Before he could relight himself, I sent him floating upward, levitating toward the ceiling myself, too. With a loud grunt, I hurled him into the ground with ground-shattering force, causing him to scrape the floor underneath until he ended up back where he started.

I made sure to send him sliding through the fires he set, even if they didn't give him the slightest lick of pain.

For the next few seconds, Rage and I locked each other into the most intense stalemate of our short lives. Every flame and fireball he shot at me, I blocked with a force field. Every miniature star and photon ball I hurled at him, he sidestepped away. Every strike he sent my way, I danced out of its path. Every strike I threw at him, he blocked by lighting himself aflame. Although our fight showed no signs of coming to an end, the two of us were enjoying it.

"Your proficiency in combat is impressive, Jessica Summer," Rage said. "Just imagine what an unstoppable duo we would make if you were mine."

"Not an ideal time for flattery, Rage," I answered back as we continued to trade kicks and punches. "Shouldn't you be worried about the consequences of the expulsion that Manzanita's handed you? And that you've blown your chances at USC by going on a killing spree just to get revenge on the girls you think should've showered you with love? Not smart of you to waste a valuable education, Garrett Lowe. No pun intended."

"Who needs school when I can have more fun butchering all those who wronged me? Besides, I'm not worried at all about any stupid expulsion. My celebrity privilege will take me into USC by itself."

"Your dad was the one who worked hard and earned millions of dollars to grant you your privilege and your precious life of glamour. You did nothing to earn it. You're just a beneficiary of celebrity success."

Rage's glower intensified as his flames spouted outward upon igniting. I once again activated my force field just in the nick of time as they spiraled out in all directions. It was even harder to breathe in this broken-down building than before as the surrounding fires and rising smoke intensified. All I could see were raging flames all around me, an eerie darkness where there weren't flames, and, from a large hole in the abandoned house's roof, a dark gray cloud where the sun should be.

I hopped upward and floated above the rumbling flames, having a hard time spotting Darren and Melissa in spite of having a bird's-eye view. The first sign I detected of them was the top of Melissa's golden blond hair and her legs popping out of her silky white skirt. Right next to her was a green T-shirt—it was Darren, wearing Manzanita school colors.

I landed next to where Melissa and Darren were chained, but just when I was about to free them, a spout of flame jutted into my face like scalding water bursting from an erupting geyser. Behind the embers, I could make out Melissa's hazel eyes looking toward me. Then a pain unlike anything I ever felt before pierced me in the chest, eliciting a deafening shriek from my vocal cords.

CHAPTER

20

Whatever stabbing sensation just struck me was no ordinary pain. It tore my skin open, sketching a hole where it hit me. I looked down at my plain white T-shirt and noticed an enormous red stain painting my chest with the utmost aggression. My mouth gaped open as it dawned on me what just happened.

Clutching my hand to my chest, I bobbed my head back up to see what was in front of me, but for a few seconds, all I could see were more menacing flames. The fire calmed down for a bit to reveal the last person I wanted to see right then. As much as I didn't want to believe that my worst fear just came to life, there it was in front of me, taunting me.

"Bet you didn't see that coming," Rage said, keeping his gun pointed at me. Somehow, Garrett Lowe was even more intimidating with a gun in his hand than he was when his body was on fire.

Rage sent another gunshot toward me, this time at my lower right leg. The combined force of the two bullet wounds caused me to fall to my knees, making it difficult for me to even stand up.

"Just a friendly reminder, by the way, Jessica," Rage said, showing off his gun with pride. "This Glock 34 pistol in my hand is the very same one I used to murder Lizzy. The same one I used to slaughter all those selfish, smug assholes that fateful May afternoon." Rage let out a sinister laugh. "I may not have intended to murder Lizzy, Jessica. But I sure as hell took pride in slaying a girl like her." In a soft but mocking tone, he continued, "Delusional feminists, always ruining everything.

When are they going to learn that this world is a man's world, and will always be one?"

Rage incited me to unleash the most furious energy beam that I could fire at him, with a frustrated scream to complement it. However, it fizzled out in a second, as my diminished strength wasn't enough for me to generate enough energy to create one.

"Look at you, Jessica. Using your anger to empower yourself in battle. You're no different from me."

I tried once again to siphon energy into an attack, but my body wasn't able to, and I grunted and clutched the area of my upper body where Rage shot me. My breaths were getting fainter, and the suffocation in my body amplified. As for Darren and Melissa, they were no closer to breaking free from their chains than they were a few minutes before.

"You can fight it off, Jessica," said Melissa. "I wish I could patch up your wounds right now, but the smoke in this building is draining me of my healing power. Surely you have some superhero durability in you. Or a healing factor. You can get through the pain. I know you've got this, girl."

Alas, my wounds continued to suck the life out of me, and the pain lingered on. For all the awesome powers it gave me, the Great Bestowal didn't bless me with bullet resistance. Heck, any kind of superhuman physical resistance. Tears began to saturate and redden my face.

"Garrett's right," I cried. "This is the real world. Bad people get their way every time. Violence, greed, and tyranny run the world. And we can't do a goddamn thing about it. Not even with incredible powers like ours." My anguish was too much for me to be able to form words for a few seconds. "Why did I even bother trying to save the day? This isn't a comic book. I was a fool to think that real life would be just like the comics."

Rage cackled again, putting more enthusiasm into his laughing this time. "Looks like the Cosmic Girl isn't so powerful after all," he said. "I was hoping for a worthier adversary than that. You sure looked like you were going to give me a run for my money. But it turns out that your strength is just a façade. I should've expected nothing more than a pathetic showing from a girl."

Rage's words provoked me once again to launch another photon ball at him, but the gunshot wounds afflicting me had sapped me of too much strength to land it on him with success. I spent more time clutching my chest, the blood coloring more of my white T-shirt. This gave Rage time to land one more bullet in my body, this time in my upper right arm, just below the shoulder. The pleasure he took in wounding me with his gun further escalated the agony I was in.

"Now . . . where was I? Oh, right." Rage pointed his Glock 34 toward Melissa and Darren. But . . . Darren wasn't there. All that was left in his place were the chains that bound him.

Rage paused, confused, before a fist pummeled him from behind at Mach speed. Despite the force and velocity of the strike, he was somehow able to keep his pistol clutched in his hand.

Though the figure who just struck from behind appeared in a flash, I didn't need to go through a fancy deduction process to determine who it was. Even without the supersonic speed, the cocky look on the man's face said it all. There he stood, in all his glory, looking like a doofus putting his hands on his hips, not even wincing from the burns that Garrett inflicted on him before his capture.

"Sorry I kept you waiting, Blondie," Darren said. "Trying to bust free from those chains wasn't the easiest task with how hard it is to breathe in this place. But I'm here now. It's an honor to be fighting by your side, hot stuff."

"Cool, thanks, Darren," I said in a blunt, monotone voice. "Less talking, more fighting now. And by the way, I have a name. Please call me Jessica." Darren flashed a rather indifferent smirk at me, as if to say, "Whatever."

Despite Darren's declaration to fight alongside me, I had nowhere close to the strength I needed to feel comfortable engaging in combat again. While Darren kept Rage at bay, I dragged myself to Melissa's position, all the while keeping my eye on Darren and Rage's battle. Unable to react on time to each one of Darren's zips, Rage flailed his gun at him whenever he tried to strike, having difficulty finding the right time to relight his body.

Although she was still struggling to break free of her cuffs, Melissa pulled away from them enough to give me the space I needed to channel a small photon beam from my index finger to break off the chains. Once she was free, Melissa skipped her way through the nearby embers, not minding if she suffered a burn that she could take care of herself. She tumbled into my arms and wrapped her own around my shoulders. The embrace we exchanged would've been more pleasant for me if my lingering wounds hadn't interfered with it.

After Melissa heard my grunts of pain, she took a look at me and glanced at the crimson red blotches painting my T-shirt, arm, and leg. "Oh God, Garrett got you really good, huh?" she asked.

"He didn't just shoot me with any ordinary gun," I answered. "He shot me with the same gun he used in the shooting. The same gun he used to take Lizzy's life."

"Damn . . . what a psychopath."

"Way to state the obvious, Melissa. Anyway, we should look for a safe place around here. I'm sure we can find a spot where you can take care of all these wounds." I looked around to see growing flames around me, but I placed trust in my inner determination to get me and Melissa around them all.

Before the two of us could reach a safe space, a spinning column of fire rolled in our direction, forcing us to jump out of its way. As I took a moment to soak in my lingering pain once more, Rage appeared behind the flames newly generated by his fire tornado, stepping past them with a cold, frightening scowl.

"Well, that's something new from you," I said to Rage. Darren was about to strike him from behind again, but Garrett blew him back with a fireball, sending him to the other side of the burning house. Of course, that didn't do anything to keep him away for long, since he just zipped forward toward where Melissa and I were sitting.

"What's it going to take to put you bitches in your place?" Rage said. "When will you learn that people like me are meant to write the fate of the world?"

"No one decides who writes fate, Garrett," I answered. "That's a role that only the gods are allowed to have. News flash, Garrett: You are no god. Nor do you deserve to be one, or act like one. Shouldn't Psion have knocked that into your head the other day? Or did you forget to take your reality pills after he took you down?"

"You're saying that I, Garrett Oliver Lowe, only son of the world-famous comic book writer Scott Lowe, have no right to decide how the world goes, determine the status quo? Indeed, my defeat to Psion was shameful for me. I do not stand up for such failure. But luckily, I learn from my mistakes. And this time, I, the Almighty Gentleman, will come out triumphant."

"Almighty Gentleman," Darren snickered. "Who gave you the right to choose that nickname?"

Rage fired a bullet at Darren's chest, but Darren's speed and reflexes allowed him to dodge it with relative ease. Rage continued to fire at him, but every single bullet found nothing but air.

"Dammit!" he yelped, tightening the clutch on his gun in frustration.

After a few split-second dashes, Darren reached my side, smirking and not having suffered a single scratch from Rage's Glock 34. I couldn't tell if that smirk was because of his eagerness to fight, or because he was quite enthusiastic to fight alongside me. Regardless of the reason, I had his back as an ally, no matter how cringy he acted.

"Blondie, can you still fight?" Darren asked. "Your wounds seem very serious."

"These bullets still hurt like a bitch," I replied, an unpleasant grunt following right after. "But no matter how much pain I'm in right now, I want to keep fighting. I have to, I'll do anything to take this bastard down."

Relighting himself on fire, Rage brought his attention to Melissa. The look he delivered to her, I doubted that he'd give the same look to Darren or any other guy. It was the type of expression that would make a slasher movie antagonist blush.

"You don't seem to have any power that can threaten me," Rage said to her. "You should make for an easy target. Start off small, then work from there. Sounds like a smart plan."

Rage put his right arm out toward Melissa's face, with small embers starting to spiral around his hand. Just as a fireball took shape upon his palm, I volleyed another blue star at his face, its brightness intense enough to impair his vision for a brief moment. Rage fell off his feet, giving me and Darren some leeway.

"Nice one, Blondie," Darren said.

"I have an idea, Darren," I declared as I still fought off the pain in my right shoulder blade. "How about you fight Garrett up close and I pummel him from long range? That should give Melissa room to try to heal me as soon as she can."

"Sounds like a plan." Darren charged toward Rage, then hit him in the jaw with a jab, his speed preventing him from feeling any significant pain from striking Rage's flaming face. As I started to get my strength back, I unleashed beams and photon balls at Rage while he focused on his more immediate tussle with Darren.

Although her white miniskirt and block-heel sandals weren't the ideal combat outfit, and she lacked the potent offensive abilities that Darren and I possessed, Melissa jumped into the fray anyway. She waited for Rage to be distracted enough to shut off his flames before finding the right time to strike. When he did, she put all the energy and fury into every punch and kick (mostly kicks, even in open-toed shoes) that she threw at him. Like Darren, she appeared unfazed by any pain her burn marks might have given her as she lashed out at Rage; of course, any pain she experienced wouldn't have mattered in the end, thanks to her Exceptional gift.

I had to admit, there was something satisfying about watching an egotistical misogynist get his ass handed to him by an attractive young blond girl in a skirt and heels. And the technique she put into her strikes was a lot more polished and less silly-looking than what I had seen from Orlando.

"And you said I wasn't threatening," Melissa said to Rage. "Maybe next time, don't be quick to judge a book by its cover."

"Nice moves, MelSny," I said. "Where did you learn all those fancy karate techniques?"

"Oh, I dunno, Jessica . . . just a little improvising, that's all."

"Huh. Sounds a lot like a friend of mine."

I'd never fought side-by-side with Darren and Melissa, nor had I fought alongside anyone else in general. Despite that, however, our chemistry fighting together was immediate, certainly better than it was at school. It did help that we had a three-on-one numbers advantage against someone who didn't even bother to look for teammates, but our shared determination against a common enemy helped, too, allowing us to put aside any animosities we had on campus.

Seconds pass, and my arms started to give out from merely standing back in the fray and peppering Rage with beams and projectiles of cosmic energy, along with deploying the occasional force field to protect Melissa or Darren from Rage's flames and strikes. I'd used up enough of my limited strength that the entire upper half of my body was going numb. As much as I wanted to, I wasn't sure I could go on any longer in the fight. But the intensity of my emotions remained as a patch of darkness started to emerge behind me. It was hard to make it out amid the smoke and blackness filling the house, but looking behind me, I could tell that what just appeared was no ordinary darkness. Looking closely, I noticed that its vicinity was even darker than the rest of the darkness into which it ripped a blank into the surrounding space.

"Dude . . . what is that behind you, Blondie?" Darren asked.

The sight of the patch of mysterious emptiness was enough to halt the fight and get all four of us in the house to stare at it in awe, even Rage. As it expanded, it started to paint a blank void in the middle of its surroundings, vacuuming up everything around it and creating a strange distortion in its vicinity. Like a fierce, unstoppable wind, the black emptiness started to exert its physical presence, creating the illusion of everything slowing down around it. On top of that, my body was now radiating a brand-new glow: a deep black aura.

"Jessica . . . your eyes . . ." Melissa said to me.

"Yeah, there's nothing but empty darkness where your eyeballs should be," Darren added. "You're one intimidating-looking Blondie right now."

Despite my eyes emanating the same deep black glow as the new aura that I was generating, I was still able to see, but with a pitch-black filter surrounding the edges of what my eyes perceived in front of them. Whatever I looked like to everyone else in that collapsing house, it must not have been the prettiest sight. Although I certainly didn't mind that for the sake of appearing as menacing to Rage as possible.

CHAPTER

21

"Something funky is going on," Darren said. "I can't reach Mach speed all of a sudden. Who's behind that dark void? It's not Rage, is it?"

"It's me," I answered. "It's coming from my powers. This is a new ability I haven't used before."

Darren noticed my empty, pitch-black eyes and the dark aura surrounding me. "So you're not going to rip apart everything around you, are you, Blondie?"

"You don't have anything to worry about, Darren. I'm doing this on my own free will. Promise."

I expanded the size of the solid black entity that I was generating, increasing its magnitude and force. It was now powerful enough to cause some of the flames in the house to dissipate, falling deep into the void of nothingness inside. The anger in me continued to intensify; the sight of Rage was all that I needed to fuel it.

"Darren, Melissa, I appreciate the help you've given me. I can tell how eager you two are to do battle. But this is my fight," I declared. "I must be the one to vanquish this monster. Let me handle him on my own."

I stepped in front of Darren and Melissa and take up my most cliché battle pose: legs spread out and arms to my side in a diagonal manner. Meanwhile, Darren and Melissa stayed in the back, now accepting their roles as spectators to our upcoming grudge match.

"So you've decided to face off against me one-on-one," Rage said. "Bold of you, Jessica Summer. Bold of you."

"Just the way it should be, Garrett Lowe," I said. "You against me, for all the marbles."

"I would like that for sure. Just one thing." Rage pointed his gun at Darren and Melissa. "Got some unfinished business to take care of first."

"Don't you dare drag them into this, Garrett. This is our fight, remember?"

"I don't think it would be right to start until those two are bleeding like stuck pigs. That's why the two of us are here in the first place, Jessica. I can't really get into a battle mood until I'm done with those two pests. And then I will get rid of their stupid friends, too."

Despite the intimidating presence of the black vortex behind us, Rage didn't flinch one bit. His ambition was just as high as it was on that fateful May afternoon.

"You might want to get out of the way, Jess," Rage said. "They're our common enemies, remember? Heartless douchebags who keep putting us down just to maintain their positions atop the high school hierarchy?"

I continued to stand in Rage's path, the only obstacle standing between him and fulfilling his ultimate objective. I wasn't flinching either, with just about all of my energy and focus pouring into the void that I was ripping into the background.

"Dammit, Jessica," Rage said. "Just let me end those two shitheads. They have to get what they deserve."

I was dead quiet, but my silence was enough to speak on behalf of my unfazed determination. I could've looked behind me to see how Melissa and Darren were during this tense moment, but the inner workings of my body, both mind and muscles, prevented me from doing so. Nothing but me, Rage, and the hole of nothingness reigning over the background.

"You don't want me to shoot them dead, do you, Jessica?" Rage said. "Just so you don't have to relive your painful memories of watching Lizzy die in front of your very eyes. I get it. I really do get it now."

Rage's words intensified my anger further, leading the void behind me to expand in size. When he fired his first shot at me, I got out of the way and let the growing black entity do its work. Not a single bullet pierced anyone. No one out of me, Melissa, and Darren suffered a wound. The bullets were just . . . gone.

I could've talked some shit to Rage, but I was too angry. Whatever this new power was, it seemed to be controlling me rather than me controlling it. Not that I minded if it was preventing Rage from landing a shot on anyone.

Before Rage could fire another bullet, the circular darkness behind me expanded once more. Then Rage's Glock 34 flew out of his right hand, never to be seen again.

Watching his gun disappear provoked Rage to immediately relight his body on fire, anger and exasperation fueling his flames. Before he could strike back at me, he noticed some of the flames on his body starting to wither away. He tried to unleash streams of flame at me, followed by fireballs. But in both cases, the flames quickly fizzled out.

The black void grew again, continuing to eat up the fire enveloping Rage's body. At that point, the void was the size of the globe in front of Universal Studios. I could sense it tearing apart and eating its surroundings, even ripping off a few sticks of burning wood and chunks of the house's already crumbling walls. But I didn't care. If this was what it was going to take to defeat Rage, so be it.

"Jessica, you're beginning to destroy everything around you," Darren said. "Get a hold of yourself."

"Don't you know what you're toying with, Jessica?" Melissa said. "Black holes are the most powerful objects in the universe. So strong that nothing can and will ever escape their grasp. You need to be careful!"

Anger and determination still flowed through my veins. As more of Rage's flames went out, I ignored Darren and Melissa's pleas, wanting nothing but for Rage to be defeated at long last. At that point, he was only covered in flames from the waist down.

"You will not . . . stop me . . . Jessica . . ." Rage said. "Those two bastards . . . all the popular jerks . . . all the slutty girls . . . who rejected me . . . they must pay . . . for everything . . . they did to me . . ."

Rage struggled to reignite his flames and unleash attacks on me. The influence of the black hole was strong enough that I was a 200-mph wind preventing him from walking any faster than a three-toed sloth.

The streak of arrogance in Rage's eyes, the smug smile on his face, they only fueled my anger further. The very sight of Garrett Lowe sparked the flow of several of my worst recent memories, flashing in my mind like a lightning-quick cinematic montage.

Garrett stalking me when I wasn't looking and making it into a video on his YouTube channel.

Holding Lizzy in my arms as she was dying.

The "Reckoning" manifesto.

Garrett wishing for me to be his because he felt entitled to my affections just because I was the type of pretty blond he dreamed of having.

Garrett bragging about taking Lizzy's life and enjoying every single second of the mass shooting he executed at my school.

As these traumatic memories continue to cycle through my brain, two simple, short words exploded out of my mouth.

"FUCK YOUUUUUUUUUUUUUU!"

The black hole became larger and even more terrifying. The black aura surrounding my body intensified likewise, and my eyes glowed the deepest, darkest black possible, just like the black hole itself. I was trying my damnedest not to let the black hole spiral out of control to the point of actually destroying everything in sight. But at the same time, I was too angry to get any hold on it. All the hurt and pain that Garrett caused me, I wanted nothing more than to channel it onto Garrett himself. Suck up every last bit of flame power he still had left.

Once I watched Garrett's last flames go out and saw his body completely free of fire, the black hole behind me shrunk down and disappeared for good. The task of closing it off was agonizing enough that I fell to the ground and came close to fainting. But I was able to do it regardless. Right when it disappeared, Garrett fell down on his arms at the same time that I collapsed from my exhaustion. Melissa and Darren ran up to me and caught me in their own arms.

When the dust settled, I scanned my surroundings and examined the full extent of the damage that my battle with Garrett brought about. All the flames and smoke in the area had now cleared up, with piles and blotches of ash the only evidence that they were ever there. But scores of bricks were torn off the walls of the deteriorating house. Several damaged cars dotted the streets. Trees were uprooted here and there. Cracks ripped through the ground. It was sinking in that the damage that my black hole caused was not limited to the house itself, but widespread through much of the small, isolated neighborhood that we were in.

I was too drained of energy to get up, unable to move a limb or even lift a finger. I was having a hard time catching my breath to the point that my breathing was now a series of wheezes.

"I did it . . . it's over . . ." I said, with heavy gasps punctuating whatever enthusiasm I could still muster.

"Are you okay, Jessica?" Melissa asked. "You might have overexerted yourself a bit there."

"I'm fine . . . I may not be able . . . to move a muscle . . . but that doesn't matter . . . too much to me . . . right now. What . . . about you . . . MelSny?"

Melissa took a brief but deep breath. "Much better now that the air around me is fresh again," she replied. "I don't know if my healing can work again now, but I'll try."

"Let's hope," I said, my voice fainter.

"You should get some rest, Jessica. And a lot of water. Other than that, I'll heal up your wounds right now. I might as well now that it's safe for me to do so."

"Thanks . . . Melissa. I could . . . use that."

To his delight, Darren held me in his arms to allow Melissa to heal the three gunshot wounds that Rage left in my body. A shiny pink aura emanated from Melissa's hands; it started off faint but gradually intensified, to my relief. One by one, Melissa dragged the aura into each of the three areas of my body where Rage shot me. After a few seconds, there was no longer a single spot of red dotting my white T-shirt, nor was there any trace of a bullet hole anywhere on my body and clothes. Of course, Darren brought his face a little too close to mine, interrupting the smile of relief I had from the wonderful sensation I received from Melissa's healing aura.

"Dude . . . that was nuts what you just did there, Blondie," Darren said, smirking. "You really can channel those black hole thingies now?"

"Okay, you can get off me now, Darren," I said. "I'm not your princess in shining armor, you know." Darren pulled his face away from mine and returned his focus to helping me out, thank God.

As Melissa and Darren struggled to help me get back on my feet, they froze up at the sight of Garrett storming toward us. Although he was down for a good few minutes, Garrett looked as if he didn't suffer any bruises or wounds at all.

"Don't think I'm done with you two yet," he said to Melissa and Darren. "I may not have my gun anymore, but in case you forgot . . . I'm an Exceptional."

Garrett threw his right hand toward the three of us . . . but not a single spark of flame came out. He tried another time to shoot a fireball, but again, nothing. Then he put his arms at his sides and squeezed his fists, expelling all the energy out of him. Still, not a single ember rose out. Realizing what happened to him, Garrett bent his arms with his palms facing upward, bobbing his head from side to side.

"What . . . my powers . . . how?" he said.

Before it fully dawned on him that he was just a regular, pathetic, disgruntled teenager again, police sirens arrived at the scene of the wreckage left around us. It wasn't long before the officers closest to us slammed a pair of handcuffs onto Garrett's wrists, able to restrain him with ease on account of the sharp contrast between their professional wrestler-sized bodies and his scrawny adolescent figure.

"I've been waiting a *long* time for this," said the pale-skinned cop to Garrett's left. Garrett tried to break free, but with such a slim body and no more powers to bail him out, it was an impossible task for him as the two officers dragged him to their police car, relishing their opportunity to return him to the county jail. They couldn't stop him from shutting his giant mouth, however.

"I'm white; I have nothing to worry about with you punks!" he told the two officers. "Do you realize that you fools are dealing with an Exceptional, the son of Scott Lowe, the world's most renowned comic book writer? You're going to regret sending me back to that cage when I get my powers back!" His crass comments were even more untimely on account of the fact that one cop restraining him happened to be a black man. How hilarious that he was going to be the one driving Garrett back to prison, too.

The remaining cops in the area stuck around to seek important details from us. The number of police cars and sirens around us served as a harsh reminder of the afternoon on which the Manzanita shooting took place. This time around, however, at least I knew that things were going to get better from there.

"Is everyone here okay?" a tan-skinned officer asked us. "No one murdered, or suffered grave injuries, or anything?"

"The two of us are fine," Melissa answered, referring to herself and Darren. "Our friend here, meanwhile, she got exhausted from . . . all the fire in the building. Had a hard time breathing in there. Also got shot three times by the same young man you guys just arrested, which only added to the exhaustion she's going through. Luckily, I can instantly heal others with a single touch, so her gunshot wounds are all gone now. You won't have to worry about them, Officer."

The officer jotted down a few notes on a thick clipboard he was carrying before continuing to speak. "Can any of you give out any more details about what happened here? That's quite a lot of damage I'm seeing around me. I hope you kids weren't getting into any naughty antics of any kind . . . there's a brand-new level of delinquency we officers have to monitor now that all these kids are roaming around town with these fancy new magic powers." His last remark made me shudder.

I raise my head up as much as I could. In a weak, raspy voice, I ceased my long, exhausted silence. "It was me," I told the officer. "In case you're not aware, I'm an Exceptional. In fact, you may know me as the 'Cosmic Girl.' I can fly, alter gravity, generate force fields, and fire beams and balls of photon energy, among many other cosmos-related abilities. And now, just moments ago, I discovered the ability to create and manipulate black holes. I spawned one in the middle of a battle that I got into with Garrett Lowe after he kidnapped my friends this morning, the same two folks holding me in their arms right now. That's what caused all the destruction within this neighborhood, and it's something I take full responsibility for. But at the same time, I did also rob Garrett of his powers, so he won't be a threat to escape from prison again and further terrorize our beautiful town."

I caught Melissa by surprise admitting to the mess that my powers ended up causing. I did mumble to her, however, that things were going to be okay.

"I can see now why others are so fearful of us causing utter wreckage anywhere we go," I continued with my ongoing statement to the officer. "But I promise you that, in spite of my immense power, I mean no harm. You and your colleagues have no reason to be suspicious of someone like me anymore."

The officer stayed mum for a few seconds to take a few notes from my description of the fight that I had engaged in. "We'll take your word for it, miss," he said. "We thank you for your efforts in helping us to re-arrest one of California's most wanted criminals. He has caused so much devastation and anxiety to the Santa Barbara community ever since the horrific mass murder he pulled off at Manzanita High School. The whole city will be relieved to hear that you took him down and played a huge role in ensuring he would go back to jail."

"All three of us are proud Manzanita Marauders, in fact," I continued. "Ever since Garrett shot ten of our fellow students dead, I have wanted to deliver justice to him. Just like a superhero would've. Suffice it to say, mission accomplished."

The officer flashed a light smile at me. "Before we leave, can I get your name, please?" he asked.

"Jessica . . . Jessica Summer."

Those were the last words I could utter before everything around me went dark.

CHAPTER

22

I awakened on a bed in Santa Barbara Cottage Hospital with Melissa and Darren by my side, still in the same clothes that I wore in the broken down house where I encountered Garrett. It was very eerie to find myself lying in the same hospital where Lizzy was pronounced dead twenty-five days ago. I didn't know what time it was, or if I had lunch yet. All I remembered about the last few hours was encountering Garrett in a final confrontation, creating a black hole to sap him of his flame powers . . . and then nothing after that.

"You may want this," Melissa said. She offered me a cup of water.

"Thanks, MelSny," I said, and took a sip. "So did the doctors diagnose me with any sort of grim condition? Have I suffered any form of permanent physical damage?"

"You're going to be fine, Blo—I mean, Jessica," Darren said, provoking a smirk in me with his well-timed last-minute name switch. "Doctors said that you just need a bit more rest. Nothing but a bit of exhaustion, really. Good thing MelSny saved them a lot of work thanks to her trusty healing touch, heheh."

"Got it. Had the feeling it would be something more, given that I crossed into unprecedented territory by spawning a black hole here on Earth, so I'm glad I dodged a bullet there . . . anyway, how long are you two going to stick around?"

"D. O. and I have a lot of catching up to do with our studies after we missed an entire day of school due to unforeseen circumstances beyond our control," replied Melissa.

"Heh. I totally understand. Got some finals to prepare for . . . and not quite the most ideal start to finals week for you two so far."

Melissa giggled. "We called your parents and your brother, so they should be coming over very soon. We let them know that you're in the hospital and updated them on your condition."

"Thanks so much, Melissa. Best of luck with your finals this week, and see you two at school tomorrow."

"You can count on that for sure. We'll see you tomorrow, too. You know where to find us, nerd."

As Melissa and Darren walked out the door of my hospital room, I flipped my attention to the small television hanging on the wall opposite my bed. As much as I didn't want to take a single peek at the TV, it was too much of a distraction to avoid giving it a glance any longer. Even better, the television had to be tuned in to my new favorite national news channel, USNC. At least good ol' Dick Jackson's face wasn't on the screen.

"Friend or foe?" asked the anchor on the screen, who was reporting live from the scene of my battle with Rage. "That's what Americans continue to ask about their Exceptional friends after police reports from Santa Barbara, California indicate that an epic fight between Exceptionals ensued on the edge of the small beachside town, culminating in the arrest of Scott Lowe's son, Garrett Lowe, better known as the infamous Santa Barbara school shooter who also goes by the alias Rage. While details continue to flow in about what happened in the abandoned house here in front of me, reports do confirm that it was an Exceptional who came to this area and encountered the eighteen-year-old murderer of ten students at local high school Manzanita High. Lowe kidnapped two other Manzanita students, leading to a clash that ended with the Exceptional stripping him of his fire abilities by summoning a black hole in the area—whatever that means."

The sight of the reporter and the USNC channel made me cringe, but I couldn't help but have a laugh at the reporter's last comment.

"Hmm, someone doesn't read enough comics or go to the movies enough," I joked.

Following the live report was a trio of interviews with local residents regarding their views on Exceptionals. Two of the interviews were with individuals who expressed open opposition to Exceptionals, while the third one was with someone trying to offer a defense in favor of Exceptionalkind, explaining some of the ways in which our powers could benefit society and open up methods of advancing civilization that weren't possible before. While watching this news report, I noticed that so much more screen time was given to the anti-Exceptional individuals and coverage of the potential threats that Exceptionals posed to society in comparison to the Exceptional defender and any other pro-Exceptional coverage.

There was nothing else in the hospital room to distract me from the news until Larson passed through the door. The two of us didn't exchange a single word as we folded into each other in an embrace.

"How have you been feeling, sis?" Larson asked. "I hope you didn't get hurt too badly."

"I'm doing better," I replied. "Just needed to get a few hours of rest, but of course, it could've been a lot worse. I did get shot a few times by Rage, but luckily, a friend of mine has instant healing powers, so she used them to heal all my gunshot wounds."

"Ooh, you scared me for a bit there when you said you got shot. Makes me glad that people with superpowers exist now, Jess."

"He had to use the same gun he used on the day of the shooting, too . . . thankfully, the black hole I used to depower him also took away his gun."

"Jesus . . . all the more reason to be thankful that we're in a world of superheroes now. And that somehow, my sister ended up becoming one of those superheroes." Larson placed his head on my neck, and I returned my brother's affections back to him as he pulled out a pair of flip-flops. The foot imprints on the flip-flops were a clear indication that they'd been worn just about every day.

"I brought you your Rainbows, by the way," he said. "Thought you'd feel more comfortable wearing them over your sneakers after you walk out of here."

"Thanks very much. My feet were suffocating under those Vans I was wearing today." I planted a light kiss on Larson's forehead. "Are Mom and Dad coming over?"

"They should be here soon. Both of them have already called off work for the rest of the day."

My parents arrived at my hospital bed at the same time that the hospital was set to discharge me. Since I hadn't eaten lunch yet, they were kind enough to bring me lunch from Dart Coffee in the form of a vegan quinoa meal and a mocha. I made sure to have my lunch before the doctor discharged me.

When the doctor who took care of me arrived to make my discharge official, I filled out a few documents before slipping on my flip-flops and heading out with my parents and Larson. Despite all the unusual shit I went through earlier, the four of us tried to keep our conversation as low-key as possible. We couldn't avoid the elephant in the room for much longer, however.

"So Larson told us that you can create black holes now. Is that true?" Mom asked, voicing a slight bit of concern for good reason.

"Yes it is, Mom," I answered. "But I don't want to get too much into detail about it with you three. The media might catch us discussing it, and you know where it would go from there. So I'd much rather keep the secrets to my new power under wraps."

"Sounds like a good idea."

Of course, as the four of us walked out of the hospital, media reporters were already all over the place to greet us. And none other than Dick Jackson was already waiting right by the hospital entrance. How these people managed to find me and track my every move was beyond me.

"Oh God, him again . . ." Dad said.

"Is this the same reporter who harassed Jessica by your surf store, Dad?" Larson asked.

"Unfortunately, yes. I should've known he wouldn't go away so easily."

"Pfft, what a dweeb. I heard he has cool teleportation powers, too, as if he couldn't find any more ways to be annoying."

Mr. Jackson didn't have his eyes on us, focusing instead on the camera in front of him. As much as I disliked him, I did appreciate the passionate dedication that he gave to his job. That must've explained why he was so relentless in pursuing me while reporting.

"Dick Jackson with USNC here in Santa Barbara, California with a breaking news report," he said. "We have just gotten word that local police have arrested Garrett Lowe, alias Rage, the culprit behind last month's Manzanita High School shooting that took the lives of ten students at the school. Earlier this morning, Lowe kidnapped two Manzanita students whom he reportedly wanted to murder on the day of his massacre, but failed to. But to the relief of the Santa Barbara community, the brave teenage girl known as Jessica Summer came to the students' rescue, putting a halt to his next intended murders and even sapping the monstrous killer of the flame abilities that he gained from the Great Bestowal."

After this brief report, Jackson turned around in a flash so he could start pestering me once again after noticing my presence. "I'm here with the Cosmic Girl herself, who tapped into the power of a black hole to defeat Rage," he said. Well, would you look at that; he knew already. "This courageous soul is a true hero to the town of Santa Barbara, and to the entirety of humankind." Then he asked me, "How does it feel to unleash the incredible force of the most powerful object in the universe?"

"It's nothing, really," I answered, trying to maintain a laid-back vibe as best I could. "I was just doing what I could to save the town and stop Garrett from laying the groundwork to spark more chaos and destruction within Santa Barbara, and maybe even elsewhere in the world. I don't know why you have to make a big deal out of it, or anything that I do. I could just take a simple breath, and you'll already be all over me, ready to interrogate me with your stupid questions. You seem to be forgetting, too, that I received some help from two of my friends who happen to be Exceptionals like me. I don't think I would have been able to defeat Rage without their assistance."

Jackson looked at me in awe for a few seconds. "You're just getting started as the savior of Santa Barbara, Jessica," he said. "Losing your best friend to Rage and then defeating him and taking away his powers? Talk about the start of an epic superhero journey! Of course, as awesome as you are, I didn't forget about that brave kid who goes by Psion, either. Our town is in good hands with you Exceptionals around." I would've loved to be humbled by Jackson's words, but the way he annoyed me, I didn't have the urge to.

"Say, speaking of Psion, why don't you go disturb him instead of wasting all your energy on me?" I suggested to Jackson in an awkward tone. "Nothing against him, of course; I'm just saying. If you're willing to bother me like this, why aren't you bothering him in the same way? Or any other Exceptional with a pulse? I already told you that I'm not trying to be a superhero or live the life of one. I just want to be a regular teenage girl."

"Jessica, you must stop underestimating yourself and realize your full capabilities. You were too shy to accept it the previous time that we met, and you still don't seem to be willing to accept it. But now you can see the true extent of your powers. And you wound up proving me and many others right with our claims about your true power. Imagine what you can do with that incredible potential—"

A miniature asteroid took shape in my right hand, and I launched it at Jackson's forehead to knock him out and shut him up. "I feel better now," I said. "Pardon me, Mom and Dad. I hope I'm not in trouble for that. Or that any superists saw that so they can use it to create more anti-Exceptional tension."

"In all honesty, that was oddly satisfying to watch, cupcake," Dad said. "Gotta find some creative way to make use of your powers, you know."

Before we could reach the car, we ran into a large flood of news reporters scattered throughout the plaza at the entrance, as well as many more waiting along the adjacent street. Yep, even with Dick Jackson knocked out, there were plenty more where that came from. I didn't even want to know what kinds of questions they had in mind for me. Or if any of them could rival Mr. Jackson in terms of Exceptional obsession.

As ready as I was to get home and return to studying for my first final, I decided to go with a last-second change of plans. As if I had a magnet for a hand, I relayed the closest reporter's microphone through the air and into my right palm using my gravity powers. It was hard to tell if the reporters around me were amazed to observe me using my powers in person, or if they were tossing some suspicion my way.

"I apologize for taking your microphone away from you, ma'am," I stated before raising my voice. "But I have plenty of things to say to you. To all you media scumbags. To those of you who have been mistaking us Exceptionals for a threat."

I sparked up my golden-yellow glow as an irritated expression emerged onto my face. In response, the journalists who were looking to swarm me retreated from their scattered formation into a more neatly arranged one. In the meantime, Mom, Dad, and Larson stayed behind, allowing me to take center stage as I shut off my solar glow to prevent myself from looking too intimidating.

"Thank you for giving me all your attention." As I raised the microphone closer to my mouth, all the reporters in the area were ready to listen to me like they would to a respected military general, no longer willing to start another ruckus. "Now, I admit that this is a rather last-minute arrangement deciding to hold this speech I'm about to make. But I find what I have to say too important to just leave on the shelf. For both Exceptionalkind and for the rest of society."

There wasn't a podium in front of me, but I stood in front of the swarm of reporters and journalists as if there was one present. Like they would in a scheduled press conference, every single camera in the area focused on me. Thus began my latest impromptu speech. At least I'd been through this situation a couple of times before over the past month, so it was nothing new for me.

"I've been obsessed with superheroes as far back as I can remember," I began. "I've grown up on their comics, watched so many of their movies and shows, and been to Wonder World more times than you can count. Superheroes are a part of my identity. And what my beloved comics and movies demonstrate time and time again is that people with extraordinary powers are the ones who save the day. Just now, life imitated art."

Heavy emotions started to get to me again, but this time around, I was able to keep them in check. "The day after the devastating mass shooting that struck my high school, Manzanita, I saw a shooting star in the sky that night and made a wish for superheroes to become real.

I wanted a world in which criminals like Garrett Lowe, the culprit behind the Manzanita shooting, would never be allowed to harm or murder others again, with superheroes to come to our rescue whenever they need to. Call it a coincidence if you may, but I fittingly discovered my own powers the day after I made my wish. And suffice it to say, I became a superhero and fulfilled my own wish. Talk about a girl living a childhood dream that she used to think was impossible. It makes for a heartwarming story, does it not?"

The reporters in the area took photos, while others hastily scribbled on their notepads. All the while, I flashed a soft smile, knowing that I might be starting to change not just the public's perception of me, but of Exceptionalkind as a whole.

"While some Exceptionals, such as Garrett Lowe himself, may indeed be bad apples, most of us mean no harm at all. And we find it appalling that the rest of society is treating us with fear and suspicion, labeling us as guilty for the mere crime of having extraordinary powers that no human being has ever had before in history. We've been dealing with a lot ever since we first discovered our powers; not all of us have been able to grasp them right from the get-go, which has caused some of us additional problems that we didn't have before. Then bam, now we're receiving the same treatment that numerous demographics such as African Americans and the LGBTQ+ community have dealt with on a daily basis for decades."

Like my speeches at the Manzanita memorial and at Lizzy's funeral, all of the words that I spoke came straight from the heart. Nothing scripted, nothing prepared. That didn't stop my words from carrying impactful weight with the dozens of journalists that I spoke to. And public speaking wasn't even a natural gift for me, as much as I'd made it look that way over the past month.

"We desire and deserve respect like the rest of you who didn't gain powers from the Great Bestowal," I continued. "Maybe instead of pigeonholing us into the concept of an imagined threat, start thinking about the good we could do for the world. Think about what humanity can now achieve that they couldn't in the past, because we now have the benefit of someone with a brain that works like a computer, or because there now exist beings who can fly at speeds faster than commercial airliners. Until the Unexceptional portion of society can come to terms with that, it looks like it will be an uphill climb for us to earn more widespread trust from them, just like it has been for groups like the ones I mention. But we won't stop fighting until we earn such respect, we can assure you that."

Before I moved on with my speech, a reporter in the crowd interrupted me. "Hello, Ms. Summer, I just have a quick question for you," he said in a rushed, rapid-fire fashion. "How do you feel about how the battle that you just engaged in against Rage could potentially impact the script of the proposed Hollywood—"

Knowing what he was about to ask me about, I ceased his question before he could finish it. "Hi, hi, sorry if I'm coming off as a bit rude, sir, but I would prefer not to take any questions until after my speech has concluded," I said, trying to hide my agitation over the reporter's rushed question. "Thank you."

I took a few seconds to settle down and catch my breath before moving on with the remainder of my speech. "Sorry about that. I've had a long day, in case you can't tell," I said to the crowd of journalists. "Anyway, where was I . . . oh yeah. To wrap up my speech, I want to start off by saying that, as much as it may surprise some of you to hear this, my trials and tribulations over the past month have allowed me to realize that that the superhero life is personally not for me. The lifelong superhero fan in me is no doubt proud to defeat the local menace who now calls himself Rage; I'm sure my favorite comic book superheroes would feel the same way if they existed in real life. But being a superhero that the public depends on to defend Santa Barbara would place too much of a load on my shoulders, something that I doubt I would be able to adjust to as a sixteen-year-old girl. To be honest, I'm certain I wouldn't be able to handle that level of attention. Being the centerpiece of a proposed movie based on a real-life tragedy I was in is enough of an unwanted spotlight for me, thank you."

My throat started to dry up from speaking for so long, as well as the unusual exhaustion I had after creating the black hole that allowed me to defeat and depower Rage, so I cleared it before continuing. "With everything I've been going through over the past month, from the suspicion I've faced for my powers to the loss of my best friend in the shooting at Manzanita High School, to the outrage that my school and I have felt over a Hollywood studio's proposal to make a movie based on the aforementioned shooting and my own life in particular, I would much prefer to be left alone rather than live under the intense spotlight that my favorite comic book superheroes often fall under."

The crowd of journalists gave me a short round of applause. It came as a surprise to me that I somehow touched them with my words, but it was flattering at the same time considering my not-so-great recent history with them and their coverage of both the Manzanita shooting and of Exceptionals.

"And one last thing: I apologize for having knocked out USNC's Dick Jackson with a miniature asteroid earlier. Just wanted to get those words out before any of your superists start to make up all sorts of things about it. But it should serve as a warning to any of you in the journalism industry that there's a chance of some not-so-ideal consequences if you decide to bother me the way that many of you often have over the past month. Don't expect that I'll be the only Exceptional in the world to feel that way, either. We're regular people, not celebrities. And we prefer to be treated as such. That's all I have for today. Thank you for your time."

A greater round of applause erupted from the crowd of journalists as I got ready to walk back to my parents and Larson. Before I did, however, I turned my attention back to the reporter who was closest to me.

"Oh, here's your microphone back by the way, ma'am," I said to her as I sent her microphone floating back into her hand. Putting aside my courteous gesture to her, I tried to ignore the flow of news reporters as they kicked off their latest attempts to interrogate me when I wasn't in the mood for it. I could already see the camera flashes behind me as the reporters' questions blended together into something incoherent. My family wasn't having any of their antics, either.

"We will not take any further questions at this time," Dad said to all the reporters pursuing us. "Thank you."

Anxious to get away from the chasing wave of reporters, the four of us resorted to power walking back to Dad's car. Despite my worries that we wouldn't get there fast enough, we were able to make it there with minimal fuss.

"So, what was with you saying that the superhero life isn't for you?" Larson asked me shortly after we get into the car. "I thought you would be all excited to be a real-life superheroine."

"To be frank, Larson, I'm a hundred percent okay with living a normal teenage girl life," I answered. "I may be an outcast on campus, and I may face a lot of mockery for being a geek, especially from my school's most popular kids. But to be honest, school *is* my happy place. It gives me both purpose and identity."

Larson giggled. "Spoken like a true nerd, Jess." My parents joined me in laughing at his attempt at humor.

"That's precisely what the most popular girl in my class would tell me," I said with a big grin. "So thanks, Larson."

"*De nada*, sis."

The four of us were silent for a few seconds, gazing at the surroundings of our beautiful, sunny beach town on the way home, reflecting the whole time. Then Larson broke the silence again.

"By the way, have you been thinking about the consequences that might result from your big battle, Jess?" he asked. "Quite a lot of property damage, I heard."

"Ah, someone had to bring that up," I answered with a nervous frown. "That's a conversation to save for another day, though."

CHAPTER

23

My routine before school was the same as usual: eat breakfast, slip on my flip-flops by the doorstep, meet up with Charlotte and Orlando at the same street corner close to our school, walk to Manzanita from there, and then lastly, pay a brief visit to Lizzy's memorial near the entrance to campus—an experience that was emotional for the three of us every time, but always worth it for the sake of honoring our fallen childhood friend. Because things were a bit different this time around, the sight of me walking down the street was enough to catch anybody's attention today, though thankfully not in the manner that I disliked.

"Hey, you're the Exceptional who defeated Rage yesterday!" a little red-haired girl said to me as she and her blond-haired friend, both of whom appeared to be somewhere from six to eight years old, ran down the sidewalk toward me.

"No way, that's the Cosmic Girl?" the blond girl said.

When the two girls stopped in front of me, I giggled and said, "Yes, that is me."

"Oh, my gosh . . . it really is you . . . a real-life superhero . . ." the red-haired girl said. It was quite flattering to me for a little girl to refer to me by that title. Talk about witnessing my wish come true. "Can you sign my backpack, Exceptional? I'll let you borrow my Sharpie."

"I'm not one for autographs, but since you asked nicely, sure." The red-haired girl gave me her Sharpie, and I used it to sign the front of her pink backpack. I proceeded to do the same with the blond girl and her lilac-colored bag.

"Thank you, Cosmic Girl," the red-haired girl said. "You just made our day."

"No problem." I flashed a heartwarming smile, knowing that I brought my own light to a pair of little girls and gave them hope for the future at a young age.

"Show us some of your powers, please!" said the blond girl.

"Okay, if you say so." I stood up straight with my arms spread out and ignited my golden-yellow solar-powered glow, causing the two little girls' mouths to gape open. Their eyes locked on to me as I floated up into the sky, and photon balls formed in the palms of each of my hands. To wrap up my superpowered spectacle, I deployed my force field bubble for a few seconds before descending back down onto the sidewalk.

"Wow, you're so much cooler in person than what I've heard on the news," said the blond girl.

"Well, that's just the tip of the iceberg of what I can do, kid. Not to brag or anything, but I'd say you just met a pretty cool Exceptional today." The two little girls clapped with enthusiasm as I placed my hands on my hips, taking up the most cliché of superhero poses.

"Ooh, speaking of, can you do the black hole thing, please?" the red-haired girl asked.

"Now, now, that would be a little too dangerous for me to pull off right here. Black holes are so powerful that not even light can escape them. So I don't want to make either of you disappear forever because you asked me to summon one. I don't think your parents would be happy with me if I did that."

"Well, I guess that's fair. But thank you for showing us your powers, Cosmic Girl. You're a real superhero now."

"Thank you. It's such an honor to hear that from you, girls. And by the way, you can just call me Jessica from now on. I don't do superhero names, personally."

"Okay then . . . Jessica. If that's what you want." The red-haired girl giggled.

"Hope we get to see you around again one day!" the blond girl said. "You seem just as cool in normal life."

"Thank you for your kind words, miss. I sure would love it if our paths crossed again, too. Enjoy your day, girls." The three of us waved goodbye to each other as I continued my walk to school, in no hurry.

I did say that I wasn't accustomed to the celebrity status I would attract as a superhero. But when those two girls expressed their idolization of me for my powers, it was a welcome change of pace from the prejudice that we Exceptionals had been receiving since discovering our powers for the first time. Having seen female superheroes get mocked regularly by geek fandom and not taken as seriously as their male counterparts, I was quite proud to play a part in being a heroic figure that women and girls could look up to as a role model.

—∞—

When I met up with Orlando and Charlotte at the school entrance and stepped onto campus for the first time, I felt less like a celebrity and more like a regular student, just the way I liked it. I anticipated the occasional VIP treatment from peers here and there, but even after the events of the previous day, this Tuesday felt like yet another school day, albeit one in the midst of our finals week. I couldn't even remember the last time that I felt such a state of normalcy in my life.

As the three of us headed to homeroom, I didn't even bring up the fact that little kids were viewing me as an idol and celebrity now. We just discussed our typical array of things: dance (mostly Sunday's dance show), the latest books we'd been reading, and which superhero would beat who in a showdown of destiny. Plenty for us to catch up on after I missed most of the previous school day; it was just business as usual as we passed by our favorite popular clique going through the school plaza.

"Hey, Blondie," Darren greeted me, as per usual.

"Hey, Darren," I greeted him back. "How are things today?"

"Oh, everything's cool, man. Except for the fact that there were several journalists chasing me and Melissa just before school started. Tried to get our thoughts on what it was like being witnesses to the epic battle between you and Rage. Pretty wild stuff this morning."

"Believe it or not, I can understand where you're coming from, dude." I flashed a wide-eyed grin in Darren's direction. "Anyway, I better head to class now. See you two later."

"See ya, nerd." Melissa said her usual greeting toward me with more affection this time. I made sure to smile back at her, too.

Turning my eyes back to Darren, I blew a kiss at him as I parted ways with him and Melissa on my way to homeroom. Yeesh, it tasted like slime spewing from my mouth doing so. Especially after seeing an even greater arrogance in his facial expression that I hadn't seen from him before.

"So, you like Darren now or what?" Orlando asked in a teasing, flirtatious tone of voice.

"Eww, no," I replied. "Just wanted to give him a proper gesture for helping me defeat Rage yesterday. Plus, a good way to get him off my ass for now. Hopefully I won't have to see his stupid face once this summer."

The school day felt as if the previous day never even happened. At least until Kenzie came around and reminded me that stuff did happen that day. When she saw my long-flowing light blond hair, she squeed like a rabid fangirl as she ran up to me just a few minutes before homeroom started.

"I wish I could've seen your epic battle yesterday morning," she said in a rapid-fire manner that would make Eminem sweat. "God, I can imagine how cool that was . . ."

Deepening her voice in imitation of a cartoon narrator, she slowed down her speech and continued, "Almost a month after the horrific shooting that claimed the life of Lizzy Manchester, the ultimate grudge match between Jessica Summer and Rage has finally arrived. An epic clash of photon balls and fireballs. Pew! Pew! Pew! Bam! And just when it seems that all hope is lost, Jessica unleashed the most menacing object in the universe: a black hole. What's this? Rage has now lost his powers? Perfect timing for the police to arrive at the scene of the fight and send him back to prison. At long last, Jessica Summer has come out victorious over her new archrival. It's a superhero tale come to life!"

I laughed the hardest that I had in a while. "You should be a comic book writer, Kenzie," I said. "It sounds like something you'd be really good at." I grinned and give Kenzie a soft pat on the back before we parted ways.

"Looks like you're famous now, Jess," Charlotte said.

"You truly are like all your favorite superheroes now," Orlando adds. "How cool is that?"

"It is cool and such, yes, but I don't really care for such recognition, to be honest. When I first got my powers, I thought many times about how awesome it would be to use them to stop crimes and disasters from happening every chance I could get. But in the end, I've realized I'm not cut out for that kind of lifestyle. I don't need to be a superhero. I just need to be Jessica Summer."

"You've got mad guts to ditch the superhero life in favor of the headache that is high school, Jessica," Orlando said. "Mad guts."

"Which only means more time for me to be an annoying shit to you two. Hate to break it to you." I gave a playful slap to Orlando's and Charlotte's backs as the three of us all laughed at once before heading to our respective homeroom classes.

—~—

I got a 98 on my English paper that I got back at second period; not a bad showing with how little time I had to finish and polish it after all the craziness I had to deal with over the past three-and-a-half weeks. Much like my performance at Sunday's dance show, I took pride in the fulfillment of satisfying months of hard work toward a project that I put up a heavy dedication to with a near-perfect grade. But despite all the satisfaction I received from my academic accomplishment, my focus turned to a more important matter during lunchtime.

After finishing my lunch, I marched over to Principal Warden's office with heavy determination. Just before I entered the door into the school's front offices, however, I halted my steps for a bit. My endeavors the previous day had been on the news, so there was no way school staff wasn't aware that I ditched school for the sake of engaging in a battle between Exceptionals that caused major property damage. I was sure that my teachers realized that themselves, too. Someone in that office was going to be mad at me knowing that I lied my way out of school yesterday.

In the end, however, I decided to stop worrying too much about that. The Manzanita shooter was back in prison thanks to my efforts, and I saved two of our students from his unquenchable desire to murder them. I was sure they'd give me a free pass because I was a local hero now.

Just brush it off, Jessica, I thought.

When I arrived at Principal Warden's office, my anxiety rose, since there was no guarantee he'd be able to speak with me before third period started. Thankfully, I could breathe easy again when the principal walked over to the door of his office on his way back from a meeting.

"Jessica Summer," he said to me. "What a surprise to see you here."

"I could say the same myself," I said with a somewhat nervous giggle. "Anyway, is it okay if I speak with you a bit? I have something important that I really wanted to talk to you about."

"Sure. Feel free to take a seat in my office, Jessica." I remained steely as I pulled up the chair on the opposite side of the principal's desk and settled myself in. Then I let out a large exhale, uncertain about how he'd react to the subject matter I was about to bring up to him.

"So I want to get to what I'm here to discuss right away, because it's a very important matter for all of us students, Exceptional and Unexceptional." Principal Warden stayed quiet, ready to listen to what I had to say to him.

"On behalf of the students at Manzanita, I would like to request that the school hand a harsher punishment to the security guards who beat Plasma Kid, the alias of student Greg Nathan, unconscious at the entrance to our school a week ago. In addition to that, I demand a reduction of Greg's multi-month punishment that many of us would agree to be too excessive and well beyond the school's instituted punishment of a week-long suspension for first-time offenders of the new rules forbidding Exceptional powers. Greg is my neighbor, and I've known him since I was a child, so I can assure you that he's a living, breathing person, and not just someone to be billed as a supposed threat. The fact that he, a student, would get a much harsher punishment than the men who *almost beat him to death*, I find to be just . . . absurd and shocking. And I'm sure my fellow students would agree with me. In all, we students who are Exceptionals are not pleased with how the school seems to be singling us out as a supposed threat to others around us. To be honest, it's been making Exceptional students scared of going to school, especially after Greg's beating. We would appreciate it if the school could be more accommodating of Exceptionals from now on; we desire the same treatment as everyone else at Manzanita and don't want to be scared of stepping onto campus because of characteristics of ours that we can't control." Thanks to the speeches that I'd given in memory of Lizzy, getting all this off my chest wound up being a lot easier than I expected.

Principal Warden nodded a couple of times. "I understand your concerns, Jessica," he said. "As principal, part of my job is to make sure that our students are comfortable, and I can understand why someone like you would be discouraged from going to school because of the incident that you mentioned. So I will make sure to discuss the matter with school staff some time in the next few days before the school year ends. You can look forward to hearing a decision from us regarding the job status of those guards soon."

"Thank you, Principal Warden. I appreciate your understanding."

As I walked out of his office, I worried about how much Principal Warden was willing to listen to me. There was a heavy burden on him to respond to the needs of a community that hadn't even existed for a full month. So would he do the right thing and be a key voice to Manzanita's Exceptional student population (as well as any Exceptional employees, if there were any)? Or was he going to side with superist voices and continue to marginalize us as a demographic for others to be suspicious of?

Joel Warden's legacy as Manzanita High School principal was on the line, and whatever decisions he made in response to the emergence of Exceptional students would have a major impact on the status of Exceptionals at our school, and possibly even elsewhere. Although I trusted Principal Warden, this wasn't the most comfortable thing to think about.

After finishing dinner, I walked by myself to the same spot on West Beach where I sat the first time I saw the shooting star that sparked the Great Bestowal. Like last time, I stuck around that spot after sunset as I waited and hoped for said shooting star to light up the night sky again. To my relief, after waiting for around half an hour after sunset, the shooting star indeed appeared in the sky above me as twilight broke. Given what I'd just been through, I was certain that Ids had been thinking about me as of late.

I walked back home right after seeing the shooting star so that I could get enough sleep for my second-to-last day of school and the two finals that I would take that day (geometry and French). Some indeterminate amount of time after falling asleep, I opened my eyes and found myself back in the Aurora Dimension. I descended from my lying position to the imaginary ground below me, with Ids already in my sights.

"Hey Ids," I said. "I did it. I defeated my worst enemy. Rage has lost his flame powers and is back in jail. My journey to avenge Lizzy and the devastation he caused to my high school is complete."

"Congratulations, Jessica Summer," Ids said. "I'm glad that my training and philosophy paid off for you. You appear to have improved as a superhero. But even with your archenemy vanquished, your journey as a superhero is just beginning. There are plenty more adventures to come for you."

"Just as all my favorite comics taught me. Though I prefer not to be called a superhero, thanks. I still would like to defend my friends and family from whatever threats come our way. But I'm more comfortable living the life of a normal teenage girl. Being a superhero would put too much pressure on me; I don't think it would be as awesome as it is for my favorite comic book characters."

"At least you're finding your identity, Jessica. All the better for you if you're able to recognize what makes you most comfortable."

This time, Ids and I weren't alone; there were three other floating entities around us. But none of them looked exactly like Ids; their looks varied—a living, floating silver aurora, a bright blob of sky-blue light, and a scarlet-red star with the same hollow eyes as Ids. Still, all of them carried some sort of strange, amorphous, phantom-esque appearance like Ids did.

"Who are these guys?" I asked Ids. "I suppose that they—"

"Yes. These are my fellow *vshqi*. I could introduce their names to you, but they would most likely be unpronounceable to a being from your planet, heheh."

"Heh, fair enough. By the way, I thought your *vshqi* saw you as some kind of joke?" I was pretty sure I botched the pronunciation of *vshqi* there.

"Not all of them. My friends here are more benevolent to me than others in this dimension. So I have my own posse that I'm lucky to have when so many look down on me."

I giggled. "Story of my life."

"The four of us have gathered today to congratulate you on your victory. Although this is the first time you've met my pals, all of us couldn't be any happier for you."

The four beings in the . . . room sent out sparks of light that flew into each other and created a spectacular firework upon making contact. The gesture appeared to me like a four-way high five, only with their powers instead of physical contact with hands. Afterward, they appeared to use whatever they had for limbs and lit them up when they made contact with their bodies. Although it was hard for me to tell for sure, such gestures appeared to bring pleasant feelings to them after performing them.

"*Zithnk*, friend!" said the blob of sky-blue light. "That's our language's equivalent of *hello*, by the way. You must be the Earth being that Ids empowered."

"Yes, that is me . . . sir," I said. "Any way I'm supposed to tell if you're men or women or anything?"

"Men? Women? We have no clue what those are," said the scarlet red star.

"They're two types of genders into which Jessica's species is classified in her world," Ids explained.

"Ah, so you guys in the Aurora Dimension don't have—"

"Yes, Jessica. Unlike in your world, there's no such thing as gender here."

"Ah. That's a little strange by my standards, but I can adjust to it," I said, giggling. Then I decided to get into a cool superhero pose and flash photon energy from my hands just to show off.

"How does it feel to have powers like ours, Jessica?" the silver aurora asked.

"It's quite awesome. It hasn't been the smooth sailing that I expected, but it's so nice to know that I no longer have to stay helpless in the face of tragedy and disaster."

Ids cleared their . . . whatever was their equivalent of a throat and bragged, "I may have had something to do with that."

"Which reminds me," I said as I turned my eyes toward Ids. "Thanks for your help, Ids. Thanks for opening up the possibilities for me. Thanks for bringing me the hope that I needed in the harsh world I live in. In the gut-wrenching times I've found myself in." Ids didn't mind a hug this time, despite not being a hugger.

"What was with that?" asked the living aurora.

"She calls it a hug," Ids answered. "It's how people show affection and gratitude where she comes from."

"These Earth folks sure are weird," said the star-looking being.

"You might want to get used to it, then," I said, giving the scarlet-red star an adorable wink. "Anyway, I better head back to my world. It was nice meeting you guys, and nice seeing you again, Ids. Farewell."

"Farewell, Jessica Summer," Ids said. "Best of luck with your journey as an Exceptional."

And so I floated back down into a lying position, closed my eyes, and returned my consciousness back to Earth.

CHAPTER

24

It was the second-to-last day of school, as well as the last day before the summer solstice, and for our African American friends, Juneteenth. I wanted to think that I'd be more relaxed now that I'd gotten through all but one of my final exams (I had my English final the following day). But going into my second-to-last fourth-period class of the year, my nervousness acted up in anticipation of the dance troupe's announcement regarding their co-captains for next school year. If I had permission to use my powers on campus, I would've hidden myself behind a force field bubble to conceal myself out of shyness and anxiety. Even then, my teammates could still notice the tension in my everywhere.

"Jessica? Are you okay?" Rachel asked me.

"Yeah, I'm fine," I answered. "It's just that . . . you know."

"Hey, nothing to be nervous about, Jess. We're all nervous, honestly. I know how hard you've been working all year long to become a captain. Don't tell the others, but I'm rooting for you."

"Thanks, Rachel. I'm just happy to finally get this over with."

Class began with the outgoing seniors making their farewell speeches to us, with none other than Megan Miller making the last of those speeches. Because Megan was a senior and I was a sophomore, I never had that much time to build the tightest relationship with her, as we'd only known each other since I started high school. Regardless, she'd been my biggest mentor during my time with the Manzanita

Dance Troupe, so it was an emotional experience for me to watch her make her departure speech, putting me on the verge of shedding tears.

"I can't believe this day has come," Megan said to the class. "It's been an honor to be an integral member of this team for the past four years; you have become my second family in the process. I've been dancing since I was three years old, and never has the art of dancing been more fun for me than it has been with all of you. Being captain was never a goal of mine when I first started; I was only doing this for the passion and the enjoyment of dance. But over time, my hard work and dedication to the dance troupe rewarded me with the role, and I feel I've never let you girls down as captain; I'm sure you can say the same, too. To all of you in this room, thank you for making my passion in life more enjoyable over these last four years. To Ms. Newton, thank you for being the best dance instructor and helping me to grow as a team member and eventual captain. And to Jessica Summer, you've grown so much since I first met you as a wee baby freshman. Through the lingering pain you felt from losing your best friend in the shooting, the rough battles you've fought, and the difficulties you've endured as a result of your new powers, you pulled through and led a fantastic grand finale. That makes me proud to have served as your mentor figure over our time together."

Wow. Megan Miller just dedicated part of her farewell speech to me. And she applauded me for my efforts through all the challenges and anguish that I went through. My reaction was to stand up and give Megan a big hug for making a special shout-out to me in her speech.

"I can't put into words how much it means to hear that from you, Megan," I said. "Since I joined the dance troupe freshman year, you've been the greatest teacher to me out of everyone in here. Suffice it to say, I wouldn't have been able to get through these last few weeks without your guidance. And it'll be sad to see you go."

"It's not goodbye; it's see you later, Jessica." Turning her attention back to the rest of the class, Megan continued, "That's the final word I wanted to bring up to all of you to conclude my farewell speech. I may be headed across the country to Juilliard, but that's not going to make me forget about you girls and the influence you've had with my dance career. I will still continue to keep you guys in my memories from the very first day I touch down in New York. Thank you."

Our class gave Megan a round of applause before Ms. Newton came back up to the front for the big announcement. Anxiety and excitement engaged in an epic tug-of-war inside me as she took center stage.

"This is it, Jessica," Charlotte mumbled to me from behind. "Good luck."

"Beautiful speech, Megan," Ms. Newton said. "And now, with all that said, it's time for me to announce our captains for the Manzanita Dance Troupe next school year. Our dance troupe captains for the 2024–2025 school year are going to be . . . Kayla Hidalgo and . . . Jessica Summer."

When I heard my name, a shriek fired out of my mouth. The thrill of achieving what I'd been working hard at for the past several months was so sky-high that it was more cloud ten than cloud nine. In spite of all the hard times that I'd gone through, all the sorrow and trauma I'd dealt with, I'd now accomplished my biggest goal of the year. All of my teammates mobbed me in celebration, and it was a moment that I didn't want to end.

When Charlotte and I walked out of dance class, the two of us jumped up and down and squeed in excitement, facing each other the whole time with our hands on each other's shoulders. Nothing around us existed at that moment; just the two of us in our own little bubble of elation.

"See, Jessica? I knew you would do it!" Charlotte said.

"I still can't believe it," I said. "All the bullshit I've had to deal with over the past month, and at long last, something goes right. Gosh, I have no words to describe how happy I am right now."

"Well, I've got some words for you, captain: This is the absolute best way for you to… *cap* off the year!" I didn't even care if Charlotte was up to her usual tricks with her lousy puns; my level of excitement was too high for me to find the time to cringe.

The two of us returned to squeeing and jumping up and down once more as Orlando arrived to join us. We didn't notice him until he spoke up.

"What's going on with you two?" he asked.

"Jessica is going to be co-captain of the dance troupe starting next school year," Charlotte replied. "She'd been working hard to earn it since the start of this school year."

"Really? Oh man, congrats, Jess!" Orlando gave me a big hug. "Such awesome news to hear."

As we started to head out of campus, a large crowd of students by the entrance—some of whom were holding picket signs—caught our eyes. Among the crowd were many familiar faces: Corbin Wong, Shelby Roy, Victor Ullman, Lorelyn "Elseven" Ash, and right next to Elseven in the front, Maryam Asghari.

"*Dorood*, Jessica," Maryam greeted me as I walked up to her. "A hearty congratulations and thank you on your triumph over the Manzanita shooter. I hope the grace of Allah—*subhanahu wa ta'ala*—has continued to remain strong with you."

"Thank you and thank you, Maryam. And of course, thank you for coming over to fix all the damage at my house the other day."

"Hey, it's my pleasure, friend. I always enjoy any opportunity to use my powers to have a positive impact on others. Since you comforted me after I saw Greg Nathan's horrific beating, I thought it was only right to pay you back the favor."

"Aww, it warms my heart to hear that, Maryam. Good thing I still had your number from our biology class freshman year." I made a small giggle and then asked, "What's going on here, by the way? Gutsy of you all to hold a gathering this big in the middle of finals week."

"Better late than never, as they say, Jessica. We're marching to promote better treatment of Exceptionalkind. Both at our school and worldwide. One more day of school left, one more chance to get the school to change their mind about our people."

"An Exceptional rights march? That's the first time I've heard of such a thing."

"Actually, plenty such protests have taken place around the world since the day of the Great Bestowal. And this one sure as heck won't be the last."

Although I could've walked up to the group of protesters and joined them in their march, I decided not to and stayed back with Charlotte and Orlando instead. My decision caught them by surprise.

"You're not going to join them, Jessica?" Orlando asked. "You know you could be part of history here, being a participant in one of the world's first-ever Exceptional rights protests."

"Man, would I love to . . ." I answered, "but to be honest, I think my time for the rest of the day would be better spent studying for my English final tomorrow. Plus, after all the wild stuff I've gone through, I think it would be better for me to keep my life more low-key for the time being. I don't care that we're in the era of FOMO; I could use some time away from the spotlight for once, so missing out on this protest won't bother me one bit."

"I think that's a fair decision on your part, Jess. After defeating the Manzanita shooter and helping the city return him to jail, you really deserve a break."

"Plus, I'm sure there'll be other Exceptional rights protests for you to be a part of in the future," Charlotte added. "We'd love to join you in any such protests that allow us Unexceptionals to participate."

"My thoughts exactly, C. C.," I said. "Why should I feel bad about missing out on this march when there are plenty more of them to come in the future? It's better to do whatever I think is best for me."

After I made my decision, Orlando, Charlotte, and I stayed where we were in order to permit the marching students to proceed forward onto the street leading out of Manzanita. As the crowd of students marched on, they started shouting chants in support of Exceptionals, with Maryam leading the chants—a megaphone on one hand, and a sign saying "Exceptionals + Freedom = Democracy" in her other one.

"What do we want?" Maryam said into her megaphone.

"Exceptional rights!" the crowd said in response.

"When do we want them?"

"Now!" The chants continued for a few more times as the crowd of students marched further onto the street and away from Manzanita's campus.

Once we had room to walk back home again, I was lucky to watch the crowd of peaceful protesters marching through the street ahead of us, with a vivid green glow originating from Maryam emanating from her end of the crowd to the other. The sight of the march placed a smile on my face throughout my entire walk back home, even after I parted ways with Orlando and Charlotte for the day. Even though I chose not to join the protesters, I was happy to be with them in spirit in support of the cause they were promoting.

A few blocks away from my house, my eyes caught a quick glimpse of a kid with noticeable injuries sitting down in the front yard of his house. The kid was around my age, and even with the bandages on his forehead, right cheek, and nose, I could still recognize his face.

"Greg," I said. "I see you're doing better now."

"Oh, hey Jessica," Greg said. "What's good?"

"Eh, nothing much. Just getting through finals week, that's all. What are you doing out here?"

"Literally just chilling, Jessica. I could be hanging out in my backyard, but I decided I like it here a lot more. It's the side of my house facing the ocean, so there's more of a chance for me to feel the ocean breeze on my face."

"I don't blame you for that. You need all the therapeutic relief you can find with how bad of a beating you took from those security guards. And living close to the ocean doesn't hurt in that regard."

"Ah yeah, that. I remember these guys at a hospital, my parents, and a few guys at school telling me that I was beaten to a pulp. That I fell into a coma for about a week. Caught me by surprise when I was first told about it, man; didn't know how to react. Everyone brought it up to me for a few days. I hardly recall anything that happened after I ran into those security guards though . . . but based on what you said about them, I suppose that's a good thing."

"You are so right about that, Greg. The less we talk about that day, the better. Did the school ever say anything about your suspension, by the way?"

"Funny you ask, because I didn't know that the school suspended me until they called me today. It sucks having to miss my finals, miss the start of the next school year and repeat the ninth grade, but hey, all the more time for me to focus on my journey as a superhero, at least!"

I grinned and let out a short giggle. "Love your optimism, Greg. I think I may know a few things about that. So I can offer you a few good tips on superheroism myself."

"Awesome, thanks, Jessica! I'm already very excited for you to share your superhero advice with me." Greg's eagerness was conspicuous through both his facial expressions and body language. "So what advice do you have on finding a sidekick? First things first: I need to hire a sidekick to help me out with my adventures."

"I hate to say this Greg, but you're asking the wrong person. Although Melissa Snyder and Darren Owens were key allies in my showdown against Rage on Monday, I never really planned to search for a true sidekick as I prepared to take him down. Exceptionals haven't even existed for a month, you know . . . so it would've been kind of silly for me to look for and choose a sidekick after discovering my powers. Not to mention all the high school crap I've had to deal with, of course. Yeah, no time to recruit a sidekick, really . . ."

"Okay, fair. Any tips on how I can figure out my crimefighting gimmick, though? Or how to find an archrival? Or—"

"Hey now, a little too many questions there. My apologies, but I can't find the answers or the time to respond to them all," I said with a giggle. "Perhaps a good first tip is that maybe you should take it a little slow. Becoming a beloved superhero isn't something that happens overnight."

"Yeah, you're right there, Jessica. I mean, that is something that Beacon taught me. Heck, even Heroman, too. And Captain Wonder, and . . ."

"I think it's safe to say that you get it, kid." I delivered a quick wink to Greg. "Anyway, I need to go back home to study for my English final tomorrow anyway. So, see you later. Glad you're doing okay."

I started to walk back home, only to stop and turn around for a moment when I remembered one more thing I wanted to tell Greg. "Oh, and I promise I won't let the word out that you're Plasma Kid," I said to him. "My apologies for finding that out on accident."

"I wasn't aware that you even knew about my secret identity. But thanks, man. My secret's safe with you, Jessica." I smiled at Greg as I waved goodbye to him.

—∞—

As I lay on the couch in front of our living room television and read *Kitsune: Youkai Showdown* issue #2, the latest comic that I picked up from Central Coast Comics after dropping off my school materials at home, Mom took a seat by me and tuned in to the local news. Inside, my nervous system cringed knowing what to expect from the latest news reports. However, the news coverage that we saw came as a pleasant surprise to me.

"Right after the end of their school day, around 3:15 p.m., students at Manzanita High School marched through the streets of downtown Santa Barbara in protest of new rules that their school passed about a week ago forbidding Exceptional students from using their magical powers on Manzanita school grounds," said the local news reporter on the television screen. "The crowd of protesters would eventually grow to include students from schools all throughout the city of Santa Barbara, as well as a collection of college students from both UCSB and SBCC. Consisting entirely of middle school, high school, and university students, the group of protesters were speaking out in support of Exceptional rights, as members of the brand-new demographic have begun to voice dissatisfaction with their place in society since first discovering their powers a little less than a month ago in the global power-granting event now dubbed the Great Bestowal."

Maybe it was me, but this might've been the first story I'd ever seen on the news that covered Exceptionals in a positive manner, so the pictures from the protest were a breath of fresh air for me. A line of protesters glowed green, indicating that Maryam was leading them with the utmost aplomb and passion. Protesting students displayed a level of freedom that they weren't accustomed to at my school, with some protesters flying above the crowd and others levitating their picket signs in the air to allow others to see them when they could easily get lost in the crowd. And the protest in Santa Barbara wasn't the only one going on that day. Brief clips of similar-looking pro-Exceptional protests showed up in the news broadcast, from New York and Chicago to Paris to even Tehran.

The stories covering the worldwide Exceptional rights marches didn't come without some negativity, however. As the news was showing, enormous police and security forces responded to the protests, including the one in Santa Barbara, with the type of brute force that was lacking against the January 6 Capitol rioters three years ago, brutally beating down some protesters and even deploying tanks and tear gas in some cases. Footage of young Exceptionals lying on the ground with officers subduing them as bits of their power sparked uncontrollably gave me harsh flashbacks of watching school security guards beat Plasma Kid to a pulp. In addition, Exceptional protesters here in Santa Barbara and throughout the country encountered nasty counter-protests led primarily by superists and right-wing groups. Footage of clashes between the two parties was plentiful throughout every single news report that I could find on my television screen. Somehow, watching it was as epic as it was disheartening, with some of the protesters using their extraordinary powers against those undoubtedly insecure average-Joe bigots. While I wasn't one to condone violence and I preferred peaceful resolution whenever possible like Maryam did, that was how you answered back against a group of cowards who just plain hated the fact that you were extraordinary.

These weren't just occurrences in our harshly divided America, either; such unnecessary violence, use of excessive force, and counter-protests occurred at pro-Exceptional protests elsewhere in the world, too. Luckily, with the help of their various abilities, most of the Exceptionals came out of the police attacks without a scratch; many of them were too much for opposing officers and soldiers to handle. Watching such footage on the news was like watching a brutal but action-packed anime on my television.

"Hey, wasn't that your school on the news, sweetheart?" Mom asked as she was watching the local news report, glimpsing the headline on the bottom that mentioned Manzanita.

"Yes, it was," I replied. "I even saw the start of the protest after school ended. Some of my friends were there."

"Ooh, I hope none of your classmates got hurt in their march. Your school has already been through enough."

"Seriously, Mom. I'm going to text my homeroom buddy to make sure she's safe. She was at the march today."

And so I pulled out my phone, letting my fingers tap away the fastest that they could.

Me

I heard they brought out heavy security forces at the protest today. Were you hurt? Did anybody we know get hurt?

Anxiety in my veins, I waited for three long minutes to get a reply from Shelby.

Shelby

I'm fine, Jessica. Not a scratch on me. No one else we're familiar with was injured, as far as I know. Not sure about the others at the protest, but I'm not too worried about them with the powers they have.

Me

Oh man, so true. We should all be grateful these powers are now a part of us.

Shelby

Haha for real. Thanks for checking in with me, nerd.

Me

No problemo. Glad you're safe. Hope everyone else was, too.

After finishing up my last text to Shelby, I remained silent for a bit. Today's news about the pro-Exceptional marches was a reminder to me that society was still treating Exceptionals like a square peg in a round hole. But no matter how much shit Unexceptionals tossed at us, we weren't going to stay silent in the face of injustice and discrimination. We'd proved that we could be heroes who defended the vulnerable. We could speak up for other marginalized groups on this planet based on our own challenges and experiences. And we were going to continue to show Unexceptionals that we could indeed change the world for the better. And in ways that wouldn't be possible without our help.

Breaking my brief silence, I asked Mom, "Where are Dad and Larson, by the way? They've been away for a while."

"Just got home, cupcake," Dad said as he entered the living room. "I bought you a special new gift that you'll love, too."

The sight of my new gift caused me to squee in joy louder than they'd ever heard me scream from excitement. It was an adorable, orange-striped tabby kitten. I hadn't had a cat since my last one, Diamante (named after the Xenos character who could turn her body into diamond, of course), passed away during the first half of my freshman year; her passing was so devastating to me that it left a hole in my heart that I couldn't fully recover from until this new cat came into my life. As a result, his arrival meant the world to me.

"Soooooo cute," I yelped in a high-pitched voice as I cuddled my new kitten for the first time. When I rubbed my face on his back, I announced, "I'm going to name him McFly. Just like the protagonist of the *Back to the Future* movies."

"We were hesitant about getting another cat after Diamante's passing," Dad said. "It made us iffy for a while about getting a new pet, but now we felt ready for another one, so Larson and I went to the local adoption center today and found this cutie."

"It's long overdue that we add another pet to the Summer family, guys," I said. "McFly should more than make up for the void that Diamante left behind. Thank you so much." I gave my dad a quick kiss on the nose, and then proceed to do the same with Larson, too.

The four of us participated in a cuddle session with McFly for the next few minutes, taking turns snuggling and petting our new family cat. Of course, it wasn't long before someone brought up the elephant in the room.

"How exactly do you think McFly is going to handle being with an Exceptional in the house?" Dad asked.

"I'm sure he's going to enjoy being with our little superheroine," Mom replied. "I wouldn't worry too much."

"Now that I think about it, I haven't even thought about how Exceptionals with pets handle keeping their powers in check around their pets," I said. "Nor have I heard about it on the news. But you can trust me to use my powers wisely around him. Don't expect him to end up like Dustin's cat in *Stranger Things*, if you know what I mean." Neither of my parents got that joke, but considering what happened to that poor cat on the show, I was glad they didn't.

"I have to admit that I'm a bit jealous I won't get to spend as much time with McFly as Jessica will," Larson said. "Damn you, college."

"Hey, I wouldn't mind bringing him along next time we visit you in Isla Vista. As long as your new place accepts pets, I'll let you get your cuddle time with him."

"Awesome. I sure hope he can handle IV."

"If McFly can deal with my powers, he'll be able to tolerate IV for sure." All four of us laughed together as we began preparing McFly's first meal as the newest addition to our family.

CHAPTER

25

Even with one more final to go—my English final— the last day of school was supposed to be a relaxing one for me. If only it were that simple.

Throughout the morning, the school's pending decision on the security guards responsible for beating Plasma Kid unconscious remained afloat in my head. It served as a distraction for me during my English exam, hindering my focus throughout the entire test. Not helping matters was the fact that I planned to see Principal Warden right after lunchtime, and since my English class was during second period, that only made the matter of the school's decision an even heavier burden in my head. As a result, I felt I didn't as well on my English test as I would've hoped, albeit still well enough to get at least a B.

The very second after I turned in my test to Mr. Bradley, I power walked to Principal Warden's office as fast as I could. Like I was hoping, I made it there just a few minutes before the lunch period started. I also made sure to text Charlotte and Orlando that I'd be joining them at the beach a little later than usual because of an important meeting at the principal's office. I assured them that it wasn't for something bad—just a little talk that I wanted to have with him on the last day of school.

"Principal Warden? Are you there?" I said as I knocked on the door to his office.

"Come in," the principal answered. I closed his door and took my seat on the chair in front of his desk.

"Hello, Jessica. What did you want to see me for?"

"Well, it's the last day of the school year, and I was just wanting to know if the school has made any revisions to the decisions they made about Greg Nathan and the security guards who beat him unconscious last week. Any word on that yet?"

"Ah. I had the feeling you were going to ask me about that. We did make the decision to terminate those three security guards, effective immediately." I almost pumped my fist and said "yes" in response to the news, but I made sure to do so in my head instead of out loud in order to appear more respectful and unbiased in front of Principal Warden.

"In addition, we've reduced Mr. Nathan's suspension to one week instead of until next October like we originally planned, and we're going to allow him to take his finals and complete the ninth grade. Because of how much time he's missed from school recovering from his injuries, he won't have to serve his suspension until the start of the next school year in August." More relief that the school listened to my requests. "Mr. Nathan still broke school rules, and he could've posed a threat to students and faculty around him by activating his powers on campus. Who knows who could've gotten hurt if there were more people in the area around him at the time he tried to use his powers at the campus entrance? For that reason, we have no plans to lift the new rules banning the use of superpowers on campus. Student safety must still be of the utmost priority at all times. No exceptions."

The second part of Principal Warden's announcement put a slight damper on the relief I felt over the firing of the security guards who brutalized Greg, but in the end, I accepted the school's decision. "I think that's fair," I said. "Speaking from the standpoint of Exceptionals, I admit that not every Exceptional on campus approves of these new rules, and most likely, they will continue to be unpopular with the student body—particularly us Exceptionals, of course. But at the same time, I do agree with the school's desire to emphasize campus security, especially in the wake of last month's shooting. Exceptionals are still a brand-new demographic, and as much as I dislike the treatment they've been receiving from some individuals and organizations, I can understand that school staff has reason to suspect that some of them might do some crazy irresponsible, maybe even harmful, things with their powers. Who knows if some Exceptionals on campus might have more nefarious intentions like Garrett Lowe did . . . while it's difficult for me to put myself in your shoes, I've been getting the notion that many staff members at our school fear a repeat of last month's mass killing, this time at the hands of an Exceptional, a scenario which could exceed the carnage of last month's shooting. I'm sure certain students may have thought about that, too. I lost my best friend Lizzy in the shooting, so I can empathize with anyone who fears a second massacre happening on our campus, especially with the recent emergence of Exceptionals."

Principal Warden nodded his head a couple of times and wore a partial smile on his face. "I'm glad you understand where we're coming from, Ms. Summer," he said. "A good note for us to end on for the school year."

"Glad we could come to a compromise today, Principal Warden. I never thought that students and staff would have an easy time getting on the same terms after the emergence of Exceptionals on our campus, but after everything that all of us have gone through . . ." I shrug my arms and then continue. ". . . here we are." I pushed my chair back in and waved goodbye to the principal as I departed his office, and the two of us flashed smiles at each other. "Thanks for taking the time to chat with me, Principal Warden. See you next year."

Before heading to my usual secret beachside lunch spot and meeting up with Charlotte and Orlando there, I made a quick stop by the cafeteria to chat with Maryam at her lunch table. As I looked for her, I got a few perverted looks and crude comments from Darren and his pals, but I just ignored them without issue, smirking on my way to where Maryam sat.

"Hey Maryam," I greeted her.

"Hello again, Jessica," Maryam said. "Such a pleasant surprise to see you here; I don't believe I see you much around the cafeteria."

"Yeah, I admit that I don't come here often for lunchtime. But I made an exception for today because I wanted to come over here to congratulate and thank you for leading the march through the streets of Santa Barbara yesterday and helping our voices be heard. I very much appreciate you playing your part in helping Exceptionals find their place in a society that fears and dislikes us."

"*Sepâsgozâram*—thank you for your kind words, Jessica. It can be tiring sometimes being an advocate for people that society seems to hold back at every doorstep. So it always brings a smile to my face when I hear someone voice appreciation for my work and any activism I participate in. It lets me know that I've succeeded in getting the word out about the causes I'm passionate about, *inshallah*. And as long as others need help, I'm going to keep fighting for them, no matter what the obstacles. Just as Allah—*subhanahu wa ta'ala*—encourages us, and just as the Prophet Muhammad—*salla allahu 'alayhi wa salaam*—taught us." The beauty of Maryam's words brought a glow of warmth to my heart.

"Just know that there'll always be others on your side. You can one hundred percent count on me to be one of those people, Maryam." I gave Maryam the same three-fingered gesture that Katniss Everdeen flashed in *The Hunger Games* as a salute. "Sorry that I couldn't join the protest you were leading yesterday, by the way. I would've loved to, but after all the troubles I've been dealing with and the grief I'm still feeling from Lizzy's death, I didn't feel ready to play a heavy role of responsibility once again; didn't feel comfortable with the possibility of finding myself in the media spotlight again, as if I haven't received enough of it already. Being the subject of a planned Hollywood movie based on the shooting and facing frequent harassment from a national news reporter will do that to you. So I hope you understand where I'm coming from."

"Hey, it's okay, Jessica. You've been through so much since the shooting, and I applaud you for taking a break when you need to. I've been through a lot too, as have all of us at Manzanita. So of course I understand where you're coming from. When you're ready to participate in Exceptional rights activism, I will welcome you with open arms."

"Thank you for your sympathy, Maryam," I said, flashing a hearty smile to her. "Anyway, have you heard yet about the school's announcement on the security guards who beat up Plasma Kid, by any chance?"

"Yes, I have. I'm glad justice finally came to those guards; it was long overdue. But the school's decision still feels bittersweet and unsatisfactory. Even our protest yesterday wasn't enough to give school staff a change of heart regarding their attitudes toward Exceptionals."

"I was also hoping for a better outcome than what the school ended up deciding, Maryam. Unfortunately for us, the real world doesn't work that way. But that doesn't mean we'll wilt in the face of adversity. Because the little guy always finds a way, no matter the odds. There are always positives to be found within the direst of situations."

Maryam wrapped her arms around me, and I returned the favor myself. Although we didn't know each other that well in person and mainly knew each other from our respective public reputations, we didn't mind clinging onto our hug for a good few seconds. And just in time for Elseven to arrive at the table after picking up her lunch for the day.

"Hey-o!" she greeted us. "What a pleasant surprise seeing you here, Jessica. You're usually not around here much."

I made a hearty giggle, as I often did whenever I spent time with Elseven. "Thought I could lend a hand of positivity to Maryam before the school year comes to a close today," I said to Elseven.

"Well, thanks for the invite then, Jessica Summer."

"Heh, nice try at sarcasm there, Elseven. I know sarcasm when I see it." Elseven giggled and wrapped her arms around me and Maryam in an impromptu three-way group hug.

"Hello, Elseven," Maryam said. "Thanks for marching by my side yesterday."

"I wouldn't have missed it for the world, Maryam. A prime opportunity to show the people of planet Earth what Elseven Ash can do. No one's going to silence me, or any other Exceptional. That isn't a bad apple like that mean Garrett Lowe, of course." I gave Elseven a high five in response to that last comment she made, both of us holding our mouths open as we did so, as if to say, "Hell yeah."

"So how come you didn't march with us yesterday, Jessica?" Elseven asked.

"Been through a lot in my life, wanted to study for my English final today, stuff like that," I replied. "I've had the need to keep it low-key these days."

"Hehe, even the Cosmic Girl needs a break every now and then," Elseven said in a teasing but fun manner. "Anyway, I heard that you hang out at some secret spot every lunch period now. Can you give me some hints about where to find it, by any chance, Jessica?"

"I could . . . but then it wouldn't be a secret anymore, would it?"

"Heh, fine then. I'll try to figure it out myself next school year."

"Let me guess, you're going to use your power to develop the ability to read minds or make others spoil their deepest secrets, aren't you?"

Elseven smirked. "I will if I can find such characters, hehe. I've got all summer to look for them, so better watch out, Jessica Summer!"

"Ooh, I better, all right. Lots of Exceptionals here to spoil my secret, so you might not be the first, Elseven." Those were the last words I said to her before I said goodbye to her and Maryam and headed back to my usual secret beach spot to have lunch and chat with Orlando and Charlotte one more time on campus before wrapping up our sophomore year.

Three days later and three days into summer vacation, it was June 23, marking exactly a month since the day that my life and the lives of those at Manzanita High School changed forever. Although campus grounds were closed for the next two months, I stopped by a dirt field between the entrance to Manzanita's campus and the adjacent shopping center to check out the memorial that our school created in honor of the ten students whose lives were cut short too early on that tragic day. And none other than Mr. and Mrs. Manchester were by my side to view the memorial with me.

The memorial was divided into ten sections by collections of painted rocks, one for each of the students who perished in the shooting. A small, wooden board with a photo of each student taped onto it, as well as piles of flowers, marked each slain student's section of the memorial. I'd placed some items in Lizzy's section myself, including a few of her old drawings of some of our favorite female superheroes such as Passion from the Xenos franchise and Vitality of the Protectors, an action figure of Rey from *Star Wars*, and the crest of Ravenclaw, our shared Hogwarts house. While I'd stopped by this memorial plenty of times before, this was the first time I did so with Lizzy's parents.

As Mr. and Mrs. Manchester grieved and shed tears, I wrapped my arms around both of them, attempting to remain stoic myself.

"I know we've told you over text already," Mrs. Manchester said, "but thank you for bringing down the monster who killed our daughter. The whole time he was on the run, you became our beacon of hope. A beacon of hope for the whole of Santa Barbara. You're a true superhero now, Jessica."

I flashed a slight smile at Mrs. Manchester's gratitude, staying silent for a few seconds. "I don't think a simple 'You're welcome' would suffice in this case, Mrs. Manchester," I said. "After everything we've been through, everything our school and town have been through, words aren't enough to express how satisfying my victory was."

Even with tears still in his eyes, Mr. Manchester started to flash a slight grin himself. "Never would I have imagined that your life would end up imitating the story arcs of those superheroes you girls loved so much," he said. "If anyone in the real world could go through a superhero origin story, I couldn't be any more grateful that it was our daughter's best friend."

"That's what I'm talking about, Mr. Manchester. If anything, I think this tragedy will make us better people in the long run. As long as we keep Lizzy in our thoughts, her memory will become even more powerful and inspirational for us." Lizzy's parents tightened their arms around my shoulders, sending the greatest sensation of warmth possible throughout my body. Then when we released our arms from each other, we stepped back and looked at Lizzy's memorial in fuller detail.

"I've come here every day that I walked to school," I said to Lizzy's parents. "I haven't had the time to really think about it, but it sure is beautiful. I don't think your daughter and the nine other victims could've asked for more."

"There will always be time to add more to the memorial, too," Mrs. Manchester said. "Imagine what this is going to look like a year from now."

"Oh man, I don't want to start thinking that far . . ." I giggled a bit. "I've had too much on my mind lately, you know . . ."

I knelt in front of the photo marking Lizzy's section of the memorial. The day it was taken was still clear in my memory: Lizzy's fifteenth birthday, last July 15. Lizzy held it at none other than Wonder World, "Where anyone can be a superhero." Charlotte and Orlando were there with us as well; it was the most fun day that the four of us ever had together as far back as I could remember. The thought that it would be the last time I'd ever get to celebrate Lizzy's birthday was the last thing that would've crossed my mind that day. It did not work out that way, and here I was. But despite the sorrow that came with such a change of fortunes, that wasn't something I'd let put me down.

"I did it, Lizzy," I said to Lizzy's photo. "My victory was for you. For the others who lost their lives on May 23. For the parents and siblings who lost loved ones. For everyone at Manzanita High School."

Lifting my lips into a smile, I imbued my hand with photon energy and emanated the resulting light above Lizzy's side of the memorial. I folded my fingers once more into the famed Katniss Everdeen salute, with each of my three fingers pointing toward Lizzy's photo. Then I proceeded to do the same with the other nine victims, walking by each of their photos and shining my light toward them.

ACKNOWLEDGMENTS

Sometimes, the most incredible ideas come from the darkest of moments. *Exceptional* is one of those ideas.

On a typical sunny afternoon on May 2014, tragedy struck the campus of my college, the University of California-Santa Barbara, as my Gaucho community found itself in the middle of a mass shooting that took the lives of six of our students. The experience of seeing the normally lively community of my beachside campus was so sorrowing for me that I felt a sense of helplessness that I had never felt before in my life. So many questions raced through my head in the days that followed. Among them were: Why do we have no choice but to be helpless in the face of tragedy and senseless violence? Why can't we have superpowers to defend ourselves from madmen like the UCSB shooter and save others from such shocking tragedies? Essentially, the same questions that Jessica asked herself after the shooting at her own school that took Lizzy's life.

As difficult of an experience as the shooting and its aftermath were, everything about the shooting sounded like the perfect formula for a novel, from the young lives lost to the shooter's backstory. Thus came the idea for *Exceptional*, something I've had in mind for many years and even imagined playing out in my mind (though with me as my own superpowered alter ego) as I went through my final days of college.

Exceptional is my retelling of the UCSB shooting and its aftermath as I would've liked it to go in my imagination. It serves as my homage to the awesome communities of UCSB and Isla Vista, and the astounding resilience that they displayed in the days and months that followed the shooting. As such, they are the ones I want to thank first for being the main inspiration for my debut novel.

Thank you to my former colleagues at Santee Public Library in Southern California—Liz, Eric, Nicole, Kevin, and more—for further enriching my interest in writing, literature, and pop culture. I'm happy to have shared my ideas for *Exceptional* with you before its publishing. Count yourselves lucky that you had a sneak peek of this book before it hit shelves!

Thank you to my writing coaches, Barbara and Tiffany, for guiding me through my first go-around with the process of writing and publishing a novel. Your advice has been indispensable in my journey to make this story a reality.

Thank you to Shannon, my good friend since college, for helping me out with my book cover. I'm glad you referred me to some handy tools I now plan to use to create covers for my future novels, not just this one.

Thank you to my best friend from college, Marc, for encouraging me to tap into my hidden writing talents instead of pursuing other fields that most likely would not have worked out for me. If you hadn't convinced me to do so, this book most likely wouldn't even exist! Glad I had you to get me on the right track.

Thank you to Jen and Marie from the Milton & Hugo publishing team for taking a chance on me. I'm miles more confident in the future of my writing career with your help and support, and I can't wait to see where our partnership takes us next.

And last but not least, thank you to my editors: Chersti, Jessica (not to be confused with our beloved hero herself), Sarah, and Elizabeth. All four of you have taught me so much about the writing process and have boosted my confidence in writing after having completed this work.

I can't believe it took so many years for me to gain the motivation to make this story a reality, but here we are. It's amazing how far I've come in these ten years since the idea for this novel came up in my head, and I'm glad to have shared the culmination of my hard work and colorful imagination with you, the reader.

www.ingramcontent.com/pod-product-compliance
Lightning Source LLC
Chambersburg PA
CBHW032036240626
47154CB00003B/936

* 9 7 9 8 8 9 2 8 5 1 3 4 3 *